A MATTER OF JUSTICE

A DI KAREN HEATH CRIME NOVEL

JAY NADAL

Published by 282publishing.com

Copyright @ Jay Nadal 2025

All rights reserved.

Jay Nadal has asserted his right to be identified as the author of this work.

No part of this book may be reproduced, stored in any retrieval system, or transmitted in any form or by any means, electronic, mechanical, photocopying, recording or otherwise, without the prior written permission of the author.

This book is a work of fiction, names, characters, businesses, organisations, places and events other than those clearly in the public domain, are either the product of the author's imagination or used fictitiously. Any resemblance to actual persons, living or dead, events or locales is entirely coincidental.

PROLOGUE

Night draped Rawcliffe Country Park in shifting shadows, the dim glow of distant street lights barely cutting through the darkness. The car park was nearly empty now, just the scuff of tyres and the low hum of an engine fading into the silence. Hidden behind a cluster of trees, the killer didn't move. The wind bit through his clothes, air carrying the scent of damp earth and decay, but he remained focused, his gaze locked on the silver Audi parked at the edge of the tarmac.

The vehicle's owner had chosen his spot with care, positioning his car away from the main area where couples gathered for late-night encounters. The killer had studied Mark Reeves' habits over weeks of surveillance. Reeves valued discretion, parking close enough to watch and occasionally taking a closer look, but always at a distance to maintain deniability if questioned.

The killer's fingers tightened around the Taser in his pocket. Five years. That was all Reeves had served for killing Rachel Fenway. The judge had accepted his barrister's arguments about remorse and rehabilitation. But the killer knew better. He'd seen Reeves laugh after sentencing, had seen him joke with his legal team about getting off lightly.

Rachel's parents had forgotten how to laugh, hollowed out by grief as they stood at her grave, month after month, laying flowers like fragile offerings to a God who never answered. The killer had watched them, seen their quiet suffering, their life sentence of loss. Meanwhile, Reeves walked free. A handful of years behind bars—nothing more than a pause. No regret. No remorse. Rachel was still dead.

And that was why he had to pay. A figure emerged from the darkness, moving between the trees towards the Audi. Reeves. The killer's pulse quickened, but his breathing remained steady. He'd planned this moment for months, reviewing every detail. The location was perfect, isolated enough that he could work undisturbed.

Reeves reached his car, keys jingling as he unlocked it. As he settled into the driver's seat, the killer watched, noticing him check his phone before starting the engine. The blue glow illuminated his face through the window.

The killer moved forward in silence, his steps measured. The idling engine masked the crunch of gravel under his boots.

Three more steps.

Two.

One.

He yanked open the driver's door. Before Reeves could react, the killer shoved the Taser against his neck and squeezed the trigger. Reeves convulsed, a choked sound escaping his throat as electricity coursed through him. His phone clattered to the footwell as his body went rigid, then limp.

Working fast, the killer secured the seat belt across

Reeves' chest, pulling it tight. He produced cable ties from his pocket, binding Reeves' wrists to his thighs. The restraints would prevent him from reaching the door handles or gear lever when he regained consciousness.

The killer stepped back to check his work. Reeves slumped forward against the seat belt, drool glistening on his chin. The restraints held firm. Everything was proceeding according to plan. Now came the next phase, ensuring Reeves understood why he'd been chosen. The killer pulled out a burner phone from his jacket pocket and waited for his target to wake.

Justice had failed Rachel Fenway. The system had failed her family. But that would change tonight. He would force Reeves to acknowledge his crime, to speak his guilt aloud before facing real consequences. This was only the beginning, the first step in balancing the scales that corrupt barristers and weak judges had tilted towards leniency.

The car park remained silent except for the idling of the Audi's engine. No other cars approached. No witnesses would interrupt what was to come. The killer's patience had ensured privacy for what needed to be done.

Reeves stirred in the driver's seat, his head lolling against his chest. The killer saw his eyes flutter open, confusion giving way to panic as he discovered the restraints. Reeves tugged at the cable ties, his breath coming in quick gasps.

"Please," Reeves croaked as he bucked in his seat. "I've got money. Whatever you want. Take the car."

The killer landed a few choice blows to Reeves' face and chest before holding the knife against Reeves' throat, silencing him. The blade caught the dim light from the dashboard. Reeves went rigid, his pulse visible beneath the steel.

"Rachel Fenway," the killer said. "Do you remember her?"

Reeves shook his head, the movement causing the blade to nick his skin. A bead of blood appeared. "I don't know who that is."

The killer increased the pressure. "The woman you killed while high on cannabis. The one whose life meant nothing to you."

Recognition flickered across Reeves' face, followed by fresh terror. "That was an accident. I served my time."

"Five years." The killer's voice hardened. "You killed her and walked free after five years. Now you will confess your true guilt."

He held up the phone, its screen casting a blue glow across Reeves' face. "Tell the truth about that night. About your lack of remorse. About how you laughed after sentencing."

"No, you don't understand."

The killer dragged the blade across Reeves' collarbone, drawing blood. Reeves cried out.

"Confess."

Tears streaked down Reeves' cheeks. "I... I killed her. I was high. It was unintentional, but I did it."

"And after? In court?"

"I pretended to be sorry." The words tumbled out between sobs. "My barrister said to act remorseful. But I wasn't. I just wanted it over. Please don't kill me."

The killer pressed the record button. "Say it again. All of it."

Reeves repeated his confession, his voice breaking. When he finished, the killer tossed the phone on to the passenger seat.

"This will be your last confession."

The killer produced a plastic bag and yanked it over

Reeves' head. Reeves thrashed against his restraints as the killer secured the bag with gaffer tape around his neck. A small port in the plastic connected to a length of tubing.

The killer attached the other end to a butane bottle. He opened the valve. The gas hissed as it flooded the bag.

Reeves' struggles grew frantic. His screams were muffled by the plastic, his fingers clawing at the ties until blood ran down his wrists. The killer watched through the bag as Reeves' face contorted, mouth gaping like a fish.

The struggles weakened. Reeves' eyes rolled back, his movements becoming spasmodic. His chest heaved in desperate attempts to draw oxygen from the toxic air.

Minutes passed. The killer maintained a steady flow of gas, counting down in his head. Reeves' body gave a final twitch and went still. The killer waited, monitoring for any signs of life.

After ten minutes, he closed the valve and disconnected the tubing. He checked Reeves' pulse. Nothing.

Justice had been served.

The killer gathered his equipment, leaving the phone and its recorded confession. He turned away from the car, the butane bottle concealed beneath his jacket.

As he walked into the darkness, the killer's thoughts turned to his next target. Reeves was the first. There were others he needed to track down. Hidden behind legal technicalities and selfish barristers. They would face true judgement soon enough.

The night air carried the promise of rain. By morning, the first drops would fall on Reeves' car, washing away any traces the killer might have left behind. But the recording would remain, ensuring everyone understood why Mark Reeves had faced final justice in a deserted car park on the outskirts of York.

1

Karen burst through the station doors, clutching a handmade "Welcome Back Jade" banner that threatened to escape her grasp in the morning breeze. She spotted Bel, Ty, Ed, and Dan huddled by reception, their faces brightening at her arrival. She'd spent half the night perfecting it, scrapping three attempts before settling on this one. The butterflies in her stomach hadn't let her sleep anyway.

"Here, let me help with that." Ty grabbed one end of the banner while Ed took the other, holding it high across the entrance.

"Did anyone spot her car?" Karen asked, smoothing down her blouse for the fifth time that morning.

"Not yet." Bel checked her watch. "She's due in five minutes."

"I brought coffee." Dan lifted a cardboard tray. "Thought she might need her usual double shot of caramel latte."

"Perfect." Karen grabbed one cup for herself, her

hands tingling with anticipation. "What?" she asked, catching Bel's knowing look.

"You've been up since five, haven't you? Planning this?"

Karen shrugged. "Maybe." She'd spent hours getting the banner right, trying to make everything perfect for Jade's return. After months without her friend and colleague, she needed this day to go well.

They positioned themselves near the doors, exchanging nervous glances as they waited. But Karen wasn't just nervous—her heart pounded like a war drum, an erratic beat she couldn't steady. After months of facing her friend's empty desk, and the gnawing, sickening guilt that this was her fault, Jade was walking back into this station. Back into this life. Each case tackled without her right-hand woman, and each night wondering if Jade would ever return, had left her feeling empty.

Karen's fingers clenched the coffee cup, the heat pressing into her palm, grounding her. She wanted this to be perfect, needed it to be. Because if Jade was back for good, maybe Karen could finally breathe again. A couple of uniformed officers joined them, followed by three support staff. Word had spread about Jade's return, and the reception area filled with people eager to welcome her back. Even Jade's friend, DC Peters from Fraud, had appeared. They all knew what this meant—not just to the team, but to Karen herself.

"You okay?" Bel asked quietly, noticing Karen tapping her foot impatiently.

"Fine," Karen replied automatically, then caught herself. "Actually, terrified. What if she's not ready? What if I push too hard?"

"She wouldn't be coming back if she wasn't ready," Bel said. "Trust her to know her limits."

Karen nodded, but the knot in her stomach remained.

The last time she'd seen Jade in this building, her sergeant had been as pale as a ghost, shaking uncontrollably after a panic attack. Karen had driven her home that day, watching her walk into her flat with shoulders slumped in defeat.

"There she is." Dan pointed through the glass doors.

Karen's heart jumped as she spotted Jade's red car pull into the car park. The familiar sight brought a lump to her throat. Jade parked in her usual spot, but stayed seated, hands resting on the steering wheel.

"She's nervous," Bel whispered.

"Give her time," Karen said, recognising the moment of struggle. She'd experienced it herself after her own trauma. "This isn't easy for her."

Through the windscreen, Karen watched Jade take several deep breaths. The minutes stretched as they waited, no one wanting to rush her.

The officers fell quiet as they watched through the glass doors. One minute passed. Then two. Karen resisted the urge to go outside—Jade needed to take this step herself.

Finally, Jade emerged from her car, straightened her jacket, squared her shoulders, and walked towards the entrance. The instant she pushed through the doors, cheers erupted from the gathered officers. Her steps faltered as she froze and took in the banner and beaming faces.

"Welcome home!" the team's voices rang out in unison.

Jade's eyes filled with unshed tears as Karen pushed through the crowd and wrapped her in a tight embrace. "I've missed you so much."

"Good to be back. Missed you too," Jade replied, her voice thick with emotion as she clung to Karen.

The rest of the team crowded round, enveloping Jade in a group hug. Even the front desk staff joined in the applause, creating a crescendo of welcome that echoed through reception.

The usually stoic Ty had suspiciously damp eyes as he clapped Jade on the shoulder. "Your desk's been gathering dust," he said gruffly. "Nobody wanted to touch it."

"Not true," Dan interjected. "I tried using it once. Karen nearly took my head off."

Karen stepped back, wiping her eyes as she watched her team surround Jade. Their genuine joy at her return shone through every smile, every touch, every word of welcome. This wasn't simply colleagues greeting a returning officer, this was family welcoming home one of their own.

Bel produced a box of tissues, passing them round as tears flowed freely. Dan cracked jokes about them ruining their tough detective image, which only made them cry harder while laughing.

"Your coffee, madam." Dan presented the latte with a theatrical bow. "Still take it with enough sugar to put you in a diabetic coma?"

Jade accepted the cup with a watery laugh. "Some things never change."

"Speaking of things that never change..." Ty gestured to her parking spot. "Still taking up two spaces with that rust bucket you call a car?"

"Leave my car alone." Jade punched his arm. "Better than that ridiculous blacked out drug dealer's car you drive to compensate for your shortcomings."

The familiar bickering sparked another round of laughter. Jade's shoulders relaxed as she fell back into the routine of team dynamics.

Karen felt the tension drain from her. This was real.

Jade was back—not just physically present, but the essence of her had returned too. The quick wit, the confidence, and the way she could hold her own against anyone.

"Right then." Jade dabbed her eyes. "Better get to work before we flood the place."

The normality of her words, the familiar dry humour, hit Karen like a physical force. This was what had been missing these past months. Not just Jade's skills as a detective, but her presence, her spirit, the way she made their team whole.

"Come on." Karen placed her hand on Jade's back. "Let's get you settled at your desk. The mountain of paperwork's been missing you."

Jade groaned. "Don't tell me you've saved it all for my return?"

"Course we have." Ty grinned. "Had to give you a proper welcome, didn't we?"

They moved as a group towards the Serious Crime Unit, other officers calling out greetings as they passed. Karen enjoyed Jade's response to each welcome, noting how her initial nervousness had dissolved in the warmth of their reception.

The familiar banter, the shared laughter, and the casual touches all spoke to the bonds that held their team together. Bonds that hadn't broken during Jade's absence but had grown stronger, waiting for this moment of reunion.

As they reached the doors of the SCU, Karen caught Jade's eye. The flash of gratitude in her friend's gaze said everything words couldn't express. They were whole again, ready to face whatever challenges lie ahead together.

"Right." Jade took a deep breath. "Let's see what horrors await me on my desk."

"Loads, good luck!" Ed grinned.

Dan added, "Plus, whatever we couldn't be bothered to do ourselves."

The Serious Crime Unit erupted in fresh applause as Jade walked through the doors. Officers rose from their desks, crowding round to celebrate her return. Karen hung back, watching her friend navigate the sea of well-wishers.

"Thanks, everyone." Jade's voice wavered as she addressed the room. "Your support these past months... it meant everything. Now piss off."

The crowd dispersed as Jade stood at her desk. She picked up a framed photo of the team from their last Christmas party, studying the happy faces. A small potted plant sat on her desk, a ribbon neatly tied around the ceramic pot. A card rested against it, the message short but powerful: "The team needs you. Welcome back." The simplicity of it hit harder than she expected. No grand gestures. No overdone words. Just quiet reassurance that she belonged. Her throat tightened as she picked it up, running her fingers over the ink as if memorising each letter.

She lifted her gaze to Karen, unspoken emotion written across her face. Who...?

"Wasn't me," Karen said, though the sentiment echoed her own feelings perfectly.

Jade settled into her chair, testing it like an old friend. Her hands ran across the surface of her desk, reconnecting with the space that had remained empty, waiting for her return.

The moment was broken by Karen's phone buzzing.

She glanced at the screen, her expression shifting as she read the message.

"What is it?" Jade asked, catching the change.

"Body found at Rawcliffe Country Park." Karen paused, weighing her next words. "Suspicious circumstances."

The room fell quiet. As Jade processed this information, Karen noted the subtle trembling in Jade's hands as she set down the photo frame.

"Want to come with me?" Karen held her tone neutral. "No pressure. You can stay here, get settled in first if you prefer, and milk all the attention," she teased.

Jade pushed back her chair and stood. "No. I need to do this." Her voice strengthened with each word. "It's why I came back."

"You sure?"

"Yes." Jade grabbed her coat from the back of her chair and pulled it on, her hands fidgeting, but her jaw tight. "I can't hide from bloody death scenes forever; I'd be a useless copper if I did."

Karen nodded and raised a brow, pride swelling in her chest at Jade's courage. "Bel, you're with us. Ed, start the paperwork rolling. Dan and Ty, I want you checking CCTV in the area once we know what we're dealing with."

The familiar rhythm of launching an investigation filled the room. Officers moved between desks, each knowing their role. Karen led the way as they headed for the car park.

"The vic?" Jade asked, her professional mask sliding into place.

"Male, found in his car. That's all I know so far." Karen replied unlocking the doors. "Izzy's on her way."

They climbed in, and Karen pretended not to notice

the white-knuckled grip Jade had on the door handle. Some battles had to be fought alone.

"Ready?" Karen asked, starting the engine.

Jade released a long breath. "Ready."

They pulled out of the station, sirens silent but blue lights flashing. Karen kept her focus on the road, giving Jade space to prepare herself. The morning traffic parted before them as they headed towards Rawcliffe.

"Karen?" Jade's voice was quiet but steady.

"Yeah?"

"Thanks. For not treating me like I'm fragile."

Karen glanced at her friend. "You're one of the strongest people I know. You proved that by walking through those doors this morning."

Jade nodded, her posture relaxing slightly. "Doesn't feel that way sometimes."

"Strength isn't about not being afraid." Karen turned on to the ring road. "It's about facing that fear and doing what needs to be done."

They drove in comfortable silence for several minutes. Jade's hands still trembled in her lap, but her eyes were clear and focused. Whatever demons she battled, she wasn't letting them win.

Blue lights flashed ahead, marking their destination. Jade straightened in her seat as they approached, her professional demeanour taking over.

"First day back and we've got a body." Jade managed a weak smile. "Some things never change."

2

Karen pulled into Rawcliffe Country Park and followed the signs for parking. Up ahead, a cluster of emergency vehicles crowded the far corner of the car park. Three police cars, two vans, and the white forensic van. The area sat next to the park and ride site, where a small crowd of onlookers had gathered behind the police tape.

She turned off the engine and turned to Jade. "Ready?"

Jade gave a firm nod, though her hands were wrapped in a tight ball and stuffed between her legs.

They made their way to the outer cordon and signed in on the scene log, where a young PC held out protective suits and booties.

"Just booties, thanks," Karen said, taking two sets for her and Jade.

"Ma'am." PC Andrews approached with an evidence bag. "Found this in the victim's pocket when we checked for ID."

Karen examined the wallet through the clear plastic. A driving licence identified the victim as Mark Reeves, thirty-four, from York. The photo showed a clean-cut man with close-cropped dark hair and an unsmiling expression.

"Any witnesses?" Karen asked.

"Not yet. Dog walker found him about an hour ago. Said the car was here when she arrived."

Karen nodded and moved towards the silver Audi. The forensic team worked in pairs around the vehicle, photographing and collecting evidence, each focusing on their designated area.

The victim sat slumped, held upright by his seat belt. A plastic bag covered his head, secured with tape around his neck. Karen's stomach clenched at the sight of dried blood on his wrists where cable ties cut into the flesh.

"Jade?" She glanced back at her sergeant.

"I'm fine." Jade's voice carried a slight wariness, but she stepped forward to examine the scene.

Izzy Armitage crouched by the open driver's door; her copper hair pulled back in a tight ponytail. She looked up as Karen approached.

"Morning. Not how I planned to start my day. Ah, welcome back, Jade. Great to see you."

"Thanks, Izzy. Good to see you, too."

"What can you tell me?" Karen asked.

"Interesting set-up." Izzy pointed to a small valve protruding from the plastic bag. "See this modification? It's what they call a suicide hood. Often connected to gas canisters."

Karen leaned closer, careful not to touch anything. "But this wasn't suicide or assisted."

"No chance. The cable ties and evidence of struggle rule that out. Plus, there's significant bruising around his neck consistent with being tasered."

Jade shifted beside Karen. "Time of death?"

"Body temp and lividity suggest between eleven p.m. and one a.m. I'll narrow it down after the PM."

Karen straightened, processing the details. The location, the modified bag, and the restraints. None of it suggested a random attack.

"Found this on the passenger seat." Bart Lynch, the crime scene manager, held up another evidence bag containing a mobile phone. "Cheap burner. Has a video file you'll want to see."

"Bag everything," Karen instructed. "I want full forensics on the car and surrounding area. Check the park and ride CCTV and canvas the businesses across the road. Someone might have external cameras covering this section."

She turned to study the wider scene. The car park backed on to dense woodland, offering multiple approach routes for someone who knew the area, yet open enough that a parked car wouldn't raise suspicion. The perp had chosen the spot well.

"A bar over there might be worth checking," Jade said, gesturing to a building across the road. "If it was open last night, punters leaving might have spotted something."

"Good thinking. Get uniform to follow up." Karen nodded, encouraging Jade's return to active investigation.

Karen crouched beside Izzy as the pathologist pointed to the valve mechanism embedded in the plastic bag.

"The killer knew what they were doing," Izzy said. "This is a professional modification. Not seen many in this country, but popular abroad. The valve creates a seal that allows gas in but prevents oxygen from entering."

Karen studied the set-up. "So, he suffocated?"

"Yes, but not from lack of air. The killer pumped a gas of unknown origin through the valve. Forensics can run samples on the residue inside the bag and do a tox report. He would have lost consciousness within minutes."

A sharp intake of breath drew Karen's attention. Jade stood rigid, her face pale as she stared at the body. Her hands clenched at her sides, but she held her position.

"The cable ties suggest he was conscious during the attack," Izzy continued. "There's defensive bruising on his wrists and arms where he fought against the restraints."

"Could he have broken free?" Karen asked.

"No chance. These aren't easy to snap. The more he struggled, the tighter they became." Izzy gestured to the dried blood around Reeves' wrists. "He fought hard, but the restraints held him."

Karen rose, positioning herself between Jade and the body. "Time frame for the PM?"

"I'll check and let you know when I get to the morgue."

The sudden sound of heavy footsteps took everyone by surprise. Karen spun round to see Jade backing away from an evidence marker she'd knocked over. Her sergeant's breathing came in sharp bursts.

"Fresh air," Jade muttered, turning towards the cordon.

Karen nodded to Izzy and followed her friend. They stopped at Karen's car, where Jade braced herself against the bonnet.

"Deep breaths," Karen said. "You're doing fine."

"Am I?" Jade's voice cracked. "I can't even look at him without..." She sucked in another breath. "Maybe I came back too soon."

"You made it through the initial examination. That's huge progress."

"But I'm not ready. I can't..."

"PC Roberts," Karen called to a nearby officer. "Contact the park and ride site. I want all CCTV footage from yesterday evening through to this morning."

She turned back to Jade. "You're here. You're pushing through. That's what matters."

Jade straightened, her breathing steadier. "Right. Yes." She pulled out her notebook. "The bar opposite. Kings Arms. Should be opening later this morning."

"Take Bel with you when it opens. Talk to the staff about last night. Anyone leaving around closing time might have seen something."

A flash of relief crossed Jade's face at the task. A chance to contribute without facing the body again. She nodded and began noting details.

Karen returned to the scene as Bart Lynch arrived carrying a bag of evidence.

"Found traces of white powder on the passenger seat," he said. "Could be a transfer. We'll run analysis."

"Good. What about prints?"

"Nothing obvious yet. The killer was careful. No doubt wore gloves. But we'll do a full sweep once we get the car to the lab."

Karen surveyed the scene. The forensic team worked their way outwards from the car in a careful grid pattern. Officers canvassed the perimeter, searching the treeline for discarded evidence.

"I want everything documented," she said. "Even the smallest detail could matter. This wasn't random."

"We'll go over every inch," Bart assured her.

Karen checked her watch. Cars would arrive soon, bringing more onlookers. They needed to clear the scene before traffic built up.

"How long until we can move the body?"

"Give us another hour to complete the external examination and photograph everything. We'll need the vehicle too. There could be trace evidence we can't spot in this light, so I'll arrange for a low-loader."

"Fine. I'll have officers maintain the cordon until you're done."

She found Jade by the police tape, interviewing the dog walker who'd discovered the body. Her sergeant's hands twitched as she took notes, but her voice remained professional.

"Ready to head back?" Karen asked as Jade finished the interview.

"Yes. The bar opens at eleven. Bel and I can handle it later."

They walked to the car, leaving behind the buzz of activity as the investigation continued. The morning sun broke through the clouds, casting long shadows across the car park.

"You did good work today," Karen said as they climbed in. "The first scene is the hardest."

Jade buckled her seat belt. "Thanks. For not making a big deal of... you know."

"That's what friends are for." Karen started her car. "Now let's see what that phone has to tell us."

3

BACK AT THE STATION, Karen gathered her team around Ed's computer. The burner phone sat connected to a laptop, its screen displaying a video file. The overhead fluorescent lights cast a harsh glare as they huddled close to listen.

Reeves' voice crackled through the speakers, raw with terror. "I killed her. I was high on cannabis when I hit Rachel Fenway. It wasn't on purpose."

A second voice cut in, a male, cold and controlled. "Tell them about after. In court."

"I faked being apologetic." Reeves' words broke on a sob. "My barrister told me to act remorseful. But I wasn't. I wanted it over."

"They forced the confession," Bel said, breaking the silence as the recording ended. "You can hear the fear in his voice."

Ed pulled up a file on his screen. "Mark Reeves, thirty-four. Convicted of vehicular manslaughter in 2018. Rachel Fenway died at the scene. He tested positive for cannabis and had no insurance."

"Eight-year sentence but released after five for good behaviour," Ty added, reading from his notes. "Released six months ago."

Karen paced behind the group. "We know this wasn't random. The killer targeted him."

"Rachel's boyfriend caused a scene at the sentencing," Claire said, scanning through court transcripts. "Trevor Elphick. The judge threatened to hold him in contempt when he shouted Reeves deserved to die."

"Could be our killer," Dan suggested. "Revenge is a powerful motive."

"Or someone else connected to Rachel," Bel countered. "Male family member, friend..."

Karen stopped pacing. "Claire, pull everything on Rachel Fenway's death. Court records, witness statements, press coverage. I need to know everyone involved in the case."

"Already on it." Claire's fingers flew across her keyboard.

"The confession video exposed Reeves' lack of remorse," Jade said. "The killer wanted him to admit the truth before dying."

Karen nodded. "A private confession wouldn't serve that purpose. They left the phone behind, so we'd find it. Everyone would know why Reeves was killed."

"Vigilante justice," Ed said. "Making him pay for escaping proper punishment."

"Is the location significant? It's remote enough for privacy, yet public enough that someone would quickly find the body," Bel added. "The killer wanted Reeves discovered. But why was Reeves there in the first place?"

Karen shrugged and turned to Claire. "Find Trevor Elphick. I need an address. I want to talk to him. And check if Rachel's parents are still in the area."

"The modifications to the bag suggest planning," Ty said. "This wasn't a crime of passion. The killer took time to prepare."

"Agreed. Ed, dig deeper into Reeves' history. Employment records, known associates, any incidents since his release. Dan, help Claire with the court records. It might be someone who held a grudge."

The team dispersed to their tasks, leaving Karen alone with Jade.

"You okay?" Karen kept her voice low.

"Getting there. The recording... hearing his fear..."

"I know. But you handled it well."

"The killer planned every detail," Jade said, shifting the focus back to the case. "The confession, the method, the location. Nothing was left to chance. Ever watched Dexter? Because it reminds me of him. Mr Preparation. Normal by day, sadistic killer at night."

Karen considered this. "Which means they might strike again if it wasn't personal. We need to find them before that happens."

"Where do you want me?"

"Help with Reeves' background check."

Jade nodded and headed to her desk. Karen remained by Ed's computer, replaying the confession in her mind. The killer's voice revealed no accent, no identifying characteristics. Only cold, controlled fury at a justice system he believed had failed.

The question was how far would they go to correct that failure?

"Right," Karen said, "we need to move fast on this. Preet, I want you checking CCTV from all the streets surrounding Rawcliffe Country Park. Focus on the hours between nine p.m. and two a.m. Look for any vehicles making multiple passes or anyone on foot who shouldn't be there at that time."

Preet nodded and grabbed her notebook. "I'll start with the approach roads and work inward. The park and ride site might have useful footage, too."

Karen turned to Claire, who sat with her laptop open. "I need you to go through Reeves' case file with a fine-tooth comb. Every detail matters, especially the sentencing remarks. And contact his next of kin. Someone needs to formally identify him."

"His parents live in Acomb," Claire said, pulling up an address. "He also has an ex-wife, Gemma Fletch."

"Take someone from family liaison with you when you visit his parents. They'll need support. I'll pay Gemma a visit next." Karen paused.

Ed raised his hand. "What about Reeves' house? If the killer stalked him, they might have left evidence nearby."

"You read my mind." Karen collected an evidence bag containing Reeves' keys. "Take Ned with you. Check everything. Computers, phones, and papers. I want to know his movements before his death."

She handed the keys to Ed. "And look for CCTV cameras. The killer might have watched the house before making their move."

"On it," Ed said, gesturing for Ned to follow him.

"One more thing," Karen added. "The car park location. It's isolated enough for privacy but public enough that someone might have seen something. Dan, contact local taxi firms. Their drivers might have picked up fares in that area last night."

Dan grabbed his phone. "I'll check with the regular firms first, then try the private hire companies."

"Good. Ty, help Preet with the CCTV. Four eyes are better than two."

Karen's phone buzzed with a text from Izzy about the post-mortem for tomorrow.

Karen gathered her coat and car keys, her mind racing through the tasks ahead. The first twenty-four hours of any investigation were crucial, but this one felt different. The killer's approach pointed to someone with a message to send. If he was a vigilante, that message wasn't finished —because men like him didn't stop. They struck again and again, until someone stopped them.

"Claire," she called over her shoulder. "When you find Trevor Elphick's address, text it to me. I want to speak to him tomorrow."

"Already found his work address," Claire replied. "He works at the Royal Mail sorting office on Leeman Road."

Preet and Ty huddled over CCTV footage, while Claire and Jade began searching through the various databases. Dan's voice carried across the room as he spoke with taxi dispatchers.

Karen and her team knew that careful and systematic gathering of evidence solved cases, not dramatic breakthroughs. Every phone call, every document, every frame of CCTV inched them closer to identifying their suspect.

Karen left and headed for the car park.

4

Karen parked her Mini outside a row of well-kept terraced houses in the north of York. Gemma Reeves' home sat in the middle of the block, its red-brick exterior brightened by window boxes bursting with pink and purple petunias.

The brass doorbell chimed inside as Karen pressed it. After a moment, footsteps approached, and the door opened to reveal a woman in her thirties, her dark hair pulled back in a messy bun.

"Gemma Reeves?" Karen held up her warrant card. "I'm Detective Chief Inspector Karen Heath from York Police."

Gemma's expression tightened. "It's Ms Wilson now. I went back to my maiden name after the divorce."

"I need to speak with you about an incident involving your ex-husband."

Gemma hesitated, then stepped back. "Come in."

She led Karen into a small but tidy lounge. Family photos lined the walls, though Karen noted none included Mark Reeves. A well-worn sofa faced a bay window overlooking the street, while mismatched cushions added splashes of colour to the neutral decor.

"Please, sit." Gemma settled in the armchair, her fingers twisting in her lap.

Karen settled on the sofa. "I'm afraid I have difficult news. A body was discovered this morning at Rawcliffe Country Park. Evidence at the scene suggests it's Mark."

The colour drained from Gemma's face. "Mark?"

"We believe so, but we need someone to identify him formally. Would you be willing to do that?"

Gemma nodded, her movements jerky. "Of course. His parents... they're not well enough."

"The circumstances of Mark's death are suspicious. When did you last see or speak to him?"

"Not since the divorce was finalised, about seven months ago." Gemma's voice hardened. "I cut off all contact when they released him."

"How was your relationship during the marriage?"

"Before the accident, things were strained. We'd been trying for a baby, but Mark had fertility issues. He refused to consider alternatives, donor sperm or adoption. Said he wouldn't raise another man's child." Gemma's lip curled. "His pride meant more than having a family."

"And after the accident?"

"He rang me from prison, expecting support. But hearing him joke about his lenient sentence..." Gemma shook her head. "He killed that poor girl and treated it like a minor inconvenience."

"How did he joke about it?"

"Said the judge must have been a pot smoker too, letting him off with eight years. Laughed about his barrister coaching him to look remorseful in court." Her hands clenched into fists. "Rachel Fenway's family lost their daughter forever, and he thought it was funny."

Karen made notes as Gemma spoke. "Did Mark mention any threats or concerns after his release?"

"No idea. Like I said, I broke all contact. The Mark I married died the night he killed Rachel. The man who came out of prison was a stranger, one I wanted nothing to do with."

"What about his lifestyle, friends, associates?"

"He never had close friends. Kept to himself mostly." Gemma paused. "Though his internet history during our marriage suggested he was into some questionable stuff. That's all I'll say about that."

Karen noted the deliberate vagueness. "Anything else you think might be relevant?"

"Just that actions have consequences. He couldn't give up his weed. I begged him. I was sure it had an effect on his... well you know. Mark spent years ignoring my pleas, but his habit caught up with him eventually on that night." Gemma's tone held no trace of grief. "When can I identify the body? I'd like to get it over and done with."

"This evening."

Karen studied Gemma's face, noting the coldness in her eyes.

"The fertility issues tore us apart," Gemma said, her voice breaking. "Month after month of negative tests. Each one felt like a failure."

"Did you seek medical help?"

"Three rounds of IVF. Twelve thousand pounds of debt." Gemma dabbed at her eyes with a tissue. "The doctors said stress could affect our chances. But Mark... he refused to deal with his emotions. Every setback made him angrier."

Karen kept her voice gentle. "How did that anger manifest?"

"He'd stay out late, refuse to talk. When I suggested counselling, he said I was attacking his manhood." Gemma's laugh held no humour. "His pride got in the way of everything. Even after the final failed round, he wouldn't consider other options."

"You mentioned donor sperm earlier?"

"I begged him to consider it. Or adoption. There are so many children needing homes." Gemma's shoulders slumped. "But Mark insisted his bloodline had to continue. Said his father would never accept a grandchild that wasn't biologically his."

The tissue in Gemma's hands shredded as she spoke. "The night Rachel died, Mark had stormed out after another argument about adoption. He went to the pub, got high, then drove home." Her voice cracked. "One woman dead, another childless. All because of his stupid pride."

Karen wrote notes, her pen pressing hard against the paper. Each detail painted a clearer picture of Mark Reeves. A man whose ego had destroyed multiple lives.

"The marriage ended that night," Gemma continued. "Though I didn't file for divorce until after his sentencing. His mother begged me to stand by him, said he needed support. But I couldn't forgive him. Not when he showed no real remorse."

Tears rolled down Gemma's cheeks. "Five years I gave him. Five years of trying for a baby, of walking on eggshells around his moods. Then, in one night of selfishness, he ruined everything."

She pressed her palms against her eyes. "The worst part? After I finally left him, my next fertility test showed improvement. The doctor said reducing stress levels could have helped. All that time, his attitude might have been part of the problem."

Karen closed her notebook. The woman before her bore little resemblance to the cold, composed person who had opened the door. Grief for what might have been had replaced her earlier detachment.

"I can arrange for an officer to accompany you to the mortuary," Karen said. "The post-mortem is scheduled for tomorrow morning."

Gemma nodded, wiping her eyes. "Thank you. I know I should feel something about his death. But all I feel is tired. Tired of Mark's choices affecting my life."

"That's understandable." Karen got out her phone. "I'll call to arrange for a car."

"Will you find who did this?"

Karen paused in dialling. "Yes. Though I sense you might not want us to."

"Mark deserved punishment for what he did to Rachel. The courts failed her family." Gemma sat up straight in her chair. "But murder is murder. Her parents didn't want revenge. They wanted justice. This killing won't bring Rachel back."

Karen completed the call, requesting a female officer to collect Gemma. As she hung up, Gemma spoke again.

"Rachel's mother wrote to me after the trial. Said she forgave Mark, hoped he'd learn from his mistake." She shook her head. "She showed more grace than he deserved. More than I could manage."

"An officer will be here soon," Karen said, standing. "They'll take good care of you."

Karen stood, sensing Gemma had shared all she would. "Thank you for your time."

At the door, Gemma stopped Karen. "Rachel Fenway was twenty-eight when she died. Had her whole life ahead of her. Whatever happened to Mark... maybe it's justice finally being served."

Karen left those words hanging in the air as she headed back to her car. Gemma's lack of surprise at her ex-husband's death was telling. Mark Reeves had inspired no loyalty, no lasting affection, only contempt for his actions and attitude.

5

Karen eased her car into the driveway of their gated community home, exhaustion settling into her bones. The sky had darkened to deep purple, stars beginning to peek through gaps in the clouds. She'd meant to be home hours ago, but work had gone crazy busy, and her visit to Gemma had lasted longer than expected.

The scent of garlic and herbs greeted her as she stepped through the front door. She paused to kick off her shoes, hanging her coat on the hook beside Zac's.

"In here," Zac called from the kitchen.

Karen padded through to find him stirring a pot on the stove, his sleeves rolled up to his elbows. The confidence in his movements, the ease with which he navigated their kitchen, made her heart swell.

"You didn't need to wait," she said, pressing a kiss to his cheek.

"Course I did." He tasted the sauce, adding a pinch of seasoning. "Besides, cooking keeps my mind busy. Stops me dwelling on tomorrow's pre-evaluation."

Karen perched on a bar stool at the kitchen island. "You're ready for it. Doctor Morales thinks so too."

"Maybe." Zac turned down the heat under the pot. "Still feels strange, thinking about going back. Like putting on old clothes that don't quite fit any more."

"But they will," Karen said. "Look how far you've come these past months."

She meant it. Their weekend walks in Dalby Forest had grown longer, Zac venturing deeper into the trees each time. Their recent trip to the Lake District proved he could handle crowds again, even if he preferred quieter paths. Most importantly, he spoke about his fears instead of bottling them up.

"The therapy has helped," he admitted, dishing pasta onto warmed plates. "Doctor Morales understands what it's like, getting back out there after trauma."

Karen reached for the cutlery drawer. "Remember our first forest walk? You jumped at every snapping twig."

"Now I only jump at half of them." His attempt at humour carried an edge of truth, but progress was progress.

They settled at the kitchen table, knees touching beneath the surface. Karen twirled pasta around her fork, savouring the rich tomato sauce. "This is good."

"New recipe. Needed something to focus on besides tomorrow." Zac pushed a piece of garlic bread around his plate. "What if I freeze up? What if I'm not ready?"

"Then we try again when you are." Karen squeezed his hand. "There's no rush. The job will wait."

"But I want to get back. Need to. Jade has. It's my turn." Determination burned in his eyes. "I'm tired of living in fear."

The raw honesty in his voice struck Karen. Six months

ago, he'd have changed the subject, retreated into himself. Now he faced his anxieties head-on.

"Remember what Doctor Morales said? Recovery isn't linear. You take steps forward, sometimes back, but the overall direction matters most."

Zac nodded, some tension leaving his shoulders. "She also said I need to trust my instincts again. They're still there, just buried under the trauma."

"And they're returning. A few weeks ago in Keswick, you spotted that pickpocket before anyone else did."

"Old habits." A ghost of his former confidence surfaced. "Though I nearly tackled the poor kid myself before remembering to alert the local police."

"But you didn't. You made the right call." Karen speared another forkful of pasta. "That's what matters. Your judgement's sound."

They ate in comfortable silence, the kitchen clock ticking away peaceful seconds. Such moments had grown more frequent: quiet dinners, shared laughter, conversations that didn't revolve around trauma and recovery.

"I've missed this," Zac said, as if reading her thoughts. "Just being us."

"Me too." Karen gathered their empty plates. "Though your cooking's improved since you've been home."

"Had to find a silver lining to all this enforced leave." He stood to help clear the table. "Even learned to make proper sauce instead of using jars."

The casual domesticity of loading the dishwasher together, of planning tomorrow's meals, felt like another step towards normality. Each small task completed without anxiety or flashbacks marked progress.

"Whatever happens tomorrow," Karen said, closing the dishwasher, "I'm proud of you. The work you've put in, and the courage you've shown is what defines you, not the trauma."

Zac pulled her into an embrace, his heartbeat steady against her cheek. "Couldn't have done it without you."

"Yes, you could. But I'm glad you didn't have to."

"Well, it would have been a tougher journey on my own."

"How about I grab a shower and we..." Karen gazed in to Zac's eyes.

Zac smiled as he took her hand and led her upstairs.

6

Karen entered the station, warmth spreading through her chest as memories of the previous night lingered. The intimacy with Zac marked another milestone in his recovery. Tender moments replacing the strain of recent months.

She strode through reception, exchanging greetings with the early shift. DC Peters waved from his desk as she passed, deep in conversation with someone about football scores. The familiar buzz of office life filled the corridors.

Her office beckoned, but the need for coffee won out. She dropped her bags by her desk and turned towards the kitchen, only to find Bart Lynch blocking her path.

"Need a word," he said, his eyes bright with fresh discoveries. "Got the initial results from the Reeves scene."

Karen gestured him into her office. "What have you found?"

"The killer was thorough. No prints, no fibres, nothing traceable on the body itself." Bart pulled out his notebook. "But the back seat tells a different story."

"Go on."

"Multiple DNA samples. Bodily fluids from at least four different people, plus a collection of pubic hairs. Our boy Reeves had an active social life."

Karen leaned on the edge of her desk. "All recent?"

"Some older deposits, and fresh ones within the last forty-eight hours. We're running full profiles on everything. Should be able to determine gender and race from the hair samples."

"So, he used the car for a shag fest."

"Looks like it, I'd say. The volume and variety of samples suggests frequent activity." Bart flipped through his notes. "No matches yet in the database, but we're early in the process."

Karen rapped her fingers on the desk. "The killer must have known about Reeves' activities. Did Reeves take his sexual partners there at night? But why when he has his own place?"

Bart shrugged. "Perhaps he didn't want to take them home? Or didn't want them knowing too much about his life? Or preferred the thrill of having risky sex outdoors? Added an edge if he thought he might get caught?"

"True."

"The killer chose the spot because he was certain Reeves would be there?"

"Makes sense. If Reeves visited often, the killer could predict his movements." Bart closed his notebook. "I'll keep you updated as more results come in."

"What about the white powder residue on the passenger seat?"

"Analysis is ongoing. Nothing toxic. More like industrial dust or debris."

Karen nodded. "And the phone?"

Bart handed over the evidence bag containing the phone. "Clean as expected. Burner, no prints. These models are popular for criminal activity. Cheap, untraceable, available without ID." Bart placed the phone on her desk. "Voice analysis is ongoing, but the killer spoke in a measured tone. No discernible accent or speech patterns."

"Deliberate?"

"Could be. The recording quality is good enough to detect if they tried to disguise their voice. They didn't. Just kept their tone neutral. The killer knew how to avoid leaving traces."

"Professional knowledge of evidence procedures," Karen mused. "Or extensive research."

Karen lifted the evidence bag, examining the phone through the plastic. "What about the hood?"

"These hoods are rare in the UK. More common abroad and probably purchased online. Someone researched this method, understood the technical requirements."

"I'll have the team run checks on where someone might get hold of one. Doubt they'd be on eBay!" She raised a brow.

"Might be from sites overseas, or an unsafe forum. Good luck with that."

Karen jotted notes as Bart spoke. The killer's preparation extended beyond stalking their victim. They'd invested time and resources into creating their murder weapon.

"The residue particles found inside the hood came back," Bart continued. "Commercial grade butane, available from any DIY or camping store. No unique markers or impurities to trace."

"Another dead end."

"In terms of source, then yes. But we know cause of death was oxygen displacement leading to asphyxiation. Tox report will show butane in blood and tissue samples."

Karen's phone lit up with a text from Jade. The postmortem was delayed. "Anything else from the scene?"

"Soil samples from the tyres suggest the car hadn't left York recently. The environmental trace is consistent with local roads."

"So, Reeves stayed in his comfort zone."

"Makes sense if he was a regular at that site. Familiar territory, known escape routes if things went wrong."

"Good work, Bart. Send me the full report when it's ready," she said. "Including the DNA analysis."

Bart nodded and left. Karen sank into her chair, processing the implications. The killer had studied their target, learning intimate details of his habits. This wasn't a random act of revenge. It was calculated, planned.

Her phone buzzed. A message from Ed about records recovered from Reeves' house. The probe continued, each piece adding depth to their understanding of both victim and killer.

The coffee would have to wait. Karen pulled Reeves' file closer, diving back into the details of his life and death. Someone had appointed themselves judge and executioner. Her job was to ensure they didn't strike again.

She opened her laptop, fingers hovering over the keyboard as she considered their next steps. The killer had chosen Reeves for a reason. Was it because of his lack of remorse, his early release, or his continued disregard for others? How many more people might fit similar criteria? Thousands!

Karen called Kelly to update her on the latest developments. The case grew more complex with each revelation, painting a picture of a killer who combined careful planning with righteous anger. A dangerous combination.

The buzz of the station filtered through her door. Phones ringing, keyboards clicking, and voices discussing cases. Her team worked their assigned tasks, following leads and gathering evidence. But somewhere in the city, their killer might already be selecting his next target.

Her computer pinged with another email. Jade rescheduling the post-mortem for later that morning. The email also officially confirmed Mark's identity since Gemma had visited the mortuary last night.

She opened the case file, adding notes from Bart's briefing. The killer's knowledge base suggested someone with an understanding of evidence procedures. An officer? Someone with a medical background?

She hoped not.

7

Karen arrived at York Hospital, her fingers tapping on the steering wheel as she searched for a parking spot. Dark clouds loomed over the squat buildings, promising rain. Her conversation with Bart lingered in her mind as she strode through the main entrance, past the early morning visitors clutching paper cups of coffee.

The mortuary lay in the hospital's basement, the fluorescent lights casting harsh shadows in the long corridors. Karen passed through the double doors into the examination suite. Music filled the space, one of Izzy's eclectic playlists that mixed classical pieces with modern rock.

Izzy stood by the examination table, her flame-red hair tucked under a surgical cap. Mark Reeves lay before her, his body already opened in a Y incision. The sharp tang of disinfectant mixed with other, less pleasant odours.

"Morning," Izzy called over the music. "You're just in time. I've removed and weighed the organs."

Karen stepped closer, pulling on a paper mask. Metal instruments gleamed on a tray beside the table, their purpose clear in the stark lighting. The examination room's clinical efficiency contrasted with Izzy's upbeat demeanour as she worked.

"What can you tell me?" Karen asked.

Izzy raised a portion of tissue. "Extensive damage to the mouth and upper respiratory tract from the butane. It triggered an inflammatory response in the lungs." She set down her instruments. "We've taken blood for tox screening."

"Bart mentioned we should find butane in the samples."

"Most likely. The gas caused chemical burns throughout his airway." Izzy moved to investigate the lower portion of the body. "But I've found something interesting."

She indicated the relevant area. "Our victim had haemorrhoids and mild rectal prolapse."

Karen raised an eyebrow. "Significance?"

"Multiple potential causes. Chronic constipation, straining during bowel movements, weak pelvic floor muscles." Izzy paused. "Or frequent anal intercourse."

"Given the DNA evidence from his car's back seat..." Karen took a moment to fill her in on Bart's findings.

Izzy raised a brow and nodded. "Exactly. The physical changes may suggest regular activity over an extended period." Izzy made notes on her tablet. "Combined with Bart's findings, it builds a picture of his sexual practices."

Karen considered this new information. "The killer targeted that car park. If Reeves used it for sexual encounters..."

"Then someone might have observed his habits." Izzy moved to examine the ligature marks on Reeves' wrists. "The bruising pattern shows he struggled against the restraints. Broke the skin in multiple places."

The music shifted to a classical piece, the violins creating an odd backdrop for their discussion of death and sexual practices. Izzy continued her examination, documenting each mark and injury with photographs and detailed notes.

"Time of death?" Karen asked.

"Lividity would suggest between eleven and one. I'll narrow it down once I complete the full workup." Izzy gestured to the bruising around Reeves' neck. "The Taser marks are consistent with a standard civilian model. Enough voltage to incapacitate but not kill."

Karen stepped back from the table, processing the implications. Their killer had planned each detail, from choosing the location to selecting their method.

"I'll have the full report ready this afternoon," Izzy said, returning to her examination. "Including detailed analysis of the rectal tissue changes."

Karen nodded, stepping closer to examine the bruising patterns Izzy had noted. "What about these marks on his face and chest?"

"A brief assault is my guess," Izzy said, pointing to several discoloured areas.

"So, he saw the attack coming?"

"For a second perhaps, but it appears as if he was taken by surprise." Izzy began examining the victim's hands. "No material under the fingernails so he didn't scratch his attacker."

The examination continued as they discussed each new finding, building a clearer picture of Reeves' last moments and the calculated nature of his killer's actions.

Izzy peered closer at the bruising patterns around Reeves' neck while Karen processed the implications of these latest findings. The back seat evidence Bart discovered pointed to frequent sexual encounters, and now

Izzy's examination revealed physical signs supporting that conclusion.

"His lifestyle put him at risk," Karen said. "Meeting strangers for sex in isolated locations."

"The car park was his preferred spot?" Izzy made another note on her tablet.

"According to Bart's analysis, the DNA evidence suggests multiple partners over time."

Izzy moved around the table, documenting additional marks and abrasions on the body.

"Someone took time to study his routine," Izzy said. "They knew when and where to find him alone."

Karen pulled out her phone and fired off a quick note. "The killer turned his hook-up spot into a trap. But why there? Why not follow him home?"

"Public location, easy escape routes." Izzy photographed a series of marks on Reeves' shoulder. "Less chance of neighbours hearing anything or CCTV catching clear footage."

"Or they wanted him found. Needed an audience for their message."

The examination continued in focused silence interrupted only by the music and the click of Izzy's camera. Each new photograph added detail to their understanding of Reeves' final moments.

"The Taser marks suggest someone strong enough to subdue him," Izzy said, showing the burns on his neck. "The angle implies they came at him from the side. Probably through the driver's door."

"Professional knowledge of vulnerable points?" Karen stepped closer to investigate the marks.

"Could be. The placement is precise for maximum effect with minimal force." Izzy turned the head to show more bruising. "They knew what they were doing."

"Military training perhaps? Or police?"

"That level of skill comes from practice. This may not have been their first time using a Taser."

Karen made another note. Their suspect pool expanded to include anyone with combat or restraint training. "What about his other injuries?"

"Defensive wounds on his forearms, bruising consistent with cable ties." Izzy lifted one of Reeves' hands. "Tore his skin trying to break free. Also bruising across his chest. Going on the angle, he pushed against his seat belt to escape."

Izzy added, "Other visitors might have seen something without realising its significance."

Karen thought of the DNA samples waiting for analysis. How many potential witnesses had passed through that car park that night?

"The blood spatter on his shirt collar came from struggling against the ties?"

"No, that's from a small cut. The pattern suggests he thrashed his head to dislodge the bag." Izzy indicated dark stains around the neckline.

"Look at these marks on his chest," Izzy said. "Antemortem bruising in a distinct pattern. The killer struck him several times before applying the hood."

"Punishment before execution," Karen said. "Making him suffer was part of the plan."

"Blows to the face but none to vital organs. They knew how to cause pain without risking premature death."

Karen nodded. The list of potential suspects grew more specific with each detail.

"Right." Karen straightened. "I need to speak with Rachel's boyfriend. He was vocal about wanting revenge after Reeves' sentencing."

"Keep me updated." Izzy turned back to her examination. "I'll send the full report once I've finished."

Karen grabbed her phone as she headed for the door. She typed a quick message to Bel: *Finished at morgue. Pick you up in 20. Time to talk to Trevor.*

The reply came as she reached the corridor: *Ready when you are. He's on shift at the sorting office.*

Karen stepped through the doors, leaving behind the sharp scent of disinfectant and Izzy's eclectic playlist. Their killer had chosen both location and method with care, transforming Reeves' sexual hunting ground into the place of his murder. Now they had to determine if Trevor's anger at losing Rachel had pushed him to take justice into his own hands.

The hospital corridors buzzed with morning activity as Karen made her way back to the car. Medical staff hurried past, their shoes squeaking on the polished floors.

Karen started her car, ready to return to the station and update her team.

8

THE ROYAL MAIL sorting office hummed with activity as Karen and Bel made their way through the entrance. Conveyor belts whirred overhead, carrying endless streams of parcels and letters. The sharp smell of cardboard and ink permeated the air.

A supervisor directed them past rows of workers sorting mail into pigeonholes. Mountains of envelopes lay in collection trays beneath the sorting stations, many covered in a film of dust and grease from the machinery.

"If my post goes missing, I'll know why," Bel said, eyeing a pile of letters trapped beneath a belt.

The supervisor led them to a small office off the main floor. "I'll send Trevor in."

Karen took in the cramped space. A metal desk, three chairs, and walls covered in health and safety notices. The industrial noise filtered through the thin walls, creating a constant backdrop of mechanical rhythm.

Trevor Elphick entered a few minutes later, his Royal Mail uniform creased from his morning shift. Dark circles rimmed his eyes, and his shoulders slumped as he dropped into the chair opposite Karen.

"Mr Elphick." Karen introduced herself and Bel. "We need to have a word with you about Mark Reeves."

His expression hardened at the name. "What's he done now?"

"He was found dead yesterday morning."

Trevor sat straighter, tension radiating from his frame. "Dead? How?"

"Murdered." Karen studied his reaction. "Given your history with Mr Reeves, we need to account for your movements that night."

He scrubbed his stubbly chin. "Murdered. Right." A bitter laugh spilled from him. "Can't say I'm sorry to hear it."

"Why's that?"

"Why?" Trevor's voice rose. "He killed Rachel. Took away everything we'd planned, everything we'd dreamed of." He pulled out his wallet and extracted a worn photograph. "This was us, two weeks before she died."

The photo showed a younger Trevor with his arms around a smiling woman with long, dark hair. Their happiness radiated from the image.

"We were going to Paris that summer," Trevor said, his voice cracking. "I had the ring picked out. Was going to propose by the Eiffel Tower. Proper romantic, like she deserved."

Karen let the silence stretch, giving him space to continue.

"Instead, I spent that summer planning her funeral." His fingers trembled as he returned the photo to his wallet. "While Reeves got what? Eight years? Out in five for good behaviour?"

"Where were you two nights ago, Mr Elphick?"

"The White Horse on Monkgate. From about eight till closing. Ask the staff. I'm a regular."

"Anyone who can verify that?"

"The landlord, Dave. Most of the usual crowd. We had the football on, City versus Leeds." He shrugged. "Nothing special, a normal night at the pub."

Bel made notes as Trevor spoke.

"Your reaction to news of his death... you seem happy?" Karen pressed.

Trevor met her gaze. "Wouldn't you be? He destroyed my life, killed the woman I loved, then walked free not long after. Fucking wanker. The system failed Rachel. Failed her family. Failed all of us who loved her."

"So, you support what happened to him?"

"Support it?" Trevor leaned forward. "I'd like to shake the hand of whoever did it. Buy them a pint. The world is a better place without him."

"That's quite a statement, Mr Elphick."

"It's the truth. Reeves deserved what he got. Rachel's parents might preach forgiveness, but I'm not that generous." His jaw clenched. "Five years in prison wasn't justice. This is."

Karen exchanged a glance with Bel. "We'll need to verify your whereabouts."

"Check the pub's CCTV. I was there all night, same as always." Trevor stood. "Now, if we're done, I need to get back to work. These letters won't sort themselves."

They left Trevor at his sorting station and headed for the exit. The drone of the facility followed them into the car park.

"Think he did it?" Bel asked as they reached Karen's car.

"His alibi needs checking. Contact the pub, get their

CCTV footage." Karen unlocked the doors. "And find out who else was drinking there that night."

"His reaction was intense."

"Five years of grief and anger will do that." Karen started the engine.

"Could have planned it despite the emotion."

"True. But our killer chose that specific location. How would Trevor know about Reeves' late-night activities?"

"Unless he'd been following him?"

"Check his phone records, bank statements. See if he's made any unusual purchases or travelled to that area recently." Karen pulled out of the car park. "And dig deeper into his background. Criminal record, military service, any training that could explain the technical aspects of the murder."

Bel nodded, adding to her notes. "What next?"

"You verify his alibi. I'll update the team on what we learned at the post-mortem." Karen turned towards the station. "Trevor's not the only one who wanted revenge on Reeves. We need to look at everyone connected to Rachel's death."

"He's got the motive," Bel said as they turned on to Leeman Road. "Royal Mail gives him knowledge of the area, ability to move around without drawing attention."

"But the technical aspects don't fit. The modified hood and the butane set-up. That requires specific knowledge."

"Could have researched it. Internet makes everything accessible."

Karen turned in to a side street to avoid roadworks.

"What about Rachel's family? Should we speak with them?"

"Eventually. But Trevor's reaction worries me. That level of satisfaction at someone's death..."

"Makes him either our killer or someone who wishes

he was." Bel finished making notes. "The pub alibi might prove his innocence."

"Might be his regular routine?" Karen tapped her fingers on the steering wheel. "Get statements from all the staff and regulars. Someone must remember if he was there for the entire match."

"If he left at any point?"

"Exactly. Check if the pub's CCTV covers the exits, not only the main bar. A determined person could slip out and back."

They pulled into the station car park. Karen switched off the engine but didn't move to get out.

"Trevor's anger felt genuine," she said. "But something about his reaction bothers me."

"The satisfaction?"

"More his certainty that Reeves deserved it. Like he'd thought about it before, played out scenarios in his head."

"Fantasy versus reality?" Bel suggested. "Lots of people imagine revenge. Few actually take it."

"Unless someone else made those fantasies real." Karen opened her door. "Check if Trevor's been in contact with anyone else from Rachel's life. Friends, family, or support groups. Someone with the skills he lacks might have offered to help."

"You think he could be involved, but not the actual killer?"

"It's possible. The murder took planning, technical knowledge, patience. Trevor's all emotion and raw grief. But he might know who did it."

They headed into the station, dodging a group of uniforms heading out on patrol.

"One more thing," Karen said as they reached the SCU. "Look into any connections between Trevor and the car park area. Did Rachel live nearby? Did they spend time there before her death?"

"On it." Bel peeled off towards her desk, already reaching for her phone.

Trevor's grief felt real, his hatred for Reeves justified. But had that hatred turned him into a killer? Or had someone else appointed themselves the instrument for his revenge?

The answer lay somewhere in the details of Trevor's life.

9

Karen headed down the corridor towards her office, case notes tucked under her arm. A flash of movement caught her eye as Jade rushed past, one hand pressed to her mouth. The sound of her footsteps echoed off the tiles as she pushed through the ladies' toilet door.

Karen paused, considering whether to give her sergeant space. The choice vanished when retching sounds carried into the hallway. She entered the toilets to find Jade bent over a toilet bowl, her body heaving.

Between spasms, Jade's breathing turned ragged and sharp. Her knuckles pressed white against the porcelain as tremors wracked her frame. Karen recognised the signs. This wasn't just physical illness.

"Easy now," Karen said. She dampened paper towels at the sink and rushed back to the cubicle. "Deep breaths."

Jade shook her head, gulping for air. Her next words came out strangled: "Can't... breathe..."

"Yes, you can." Karen crouched beside her, resting a hand on Jade's back and rubbing it softly. "Focus on my voice. Breathe with me. In through your nose, out through your mouth."

She demonstrated, making each breath audible. After several shaky attempts, Jade's breathing began to sync with Karen's rhythm. The tremors eased.

"That's it." Karen pressed the damp towels into Jade's hands. "Small sips of air. You're safe."

Jade slumped against the cubicle wall, pressing the cool towels to her face. Tears leaked from beneath her closed eyelids.

"Fuck. I don't understand," she whispered. "I was at the incident board looking at Reeves' photos from the crime scene. They weren't even that graphic. Nothing I haven't seen before."

"Trauma doesn't always make sense." Karen settled on the floor beside her. "Sometimes it blindsides you when you least expect it."

"But I was handling it. The scene yesterday, the post-mortem notes..." Jade's voice cracked. "Then one bloody photo and I'm falling apart."

"You're not falling apart. You're processing."

"Is that what this is?" Bitter laughter caught in Jade's throat. "Because it feels like failure."

"No." Karen's tone brooked no argument. "Failure would be pretending you're fine when you're not. This is you being honest about your struggles which takes more courage."

Silence filled the space between them, broken only by the distant sounds of office life continuing beyond the bathroom door. A passing conversation. Footsteps. Jade's breathing steadied further as the panic attack released its grip.

"I came back too soon," she murmured.

"Maybe. Maybe not." Karen shifted to face her. "There's no perfect time."

"Doctor Morales says that too." Jade wiped her eyes. "I thought I was ready. The therapy helped. I felt stronger..."

"You are stronger. But strength isn't about never breaking; it's about how you put yourself back together."

Jade's fingers twisted in the damp paper towels. "What if I can't do this job any more?"

"You can. But you don't have to prove it all at once." Karen paused. "When I came back after my attack, I had moments like this. Times when the smallest trigger sent me spiralling. It happened in London too."

"How did you handle it?"

"By accepting recovery takes time. By letting people help instead of hiding my struggles." Karen touched Jade's arm. "And by remembering that trauma changes us, but it doesn't define us."

Fresh tears flowed down Jade's cheeks. "I hate feeling this vulnerable. This weak."

"There's nothing weak about surviving trauma. Nothing weak about facing your fears and showing up anyway." Karen squeezed her arm. "The old Jade wouldn't have admitted to struggling. That's progress."

"Doesn't feel like progress when I'm throwing up in the loo."

"Better than throwing up at your desk." The jest earned a watery chuckle from Jade. "Come on. Let's get you cleaned up."

They rose from the floor, joints protesting against the hard tiles. Jade splashed cold water on her face while Karen retrieved a spare toothbrush and paste from her office emergency kit.

"I keep telling myself I should be over it by now," Jade

said, accepting the bottle of water. "That other officers bounce back faster."

"Stop comparing your recovery to others. Your journey is your own." Karen leaned against the sink. "And anyone who claims they bounced straight back is lying to themselves and everyone else."

Jade finished rinsing her mouth. "I don't want to let the team down."

"You're not. We need you healthy more than we need you pushing yourself to breaking point." Karen straightened. "Take the rest of the day off. Get some proper rest."

"But the case..."

"Will still be here tomorrow. Recovery isn't a sprint, remember?"

Jade nodded, exhaustion clear in the slump of her shoulders. "Thanks. For understanding."

"Always here for you." Karen pulled her into a brief hug. "Call me if you need anything. Day or night."

"Even at three a.m.?"

"Even then. Though I might be a grumpy bitch."

A hint of Jade's usual smile flickered across her face. "Might be?"

Karen laughed and steered her towards the door. "Go home. Sleep. Tomorrow's another day."

She stood in the SCU doorway as Jade gathered her things and left, other officers offering quiet greetings as she passed. The mask of professional competence settled back over Jade's features, but Karen noted the lingering tension in her movements.

THE SCU BUZZED with activity as Karen passed and

returned to her desk. She sank into her chair. Her team worked on their assigned tasks.

Thirty minutes later, a message from Jade arrived: *Made it home. Going to sleep.*

Karen quickly wrote a reply: *Good. Take care of yourself x*

A knock on her door pulled her attention up. Bel stood there; folders nestled under her arm.

"Everything okay?" Bel asked. "Saw Jade leaving."

"She needs time." Karen gestured for Bel to sit. "The photos from the scene hit harder than expected."

"Should we be worried?"

"No. She's processing. That's healthy, even when it doesn't feel like it."

Bel nodded, understanding in her eyes. They'd all seen colleagues struggle after trauma. Some bounced back, others left the force. The job exposed them to humanity's darkest aspects. Not everyone could carry that weight.

"The team's asking questions," Bel said. "About whether she's ready."

"She will be." Karen straightened the files on her desk. "Remember Thompson after the Harrison case?"

"Three months of claiming he was fine, then broke down during a routine interview."

"Because he wouldn't admit he needed help. At least Jade's being honest about her struggles."

The conversation paused as PC Peters passed Karen's office, reports in hand. When he moved out of earshot, Bel leaned forward.

"What do you need us to do?"

"Treat her as normal when she returns. No tiptoeing, no special treatment." Karen tapped her pen against the desk. "But keep an eye out. If she seems overwhelmed, create space for her to step back without making it obvious."

"And you? How are you handling this?"

The question caught Karen off guard. "Me?"

"Supporting Jade through her recovery while dealing with your own trauma. Plus Zac's situation." Bel's expression softened. "That's a heavy load."

Karen set down her pen. In the rush of work and others' needs, she rarely considered her own emotional state.

"I'm fine." The words came without thought. Then, more honestly: "Most days. Sometimes it all hits at once. Jade, Zac, and the memories. But that's normal, isn't it? Part of the healing process."

"As long as you're not carrying it alone." Bel stood. "We're here for you too, you know. Not only as colleagues."

"I know." Karen managed a smile. "Thanks."

After Bel left, Karen stared at the photo of her team on her desk. Taken at last year's Christmas party, before the events that changed everything. They looked happy, unaware of what lay ahead.

But they'd survived. Changed, perhaps scarred, but still standing. Still fighting for justice, still supporting each other through dark times.

Her phone buzzed again with another message from Jade: *Thank you. For everything x*

Karen typed back: *Always. Now get some rest xx*

She returned to her work, but her thoughts lingered on Jade.

Karen picked up her phone to check on Zac ahead of his session. The case could wait five minutes. Right now, being human mattered more than being a detective.

10

Karen left her office and gathered her team at the front of the SCU near the incident boards. Officers settled into chairs or perched on desk edges, notebooks ready. A hush fell over the group as they waited for her update.

"Right, listen up," Karen said. "Post-mortem results confirm cause of death as asphyxiation from oxygen starvation and more than likely exposure to butane gas. But there's more. The back seat of Reeves' car contained DNA evidence from multiple sexual partners."

Claire raised her hand. "That location's a known dogging site. Both straight and gay couples use it after dark. Local residents complained about the noise and abandoned condoms. The council installed extra lighting last year, but it didn't help."

"Reeves was a regular visitor?" Ty asked.

"The evidence suggests frequent activity," Karen said. "DNA from several people, plus hair samples. Bart's team is running a full analysis. The samples date back weeks, suggesting a pattern of behaviour."

"Gross." Bel pulled a face of disgust. "But why use his car? He had his own place."

"Maybe he enjoyed the thrill," Dan said. "Or didn't want people knowing where he lived. Could have been married visitors who needed discretion."

"Either way," Karen continued, "we need eyes on that site. It's possible someone saw him there before he died."

Dan's hand shot up. "I volunteer for surveillance duty."

"Me too," Ty added, grinning. "Happy to take one for the team."

"Thought you might." Karen shook her head at their enthusiasm. "But this is serious. We need to identify regular visitors who may have seen Reeves or something odd. This isn't about catching people in compromising positions, but we'll arrest them if we find anyone committing a lewd act in a public space."

Ed cleared his throat. "Speaking of suspicious, the house search turned up interesting items. Multiple sex toys in his bedside drawer. We've bagged them for DNA testing. The drawer had a false bottom too, hiding more explicit material."

The team exchanged glances as Ed continued. "More importantly, Reeves had CCTV cameras covering his property. The footage shows someone conducting surveillance in the days before his death. They stood in the shadows across the street for hours."

"Can we identify them?" Karen asked, moving closer to examine the grainy images Ed held up.

"No. Too far for clear images. Always kept out of direct sight. Professional approach, like they understood camera angles and blind spots."

Ty stood and moved to the incident board. "Park and ride CCTV shows several vehicles arriving between ten and midnight. They disappear from view behind the building, but we've got registration numbers to trace. Three cars made multiple visits that week."

Karen nodded. "Good. Cross-reference those plates with Elphick. Check the timing against Reeves' known movements."

"They knew Reeves would be there," Bel said.

"Which means they'd studied his habits," Karen replied. "Pull reports of any suspicious behaviour. Someone lurking in the shadows may have drawn attention."

Bel nodded and made a note.

"Ed, dig deeper into those CCTV files," Karen instructed. "I want to know how long that surveillance went on. Check traffic cameras in the surrounding streets too. Our watcher had to arrive and leave somehow."

"What about Trevor's alibi?" Karen asked, flipping through her notes.

"The White Horse confirmed he was there for the match," Bel said. "They are forwarding the CCTV as it covers both exits. He might have slipped out unnoticed. An officer is going there later to get statements from the staff about his behaviour that night."

Claire raised her hand. "I've been looking into Rachel's family. Her parents moved to Scotland after the trial, but they still visit her grave monthly. The groundskeeper remembers them, says they spend hours there talking to her."

"Keep digging," Karen said. "Anyone who knew about Reeves' activities could have passed that information to our killer. Check social media too and see if anyone discussed the dogging site online."

The meeting continued as they discussed theories and assigned tasks.

"Just a moment," Karen said as the team prepared to disperse. "The killer's knowledge of evidence procedures suggests training or experience. Check for anyone in Rachel and Trevor's circle with a police or military background. The clean crime scene wasn't luck. He knows how forensics works."

Officers returned to their desks, the quiet buzz of investigation filling the room. Karen remained at the incident board, reviewing the crime scene photos. The killer had turned Reeves' sexual hunting ground into a stage for public justice.

Bel approached with a fresh cup of coffee. "What are you thinking?"

"That our killer is patient," Karen said. "He learns routines, chooses the perfect spots. This wasn't just murder; it was a statement."

"But for who? Rachel's family? The justice system?"

"Maybe both." Karen accepted the coffee. "Check if any similar cases have gone unreported."

Karen returned to her office, the sound of her team at work following her down the corridor. They had a location, a timeline, and evidence of premeditation. Now they needed a name.

Her phone buzzed. A message from Jade: *Feeling better. Back tomorrow.*

Karen typed a quick reply: *Good. Take care of yourself. Team's got things covered here.*

She turned back to the case files, but her mind kept returning to the surveillance footage. Someone had studied Reeves, learning his habits and vulnerabilities.

11

Zac sat in Dr Morales' office, the familiar space pressing in around him. He'd spent months here, peeling back the layers, exposing the raw, jagged edges of himself. It had become a refuge, but today, it felt different. Like he was standing on a cliff edge, staring down at the life he was supposed to reclaim.

"You seem different today," Dr Morales said, her pen poised above her notepad. "More energetic."

"I got the evaluation date for returning to work." Zac leaned back in his chair and let out a heavy breath. The words felt heavier than they should. Like saying them out loud made them more real. More dangerous.

"Are you okay?"

"Ready. Nervous. Both at once." He rubbed his hands against his jeans. "Some days I can't wait to get back. Others, the thought of walking through those doors..."

"That's natural." Dr Morales set down her pen. "You've made solid progress."

"Karen says the same thing." A smile crossed his face. "She notices the changes in how I handle crowds now and take longer walks. Last week we went to York on market day. The noise, the people... six months ago it would have sent me running."

"What helped you cope?"

"The breathing exercises. Focusing on specific details instead of letting everything overwhelm me." Zac paused. "And Karen. Having her there, knowing she understands if I needed to leave."

Dr Morales nodded. "You've developed powerful coping mechanisms. But I sense something still troubles you."

The smile faded from Zac's face. "Karen's case. A body found in a car park." He pressed his fingers against his thighs. "When she told me, my first thought was, 'what if she's next?'"

"Tell me more about that fear."

"It's constant. Every time she leaves for work, I imagine all the ways she could get hurt." His voice tightened. "The phone rings, and my heart stops. Is it the station? The hospital? The morgue?"

"These anxieties are common among police families," Dr Morales said. "Especially after trauma. How do you manage them?"

"I text her throughout the day. She updates me on her location." He ran a hand across his stubbly chin. "But it's not enough. The fear sits in my chest, squeezing tighter until she comes home."

"Yet you support her continuing her work."

"Because it's who she is. The job... it's part of her." Zac stood and paced the office. "But after what happened to us, knowing the dangers..."

Constantly reliving the moment when everything unravelled.

"What specific dangers concern you most?"

"All of them. The obvious ones are violent suspects, weapons, and confrontations." He stopped by the window. "But the unpredictable ones, too. The routine call that turns deadly. The hidden threat no one sees coming."

Dr Morales let the silence stretch. "Like what happened to you?"

"Yes." Zac returned to his chair. "One moment I was at home, the next..." His hands trembled. "Karen faces those risks every day. How do I live with that?"

"By separating rational concerns from trauma responses. When these fears surface, question them. Is this a realistic worry or an echo of your experience?"

"Most times it's both." Zac exhaled. That was the worst part. It wasn't paranoia. The job *was* dangerous. People died. He nearly had, too. "The job carries real risk, but my mind amplifies them. Turns every possibility into certainty."

"What helps ground you in those moments?"

"Focusing on facts. Karen's training, her team, the procedures that keep officers safe." He rubbed his neck. "And remembering she's skilled at what she does. The same strength that helped her survive our ordeal protects her at work."

Dr Morales made a note. "You're developing a balanced perspective. Acknowledging the risks while recognising the safeguards."

"But will it be enough? When I'm back at work, facing my own dangers while worrying about hers..."

"That's why we're developing these coping strategies now." Dr Morales straightened in her chair. "You'll need them for both situations, managing your anxiety about Karen's safety and handling your own return to duty."

Zac nodded. "The department's been supportive.

Offering a phased return, letting me choose which duties I feel ready for."

"And what do you feel ready for?"

"Desk work at first. Crime analysis, case review." His expression hardened. "But eventually, full duties. I can't let this shit get me down."

"That's significant progress from our early sessions," she said. "You're not simply surviving now, you're planning for the future."

"Karen believes in me. Even when I doubt myself." Zac's voice softened. "She understands the struggle because she's been through it. After her attack in London, the recovery process..."

"Her experience helps, but your journey is your own."

"I know. Sometimes I feel guilty, leaning on her strength while she deals with her own trauma."

"Have you discussed these feelings with her?"

"Some of them. We talk more now about everything." Zac's tension eased. "That's another change. Before, I bottled everything up. Now we face it together."

She closed her notebook. "You've built a firm foundation for returning to work. The anxieties may never disappear altogether, but you have tools to manage them."

Zac stood and pulled his shoulders back. "One day at a time, right?"

"Exactly. Focus on small victories. Each step forward strengthens your resilience."

He gathered his coat and left, stepping into the cold air outside. But as he walked towards his car, the same thought coiled in his gut like a serpent.

What if I'm not strong enough? Outside, he picked up a text from Karen: *Hope session went well. Love you xx*

Zac smiled, typing his reply as he walked to his car.

The session had run over, but Dr Morales never rushed these breakthrough moments.

His phone vibrated again with a reply: *Back late. Don't wait up xx*

The familiar spike of anxiety hit his chest. His fingers hovered over the keys, tempted to ask for details, location, backup plans. Instead, he typed: *Stay safe. Call if you need me xx*

Progress meant fighting these impulses, trusting Karen's judgement without letting fear dictate his responses. He slid into the driver's seat, gripping the wheel as he recalled Dr Morales' words about distinguishing rational concerns from trauma responses.

The drive home gave him time to reflect on their session. Managing his own return to work while supporting Karen's career. Balancing vigilance with trust. Finding the line between protective instincts and paranoid fears.

As he arrived home, he saw the lights were on in the hallway, lounge, and upstairs bedrooms as usual. He smiled. Summer was forever leaving lights on in every room. In her little world, electricity was free! But he wouldn't have it any other way. His daughter's presence anchored him, gave purpose to his recovery. She needed him capable of facing the world without flinching at every shadow.

"Dad?" Summer called from the kitchen as he entered. "There's a letter from the force."

Zac found her at the counter, homework spread across its surface. The official envelope lay unopened beside her textbooks.

"Probably about the evaluation," he said, picking it up.

"Are you nervous?" Summer closed her book. "About going back?"

"A bit." He sat beside her. "But Dr Morales thinks I'm ready."

"What about Karen's work? You still worry."

Zac met his daughter's concerned gaze. "I'll always worry about Karen. Just like she worries about me. It's part of loving someone in this job."

"But you're handling it better." Summer's observation carried the simple clarity of youth. "You don't check your phone every five minutes any more."

A chuckle escaped as he rolled his eyes. "That obvious, was it?"

"You used to jump every time it buzzed. Now you wait before checking." She shrugged. "Small things, but I notice."

Her words echoed Dr Morales' advice about celebrating small victories.

"The therapy helps," he said. "Teaching me to manage the fear instead of letting it control me."

"Does Karen know? About your progress?"

"We talk more now." Zac toyed with the envelope's edge. "About everything. The fears, the nightmares, and the good days and bad."

"That's why you're better together," Summer said. "You understand each other's struggles."

Her insight struck him. Yes, he and Karen carried similar scars, but their shared experiences strengthened their bond rather than weakened it. They supported each other through the dark moments, celebrated the victories, faced each challenge as a team.

The letter could wait. Right now, this moment with his daughter mattered more. Her faith in his recovery and her understanding of the complex dynamics between him and Karen reinforced his determination to return to duty.

"Want to order a takeaway?" he asked. "Your choice."

Summer brightened. "Pizza? We can save a bit for Karen if she's working late."

"I'll never say no to pizza!"

As Summer searched for the menu, Zac's phone buzzed again. A text from Dr Morales: *Remember progress over perfection. One step at a time.*

He typed a quick acknowledgement thanking her.

The pizza arrived as darkness fell. He and Summer ate at the kitchen table, her chatter about school filling the space. Normal moments like these had seemed impossible during his darkest days. Now they grounded him, proved life continued despite trauma's lingering shadows.

Later, after Summer had gone to bed, Zac sat in the quiet house. Karen's text about running an op nagged at him, but he resisted the urge to check her location or send another message. Trust meant accepting the risks while believing in her ability to handle them.

12

Karen tapped on Detective Superintendent Kelly's open door. Her superior glanced up from a stack of reports, reading glasses perched on the end of her nose.

"Do you have a minute, ma'am?" Karen asked.

Kelly removed her glasses and gestured to the chair opposite. "Update on Reeves?"

Karen settled into the seat, spreading her notes on Kelly's desk. "Post-mortem confirms death by asphyxiation. Bart found DNA evidence suggesting regular sexual activity in his car. The location is a known dogging site."

"Hence, your planned operation tonight?"

"We need eyes on that location. Multiple cars visit after dark. Someone might have seen Reeves or noticed anything suspicious."

Kelly leaned back. "Resources?"

"A couple of unmarked cars plus support units nearby. We'll move in when they're in full swing. If you know what I mean, take statements, check for potential witnesses."

"And arrest anyone caught in the act," Kelly added.

"Of course."

Kelly studied Karen's face. "Your team can handle this? It's an unusual situation."

"Dan and Ty volunteered." Karen allowed a small smile.

"Keep them focused. This isn't about catching people with their trousers down. We need information about Reeves."

"Understood."

Kelly nodded, trust clear in her expression. "Good. What about Trevor Elphick?"

"Claims he was at the pub during the murder. We're verifying his alibi, but something feels off about his reaction."

"How so?"

"Too pleased about Reeves' death. Said he'd buy the killer a pint."

"Grieving boyfriend or potential suspect?"

Karen spread her hands. "Could be both. We're digging deeper into his background."

Kelly removed her glasses. "Keep me updated. And Karen? Be careful tonight. These situations can turn volatile."

"We'll take precautions." Karen gathered her notes. "Uniform backup will be close if needed."

Back in the corridor, Karen found Jade waiting by the stairs. "Fancy grabbing dinner before the operation?"

"Starving," Jade replied. "That restaurant round the corner?"

"Sounds good. I'll grab my coat and bag and meet you downstairs."

A Matter Of Justice

THEY WALKED the short distance to Miller's, a favourite spot for station staff. The early evening rush hadn't started, leaving plenty of empty tables. They chose a quiet corner away from the windows, shrugging off their coats in the warmth.

Susan, their regular waitress, approached with menus, though both knew them by heart. "Evening ladies. The usual?"

"Not tonight," Karen said. "I'll have the lasagne. Extra garlic bread."

"Jacket potato for me," Jade added. "Cheese, beans, and coleslaw."

"Brave choice before an operation," Karen said after Susan left. "Those beans might cause issues in a confined car."

Jade cracked a genuine smile. "Better than your honking garlic breath."

"Well lets hope we don't have to arrest someone and put them in the back seat. With your farts and my bad breath, they'll be dead before we get them into custody!"

Karen noted how Jade drummed her fingers on the table. A nervous habit she'd developed since her return. The familiar atmosphere of the coffee machine's hiss, the clatter of plates, and the murmur of conversation provided a comfortable backdrop for their talk.

"How are you holding up?" Karen asked, taking a sip of her Coke.

"Better." Jade's hand stilled. "Bit of a blip. Won't happen again."

"It might. That's normal."

Jade shifted in her seat, focusing on arranging her cutlery for the tenth time. "Can't afford to fall apart on the job."

"You didn't fall apart. You recognised your limits and stepped back. That's progress."

Their food arrived, steam rising from the plates. The lasagne's rich aroma filled the air, layers of pasta and meat sauce topped with bubbling cheese. Jade picked at her potato, pushing beans around with her fork, the coleslaw untouched.

"Remember my first week in York?" she asked, breaking the silence. "That domestic gone wrong?"

"The Morrison case. You tackled the husband before he could grab another knife."

"No hesitation then. Just instinct and training." Jade stabbed a bean. "Now I second-guess everything."

"Your instincts are still there. The training hasn't vanished. You're dealing with a tough experience."

Karen cut into her lasagne, the pasta layers collapsing into a messy heap. She remembered her own recovery, the way simple tasks became mountains to climb.

"Trevor bothers me," Jade said, pushing a forkful of potato around her plate. "From what you've told me about him, his anger feels genuine, but something's not right."

Karen welcomed the shift to work discussion. "His alibi needs verification, but from what we know already the landlord says Trevor was there until closing."

Jade shrugged. "Trevor's grief is raw, uncontrolled. The killer was methodical."

"Could be working with someone. His anger combined with another's skills."

Their conversation flowed between case details and personal matters. Karen mopped up the sauce with garlic bread as they discussed evidence and theories. She recognised their old rhythm returning. The easy exchange of ideas, the shared understanding of both police work and its emotional toll.

"Summer asked about police cadets again," Karen said, pushing her empty plate aside.

Jade grinned, though her own meal remained half eaten. "Future detective in the making?"

"Zac's not keen. After everything that happened..."

"He'll come round. She's got copper instincts... notices things others miss."

The restaurant had filled up around them, the dinner crowd trickling in.

Karen spotted the slight tremor in Jade's hand as she lifted her glass. Her friend masked it well, but signs of her struggle remained. The barely touched food told its own story.

"The team's glad you're back," Karen said. "It wasn't the same without you."

Emotion flickered across Jade's face. "I missed this. The work, the banter. Even the horrible coffee."

"Nothing's changed there. Dan still burns every pot he makes."

Susan cleared their plates, raising an eyebrow at Jade's leftovers, but saying nothing. The warmth and familiar routine of sharing a meal had eased some tension from Jade's shoulders, though Karen noticed how her eyes tracked each person entering.

"Head back?" Jade said, reaching for her coat.

Karen didn't mention the uneaten food or the way Jade's eyes darted towards the exit.

"Thanks for dinner," Jade added. "It felt... normal."

"Any time."

They stepped into the evening air, street lights casting long shadows. Karen pulled her coat tighter against the chill.

"You don't have to do the operation tonight," she said.

"I want to."

Karen squeezed her friend's arm. Together they walked back towards the station, their footsteps echoing off buildings. The station lights blazed against the darkening sky. Soon they'd coordinate tonight's operation, direct officers, gather evidence. But this quiet moment between friends mattered just as much as any investigation.

13

A STILLNESS SETTLED over Rawcliffe Country Park as Karen parked her unmarked car behind a cluster of trees. The absence of moonlight created a perfect cover for surveillance, though the darkness held its own risks.

"Everyone in position?" Karen spoke into her radio.

"Dan and Preet at the south entrance," came the first response.

"Ty and Ed covering the east side," crackled another voice.

Two more unmarked cars borrowed from the night shift confirmed their locations at strategic points around the perimeter. The operation required careful coordination. Enough officers to control the situation without spooking potential witnesses too early.

"Right," Karen said, addressing the team through her radio. "Our priority is to gather information about Mark Reeves. Anyone who frequented this spot might have seen something significant. But remember we also have a duty to prevent public indecency. If we catch people in the act, we'll make arrests."

"Question." Preet's voice carried a hint of amusement. "How close do they need to be to constitute a public act? Like, if they're sitting in their cars..."

"Use your judgement," Karen replied. "But if clothes are off or *bits* are exposed, that's an automatic arrest."

"What if they're dressed but having a *shuffle*..." Dan started.

"Focus, people," Karen cut him off. "This is still a murder investigation."

Jade shifted beside her, peering through the windscreen at the empty car park. "Never thought I'd spend my evening hunting doggers."

"Brings a whole new meaning to night shift," Ty quipped over the radio.

"Just think," Ed added, "if anyone asks what we did at work today..."

Karen suppressed a smile. Their banter masked the serious nature of their task, but she needed them sharp. "Remember no one approaches alone. We move in together."

"Speaking of aggressive," Jade said, "heads-up. First customers arriving."

Two cars entered the car park, parking at opposite ends. Their headlights extinguished, leaving only the dim glow of dashboard displays. Minutes passed as more vehicles arrived, creating a loose circle in the darkness.

"I count six cars now," Ed reported. "Two couples have moved to the back seats."

"Movement near the treeline," Preet added. "Multiple males on foot."

Karen sat up, counting the shadowy figures converging on one of the parked cars.

Through the darkness, they made out several men

gathering round a vehicle, their attention focused on activities within.

"Well," Jade muttered, "looks like someone's getting an audience. Half a dozen blokes, todgers out, having a cheap wank and a free BJ if they're lucky."

"Christ," Dan's voice crackled over the radio. "Is this what we signed up for?"

"Told you it'd be educational," Ty replied.

"That's our cue," Karen said. "All units move in. Block the exits first."

Police vehicles surged forward, their headlights blazing to life. The sudden illumination triggered chaos. Car doors flew open as people scrambled to escape, several still adjusting clothing. The men by the rocking car scattered like startled pigeons.

Officers emerged from their vehicles, torches cutting through the darkness. Most suspects froze, caught in the beams of light. A few tried running but found their paths blocked by positioned units.

"Police! Stay where you are!" Ty shouted.

Karen stepped out, projecting authority. "Everyone stay calm. We need your help with an ongoing murder investigation, and while you're here in a compromising situation, we'll have to take your details and statements."

The next hour passed in a blur of documentation and interviews. Some people cooperated, faces burning with shame. Others grew belligerent, demanding legal representation. Through it all, Karen's team stuck to their plan, though she caught occasional smirks and raised eyebrows.

"Got one who knew Reeves," Ty called out. "Regular visitor, apparently."

Karen moved to join him. A middle-aged man in an expensive suit sat in his car, his composure at odds with the situation. His wedding ring glinted in the torch beam.

"Tell DCI Heath what you told me," Ty prompted.

The man cleared his throat. "Mark came here often. Always parked in that far corner, away from the main group. Preferred to keep his distance but close enough to see the action, and when he thought it safe, would come over."

"Did you notice anyone paying particular attention to him?" Karen asked. "Anyone who seemed out of place?"

"Last week, there was someone different. Kept to the shadows, never approached anyone. Just stood there for hours, staring towards Mark's usual spot."

Karen exchanged glances with Ty. Their killer had studied their victim's habits, learning his patterns before striking.

"Can you describe this person?"

The man shook his head. "Too dark. But they lingered. Not in a panic or rush, if you get my drift. Made a few regulars nervous."

"Did they interact with anyone?"

"No. That's what stood out. Most new people here, they're obviously excited, nervous, and a bit hesitant to join in. This one just observed from the trees over there," he said, pointing to a treeline. "Made me nervous to be honest."

Karen pressed for more details, but the man's knowledge was limited. Still, it confirmed their theory the killer had conducted surveillance before acting.

Preet approached with another witness. "This gentleman says he saw Reeves here three nights before his death. Claims he wasn't alone."

The new witness, a nervous man in his thirties, kept glancing over his shoulder as he spoke. "Mark met someone. A man. They talked for a while, had a kiss, then drove off together. When he came back alone an hour later, Mark seemed upset."

"Could you identify this man?" Karen asked.

"No, but he was tall. White, athletic build. Maybe thirty to forty."

By two a.m, they'd processed everyone at the scene. Multiple arrests for public indecency, but more importantly, several witnesses who'd seen Mark Reeves in the weeks before his death.

"Well," Jade said as they prepared to leave, "that was an education."

"Could have done without some of those mental images," Dan added, shuddering. "The couple in the red Focus..."

"Don't," Ty cut him off. "I'm trying to forget."

Karen gathered her team for a final briefing. Despite the operation's unusual nature, they'd gathered valuable intelligence. The killer's preparation phase was coming into sharper focus.

"Good work tonight," she told them. "Write up your reports while everything's fresh. We'll review all statements in the morning."

The team dispersed to their vehicles, their typical banter returning now the job was done. Karen lingered, scanning the car park one last time. Somewhere in the darkness, a killer may have stood, planning their act of revenge.

"Ready?" Jade asked from the car.

Karen nodded and slid behind the wheel. The night had provided new leads but also raised fresh questions. Who was the mysterious observer? What had upset Reeves during his meeting with the unknown man?

14

THE KILLER STOOD in the stairwell of the multi-storey car park, his dark clothing blending into the evening gloom. His focus remained fixed on the second-floor windows of the apartment block opposite. Through the lit windows, James Morton moved from room to room, oblivious to the eyes tracking his movements.

A light drizzle misted the air, but the killer's position kept him dry as he documented Morton's evening routine. Phone in hand, Morton paced his living room while eating a takeaway. At eight, he settled on his sofa for an hour of television before his nightly shower.

The routine never varied. Morton lived his life by precise patterns. A creature of habit whose predictability made him vulnerable. The killer had spent weeks learning, building a detailed picture of Morton's existence. Every visitor, every departure and arrival had been noted and timed.

The street remained quiet, broken only by the occasional footsteps of a passing pedestrian. A young couple strolled past, absorbed in conversation, close enough for the killer to hear every word. They never glanced up. No one ever did.

The past weeks had revealed Morton's secrets. Late-night visits to prostitutes. The visits to schools and playgrounds, slowing his pace as he watched through the railings. The courts couldn't stop him, but justice wouldn't be denied.

His patience paid off as Morton's bathroom light flicked on right on schedule. Steam fogged the window. Morton's evening shower, always between nine and nine thirty. The killer checked his equipment one last time: cable ties, bleach, spare phone to record. Everything ready.

He left and crossed the empty street and buzzed Morton's neighbours' apartments until someone answered.

"Amazon delivery," he said, keeping his voice pleasant. The door lock clicked open.

The killer climbed to the second floor, his footsteps silent on the carpeted stairs. He positioned himself beside Morton's door, listening to the shower running inside.

Five minutes passed before the water shut off. He knocked on the door. Waited for a few seconds. Knocked again. Another three before footsteps approached. Timing was everything. Too early, and Morton might raise the alarm. Too late, and he risked other residents discovering his presence.

Morton opened his door, hair still damp, wearing a T-shirt and joggers. The killer shoved him backwards into the apartment. Morton stumbled, protesting, eyes wide with shock. Before he could shout, the killer's fist connected with his solar plexus. Morton doubled over, gasping.

The killer kicked the door shut and followed up with a

flurry of punches before dragging a dazed Morton towards the living room and heaving him up on a dining chair, zip-tying his hands behind the back of the chair. Morton struggled to catch his breath as the killer secured his ankles to the chair legs. The ties pulled tight enough to cut into flesh. Pain focused the mind, made confession easier.

"Please," Morton wheezed. "Take whatever you want."

The killer turned up the television volume until the sound filled the room. He pulled out his phone and held it up to Morton's face. The screen's light cast a bright glow across Morton's features, highlighting the fear in his eyes.

"Scream or shout for help and I'll slit your throat right now and gut your innards and lay them on the floor for your neighbours to find. Understood?"

He gulped before nodding, his eyes misting over.

"James Morton. Former teacher. Convicted sex offender." The killer hissed. "Multiple allegations. Only one conviction thanks to legal technicalities."

Morton's face drained of colour. "That was years ago. I served my time."

"Time?" The killer's hand shot out, gripping Morton's jaw. "Your victims serve a life sentence of trauma while you walked free after eighteen months."

"I... I'm reformed. In therapy. Following all court orders."

The killer's backhand snapped Morton's head sideways. Blood trickled from his split lip, dripping on to his T-shirt. Each red spot marked another lie, another attempt to evade responsibility.

"Confess. Tell the truth about all of them. Every victim whose accusations got buried in paperwork and legal loopholes."

Morton shook his head, tears streaming down his face.

The killer produced a bottle of bleach and unscrewed the cap. The sharp chemical smell cut through the room. Morton's eyes fixed on the bottle, understanding dawning in their depths.

"Confess, or I pour this down your throat."

"You're insane. I won't..."

The killer pinched Morton's nose shut and waited. When Morton gasped for air, he poured a small amount of bleach into his open mouth. Morton gagged and choked, the liquid spilling down his chin. The chemical stench filled the air as Morton's body convulsed against the restraints.

"Ready to confess?"

Morton nodded frantically. The killer released his nose and started recording, knowing time wasn't on his side before the bleach took effect.

Through sobs and retches, Morton detailed his crimes. Students he'd groomed. Evidence he'd destroyed. The witnesses pressured into silence. The killer recorded every word, every admission of guilt the courts had never heard. Each confession added weight to the justice being delivered.

When the confession ended, the killer put down his phone as Morton threw up. His face red, sweating, and contorted in pain. He gripped Morton's hair, yanking his head back. The terror in Morton's eyes spoke of true understanding, not of death, but of judgement.

"This is justice," he said, and poured the remaining bleach down Morton's throat.

Morton struggled against his bonds as the chemicals burned through his system. His screams disappeared beneath the television's volume. The killer stepped back and let the poison do its work. Morton sprayed vomit over the carpet, and his throat gurgled. His face twisted in pain as the bleach scorched the inside of his mouth. He tossed his head from side to side. This death, like the others, served a greater purpose. Each execution balanced the scales that corrupt courts had tilted.

Minutes passed. Morton's struggles weakened. His skin turned grey, foam flecking his lips as the chemicals destroyed him from within. A final shudder ran through his body before he slumped forward in the chair.

The killer dropped the empty bleach bottle. His second act of justice complete, he left Morton's apartment and descended the stairs. The night air felt clean after the chemical stench of death. He walked away from the building, already planning his next target. The list of those who had avoided due punishment remained long.

15

Karen's phone pierced the darkness. She fumbled for it, squinting at the screen. Detective Superintendent Kelly's name glowed back at her. She let out a heavy sigh, knowing a call at this time of night meant bad news.

"Another body," Kelly said without preamble. "Apartment block off Gillygate. Details coming your way."

Karen swung her legs out of bed, careful not to wake Zac. "On my way."

The city streets lay empty as Karen drove towards the address. Red and blue lights strobed against brick buildings, marking her destination. Three police cars, a white SOCO van, and an ambulance crowded the kerb.

PC Roberts stood at the cordon, logbook in hand. Karen signed in and pulled booties over her shoes before ducking under the tape. The stairwell echoed with voices and footsteps as she climbed to the second floor.

The acrid stench hit her before she reached the landing. Ammonia fumes burned her nose and eyes. She retrieved a face mask from the scene guard stationed outside the flat.

Bel met her in the doorway, voice muffled behind her own mask. "Neighbour found him. Door was open when she left for her early morning shift at work."

Karen entered the flat. SOCOs in white suits moved through the rooms, photographing and bagging evidence. Music drifted from the television, filling the space with artificial cheer that jarred against the grim scene.

James Morton sat slumped in a dining chair, arms bound behind his back. His head lolled forward at an unnatural angle, chin pressed against his chest. Blood and chemicals soaked his grey T-shirt, creating dark patterns that spread across the fabric. The acrid smell grew stronger as Karen approached.

Morton's bare feet pressed flat against the floor, suggesting he'd been conscious and struggling when restrained. Deep ligature marks scored his ankles where cable ties cut into flesh. Blood had congealed in dark pools beneath the chair.

The worst damage centred on his face. Chemical burns created a macabre mask, the skin red and blistered around his mouth and nose. His lips appeared swollen and distorted, split in several places. Clear fluid mixed with blood had dried on his chin and neck. His eyes remained half open, bloodshot and bulging.

"Jesus," she muttered. "What do we know about him?" Karen asked, fighting the urge to step back from the horrific sight.

"James Morton, forty-five. Released from prison eight months ago. Sex offender with multiple allegations, but only one conviction due to legal technicalities."

Karen circled the body, noting every detail. Bruising on Morton's face and arms suggested a beating before death. The cable ties had cut deep furrows into his wrists, evidence of his final struggles.

The dining chair stood in the centre of the living room, surrounded by spattered chemicals and blood. Nothing else appeared disturbed. No signs of robbery or random violence. The killer had come with a specific purpose.

"Cause of death?" Karen asked, though the evidence seemed clear.

"Chemical burns to mouth and throat. Looks like he was forced to drink bleach." Bel gestured to an empty bottle on the floor. "Found this under the table. Industrial strength."

A box of cleaning supplies sat in the kitchen, suggesting the killer brought their own chemicals rather than using what was available. The level of planning chilled Karen's blood.

"Time of death?"

"Izzy was here earlier and based on body temperature and rigor, estimated between ten and midnight."

Karen reached for her phone and dialled Ed who was covering the red-eye shift. "I need everything on James Morton. Focus on his conviction and the cases that didn't make it to court."

She hung up and turned back to the scene. A SOCO held up a mobile phone in an evidence bag. Karen's stomach tightened. "Another confession?"

Bel nodded. "Same type of burner phone. Found on the floor near the body."

Karen studied the flat. The living room showed signs of a normal evening. Takeaway containers on the coffee table, cushions in a heap on the sofa, and the remote control placed beside the TV guide. Morton's phone and wallet lay untouched on the kitchen counter. No drawers pulled open, no ransacked cupboards.

"The neighbour?"

"Mrs June Wallis from next door. She's with family liaison now. Says she heard the TV but thought nothing of it. Volume's often loud late at night."

"The killer used it to mask any noise." Karen moved to examine the front door. No damage to the lock or frame. "Forced entry?"

"None. Mrs Wallis mentioned residents buzzed people in often. Delivery drivers, takeaways."

The implications sank in. The killer had gained entry through deception, counted on Morton or another resident to create an opportunity.

A crime scene photographer documented the body from multiple angles. Flash bounced off the chemical residue coating Morton's chin and neck, highlighting the gruesome details of his last moments. The clicks of the camera punctuated the TV's endless chatter.

"Two victims in a few days," Bel said.

"Both forced to confess before dying." Karen pulled off her mask and stepped into the hallway's clearer air.

"Reeves killed someone while high. Morton was a sex offender. Very different crimes."

"Both murders show a lot of planning and balls!"

"And he leaves phones to make sure we find their confessions, so he doesn't want to hide his crimes." Bel made notes in her book. "He wants us to know why they were chosen."

The sound of footsteps drew their attention. Bart Lynch approached, tablet in hand. "No prints on the cable ties or bottle. Killer wore gloves. But we found trace evidence on the victim's clothes. Might give us something to work with."

"Good. Now prioritise the phone. I want that confession analysed against the first one."

"Already flagged it for voice comparison." Bart tapped his tablet.

Karen nodded and turned back to Bel. "Get uniform going door to door. Someone must have seen or heard something beyond the TV. I didn't see any CCTV covering the main door?"

Bel shook her head.

Karen read a text from Ed about Morton's basic history. "Our victim had multiple allegations against him, but most cases fell apart before trial. Legal technicalities, witness intimidation, lack of evidence."

"Just like Reeves, gaming the system to avoid proper punishment."

"And paying the price now." Karen went back to study Morton's body as SOCOs prepared it for removal. The chemical burns told a story of terrible cruelty. Forced to drink bleach while conscious, experiencing every moment of agony. The killer wanted his victims to suffer before death.

As uniformed officers knocked on neighbouring doors, an unsettling truth sat with Karen. Somewhere in York, a vigilante studied their next target and planned their next execution. Two confessions marked only the beginning.

Karen stepped aside as the mortuary team arrived with a body bag. They worked with care to transfer Morton from the chair, his limbs stiff with rigor mortis.

The investigation moved forward, but time pressed against them. Two murders in three days. How long before he chose his next target? How many others might be on his list? These were the questions that swam around her mind as Karen paced around the communal hallway.

16

The flat's oppressive atmosphere lingered as Karen and Bart reviewed the crime scene. Evidence all round them told its story. The stench of chemicals burned their nostrils despite the face masks.

"Chemical residue pattern suggests a struggle," Bart said, gesturing to the splatter marks around Morton's chair. "See these scuff marks on the floor? The chair shifted during the violent struggle."

"Any traces in the bathroom?" Karen asked, bending to examine the marks.

"Shower still damp when officers arrived. Morton may have answered the door not long after taking a shower." Bart consulted his tablet. "Door frame shows no sign of forced entry. No damage to the lock mechanism."

"So, he let the killer in willingly?"

"Or buzzed them up thinking they were a delivery. Common tactic in these blocks." Bart pointed to more evidence markers. "Found partial boot prints in the hallway."

Jade entered the flat, her steps slow as she took in the

grim scene. The contrast to her reaction at Reeves' murder marked clear progress in her recovery. She pulled on latex gloves, ready to join the search.

"Morning," she said, voice muffled behind her mask. "Uniform's finished the initial door knock. No one heard anything over the TV."

"Let's go through everything," Karen instructed. "Bedroom first. We need to understand who Morton really was."

The team spread out, examining Morton's possessions. His wardrobe revealed bland clothing. Cheap suits, casual wear, nothing remarkable. The bedside drawer contained condoms and lubricant.

"Got something," Bel called from the bathroom. She held up a packet of pills. "Viagra. Multiple prescriptions from different doctors. He's been shopping around for medication."

Karen nodded. "Bag it. Check the dates and see if this started after his release."

In the living room, Jade knelt by the sofa. "There's a laptop down here." She retrieved the device from between cushions and fired it up. "No password protection. Sloppy for someone with his history."

The screen lit up, revealing Morton's digital world. Jade clicked through folders, her expression hardening. "Found his stash. Hidden folder of images of children and drugged women. The timestamps are recent. Sick bastard never stopped."

Karen peered over Jade's shoulder at the disturbing content. "Document everything. We'll need the tech team to do a full analysis. The abuse continued right until his death."

"His email's full of spam," Jade continued, scrolling through messages. "Lots of offers for hook-ups, escort services. Multiple dating site subscriptions under different names."

"The killer knew who they were targeting," Bel said, examining a stack of letters on the kitchen counter. "Morton never stopped his behaviour; he got better at hiding it. Bills here show regular payments to adult websites."

Karen stepped back, processing the evidence.

"His browsing history's disgusting," Jade said from the laptop. "Forums dedicated to sharing exploitation photos. Private chat rooms. He was part of a network."

"Bag the laptop," Karen instructed. "Tech team can pull his browsing history, contacts, anything that might connect to other offenders. Those chat logs could reveal more potential victims."

A SOCO team member approached with another evidence bag. "Found these behind the radiator in the bedroom. USB drives."

"More evidence of his sick habits? He's done us a favour," she whispered.

They examined every drawer and cupboard until the search was complete. SOCOs photographed each piece of evidence before sealing it in bags. The morning light crept through windows, casting a fresh perspective across Morton's final confession scene.

"His phone records might be interesting," Bel said. "If he was meeting people from these websites..."

"Agreed. Get those records requested." Karen pulled off her gloves. "Jade, fancy breakfast? I need a break from this."

"God, yes." Jade stood, stretching cramped muscles. "That greasy spoon round the corner? My stomach's thinking my throat's been cut."

"Perfect." Karen turned to Bel. "You okay managing here?"

"No problem. Door-to-door enquiries extended to neighbouring buildings. I'll text if anything crucial comes up."

They left the oppressive atmosphere of Morton's flat, grateful for the fresh air after hours surrounded by death and degradation. The café beckoned with promises of coffee and normality. A steady stream of customers filled the small space, their ordinary morning routines a stark contrast to the horror scene Karen and Jade left.

"You handled that well," Karen said as they claimed a corner table. "Better than Reeves."

Jade shrugged. "Different this time. Easier to focus on the evidence when the victim's a predator. The children in those photos... and the women." She clenched her fists. "Part of me thinks the killer did the justice system a favour."

"I understand the feeling. But we can't choose which murders to solve based on the victim's character."

Their coffee arrived, strong enough to strip paint. Karen wrapped her hands around the mug, letting its warmth seep into tired muscles. The café bustled with morning commuters, their mundane conversations a welcome distraction.

"The killer's escalating," Jade said, stirring sugar into her coffee. "A couple of days between victims. More violence in the second murder. Reeves was clinical. Gas, quick death. Morton suffered."

"But the same method. Forced confession, recorded

evidence, public display of justice. The killer wanted us to know why they chose these victims."

The waitress brought their food. A full English for Karen, scrambled eggs on toast for Jade.

"Morton never stopped offending," Jade said between bites. "Just became more careful after prison. Those images were recent."

"The killer knew that. Chose him because the system failed to stop him." Karen speared a sausage. "Question is how many others are on their list?"

"Could be dozens. Plenty of criminals game the system, get off on technicalities. Defence lawyers find loopholes, evidence gets thrown out..."

A text from Bel informed Karen about a neighbour hearing voices in the hallway around nine thirty. Nothing concrete, but timeline confirmation helped.

They finished eating, the greasy breakfast providing fuel for the day ahead.

"Back to the station?" Jade asked, dropping payment on the table.

Karen nodded.

Outside, the city continued its normal rhythm, unaware of the vigilante justice being delivered in its shadows.

The return to the scene gave them time to plan the next steps.

"The team are going to have a tough time going through that laptop," Jade said as she fished out her car keys from her pocket. "Those images..."

"Agreed." Karen said as she split off and headed to her car.

17

Karen and a few others stood round Ed's computer. At her request, he connected it to the large wall-mounted screen, expanding the horror they were about to witness. An air of silence spread among those gathered as they prepared to analyse the second phone confession.

Ed raised the volume. "Ready?" he asked as he looked over his shoulder, his finger hovered over the play button.

Karen's stomach knotted. The first confession had been brutal enough. This one promised to be worse. She glanced at her team, positioned around the room in chairs or leaning against desks. They braced themselves for what was to come.

The screen flickered to life. Morton's face filled the frame, blood trickling from his split lip. His eyes bulged with terror as the killer's voice cut through: "Tell them everything. Every victim. Every accusation you buried."

Claire balled her hands into her lap. Preet fidgeted in her seat, crossing her arms tight across her chest. The tension in the room rose as Morton's ordeal began.

The video shook as Morton convulsed, vomit spewing

down his chin. His skin turned an angry red, blisters forming around his mouth from the chemical burns. Karen forced herself to keep looking as Morton's body twisted against the cable ties binding him to the chair.

"Please," Morton choked out between retches. "It hurts. I need help." Blood mixed with spittle sprayed from his lips. The bleach had begun its work, corroding his flesh from the inside.

The killer remained silent. Morton's head snapped back as another wave of pain tore through him. Tears cut tracks through the blood and chemicals coating his face. His fingers clawed at the chair, nails splintering against the wood.

"The children," he gasped. His neck tendons strained against his skin. "I... I groomed a few of them. Made them trust me. Then..." His words dissolved into muffled screams that filled the room.

Several officers turned away. Dan pressed his fist against his mouth, face pale. Claire stared at her shoes, unable to look at the screen. Ty pushed back from his desk, shaking his head in disgust.

The confession continued in excruciating detail. Morton thrashed in the chair. Pain tearing through his body. Blood vessels burst in his eyes, turning them crimson. Between bouts of vomiting and desperate gasps for air, he detailed his methods, his victims, the evidence he'd destroyed. The killer kept him talking through the agony, demanding names and dates.

"Ages," the killer pressed. "Tell them how young."

Morton sobbed, mucus and blood streaming from his nose. His confession grew more depraved with each revelation. The team's horror mounted as the extent of his crimes became clear.

Ed's hand trembled on the mouse as Morton

described grooming techniques, the trust he'd betrayed, the lives he'd destroyed. The fluorescent lights buzzed overhead, a low counterpoint to Morton's suffering.

The chemical burns spread across Morton's face as he spoke, his features distorting. His lips swelled, cracking open in new places. Each breath seemed to cause fresh agony.

Bel turned and walked to the window, her back rigid. Two junior officers left the room. The ones who remained sat frozen, unable to look away from Morton's punishment.

Karen studied every detail, noting the killer's methods, the way he prolonged Morton's pain while ensuring the man remained conscious enough to confess.

When the video ended, silence gripped the room. The blank screen reflected their stunned faces. Karen's jaw tightened. "Same voice as the Reeves confession."

"Identical," Ed confirmed, his voice hoarse. He cleared his throat. "The tech team's running it through voice analysis software, but I'd say the speech patterns match."

"The level of violence increased," Bel said, still facing the window. "Reeves died from gas inhalation. Morton suffered."

"Different crimes, different punishments," Ty suggested, rubbing his face. "The killer switched up the method."

Karen paced the length of the incident room, her footsteps loud in the quiet room. "Or they're escalating. Testing different techniques. Learning what causes maximum pain."

"Both victims received sentences the killer considered too lenient," Claire said, colour returning to her cheeks. "But Morton's crimes were mainly sexual offences against children. That could explain the heightened brutality."

Ed retrieved the file. "Speaking of Morton's crimes, his record's extensive. Multiple allegations spanning fifteen years against both women and children. But only one conviction stuck."

"Why?" Karen asked, gathering her thoughts.

"Legal technicalities mostly. Evidence ruled inadmissible. Witness statements thrown out on procedural grounds. His legal representative knew the system's weak points."

Preet leaned forward, her arms still crossed. "What about the successful conviction?"

"2019," Ed read. "Guilty plea to possessing indecent images. Eighteen months, released after twelve for good behaviour."

"That's it?" Dan's voice cracked. "After all those allegations?"

"The system failed," Claire said. "Like with Reeves."

Karen faced her shaken team. "Both victims served time at HMP Bullingdon. Their prison terms coincided for five months."

Officers shifted in their seats, the brutality of Morton's confession still hanging in the air. The wall-mounted screen loomed dark behind them, a reminder of what they'd seen.

"Could be where our killer spotted them," Ty suggested, his voice steadier. "A prison officer or someone else with access to inmate records?"

"Or someone connected to their victims," Bel said, turning from the window. "A relative seeking revenge?"

Karen disagreed. "The methodology's too sophisticated. This killer understands evidence procedures, knows how to avoid leaving traces. That suggests professional knowledge."

"What about Morton's victims?" Claire asked. "Could a parent learn the skills needed for revenge?"

"No. I haven't found anything yet to connect a parent of one of Morton's vics to Reeves," Ed said.

Silence fell over the team. The echo of Morton's screams lingered in their minds.

"That prison connection is significant," Karen remarked. "But is it the source or a coincidence? Check employee records from when both men were inside. Focus on officers, medical staff, anyone with regular inmate contact."

"What about other prisoners?" Preet asked, her voice stronger. "Someone inside might have arranged these hits."

"Good point. Pull the complete lists. Check for anyone who overlapped with both victims."

Karen moved to the evidence board, studying the crime scene photos. The images felt distant from the raw horror they'd just witnessed. "This killer's patient. He waited."

"And technical knowledge," Bel added, rejoining the group. "The suicide hood and chemical burns, they understood the effects of their methods."

"Military training?" Ty suggested. "Or medical background?"

"Could be. Or law enforcement." Karen's stomach tightened at the possibility. "Someone who knows how evidence gets processed, how investigations work."

Ed's computer pinged with a new email, making several officers jump. "Bart's got preliminary results from Morton's laptop. Multiple chat logs, dating site profiles. He was active in paedophile forums right up until his death."

"The killer knew that," Claire said, colour draining

from her face again. "Chose him because prison didn't change him."

"And made him confess it all on camera." Karen's jaw clenched.

The team worked in subdued silence, processing the evidence.

"One more thing," Karen said. "Check death records from Bullingdon during their time inside. Any suspicious incidents, unexplained fatalities. If our killer started there, he might have practised first."

Karen remained at the evidence board, examining the photos of both crime scenes. Morton's confession had revealed their killer's evolution. Each execution delivered a message not just to the victim, but to the system that had failed to punish them properly. Morton's tortured confession would haunt them all.

Karen's phone buzzed, a message from Kelly requesting an update. A double homicide within seven days demanded answers. Karen had a hunch that it wouldn't be long before he surfaced again.

18

Karen settled at her desk, staring at the case notes spread out before she picked up her mobile and dialled Zac's number.

"Hi," he said, clearing his throat.

"Hi. Sorry I left without saying goodbye. Didn't want to wake you."

"Everything alright?"

"Another body. Had to get to the scene." Karen leaned back in her chair, closing her eyes. "How are you feeling?"

"Better. Summer's in her bedroom. We might go for a walk later, get a bit of fresh air."

"That's good." Karen's lips curved into a smile. "The exercise will do you both good." She paused, hearing rustling on his end. "What are you doing?"

"Making tea. I woke not long after you left. The bed felt empty. Didn't feel right."

Karen's chest tightened at his words. "Sorry. I miss you. I would have loved another cuddle like the other night. Loved it."

"So did I." She heard the smile in his voice. "First time in ages it felt... normal."

"Normal is good." Karen twisted a strand of hair round her finger.

The kettle clicked off in the background. "Though I noticed you checking on me twice not long after we turned off the light."

"Old habits."

"I know. But I'm getting better, Karen. You don't need to worry so much."

She wanted to believe him. God, she wanted to. She wanted to let the relief settle in, to trust that things were finally moving forward. That he really was getting better. But the fear clung to her, sharp and stubborn, refusing to loosen its grip.

Because what if he wasn't?

What if this was just another fragile moment of calm before the next storm?

She couldn't expect things to be normal again. Not yet. Not when the memory of him crumbling was still so fresh, so real. She was supposed to be strong for him, to trust in his progress, but some nights she lay awake wondering if she could.

"I'll always worry about you. It's part of the job description."

Zac chuckled. "Which job? Detective or fiancée?"

"Both." Karen smiled, remembering how peaceful he'd looked sleeping beside her. "Have you thought more about the return-to-work meeting?"

"Yep. Part of me can't wait to get back, but another part..."

"Is scared?"

"Yeah." He sighed. "Bit nervous."

"Then we'll deal with it together. No pressure, no rush."

"The thing is," Zac continued, "I need to work. Need to feel useful again. Sitting here all day... it's not me. I want my life back."

"I know. And you're getting there."

"Maybe. Some days it feels like one step forward, two steps back."

A cupboard door closed in the background. "Summer's been amazing through all this. Patient, understanding. She deserves better than a dad who not so long ago couldn't leave the house without having a panic attack."

"Hey, don't do that to yourself. Summer understands. She's lucky to have you."

"I love you, you know that?"

"I know. Love you too." Karen's other phone rang. "Listen, I need to take this. Talk later?"

"Of course. Stay safe."

"Always do. Give Summer a hug from me."

Karen ended the call and picked up her desk phone. "DCI Heath."

"Karen, it's Callum from forensics. I have those initial results you wanted."

She grabbed a pen. "Go on."

"The killer's consistent. Used identical burner phones at both scenes. No prints, no DNA on the phones or the duct tape from the Reeves murder. This person understands evidence procedures."

Karen's stomach tightened. "What about CCTV?"

"Working on enhancing the footage from Reeves' house, but it's grainy. Might take a few days to get anything useful."

"Anything from Morton's street?"

"Officers found three cameras on neighbouring properties. We're collecting the footage now, but given how the killer's operated so far..."

"He'll have avoided them," Karen finished. She pinched the bridge of her nose. "What about the bleach bottle?"

"Strong bleach, available anywhere. No prints on that either. The molecular analysis shows it's a common brand stocked by most supermarkets."

"Keep me updated on the CCTV enhancement. Even a partial image could help."

"Will do. Oh, and Karen? The voice analysis from both confession recordings confirms it's the same person. Male, likely mid-thirties to forties, slight Manchester accent."

"Good work. I'll wait for the complete report."

After hanging up, Karen stood and moved to her window. Outside, officers hurried between buildings, going about their duties. The killer moved among them like a ghost, leaving no trace, staying off camera, understanding exactly how evidence could betray him.

Her phone buzzed with a text from Bel: *Officers finished the door to door near Morton's. No one saw or heard anything unusual.*

Karen typed back: *Keep pushing. Someone must have noticed something.*

The door opened and Jade entered, carrying two cups of coffee. She placed one on Karen's desk. "Thought you could use this."

"Thanks." Karen took a sip. "Callum just called. No physical evidence, again."

"Nothing?"

"Not a sausage." Karen returned to her desk. "Too forensic savvy."

"Former or serving officer?" Jade asked.

"Could be, but I hope not. The Met had a string of

bad apples in recent years and the public and political fallout was horrendous. I don't want that grief here. Might be someone who works in the justice system." Karen pulled up the crime scene photos on her computer. "Look how the scenes are staged. Everything's deliberate."

Jade studied the images. "The confessions feel staged too. Like performances."

"Exactly. Our killer wants to send a message." Karen clicked through the photos. "But they're careful. No mistakes, no traces, and no witnesses."

"What about the bleach bottle?"

Karen relayed Callum's feedback to her and then shut down the photo viewer. "We need another angle. The physical evidence isn't getting us anywhere."

"The connection has to be through the courts or prisons," Jade said. "Both victims went through the system. Police, courts, prison. Could be a bent screw? Or someone who saw both trials?"

"True. But hundreds of people work in the courts. Judges, lawyers, clerks, admin staff." Karen took another sip of coffee. "And that's not counting everyone who attends trials."

"We could cross-reference court staff with people who have law enforcement or forensic training?"

Karen nodded. "Good thinking. Make yourself useful, use my laptop. Start with anyone who had access to both cases."

"He won't stop?"

Karen pulled her shoulders back as she stood to straighten her back. "The super wants an update by the end of the day. What do I tell her? We've nothing solid."

"We've got theories," Jade replied. "The killer's connection to the justice system, their knowledge of police procedures, the pattern of targeting people who escaped proper punishment."

"Theories won't catch them before they kill again."

A few minutes later, Jade blew out a whistling sound. "Different investigating teams dealt with each case, and I can't find any officers who were on both, so it may not be a serving officer. I'll run a search for former officers and SOCOs who've left or retired."

Karen leaned in. "And the courts?"

"I'll get everything I can on court employees."

"Focus on those who were there long enough to deal with both cases."

"Will do. Let me head back to my desk. Staring at the laptop screens gives me a crappy headache."

"Let me know if you find anything," Karen said as Jade disappeared through the door.

19

Night shadows cloaked the residential street as the killer stood behind a parked van. The darkness provided perfect cover while he noted his target's movements through the lit windows of the semi-detached house opposite. His black tracksuit blended well with his surroundings as he maintained his vigil.

Alan Phillips moved between rooms. Through the bay window, the killer noted Phillips' habits. Takeaway dinner eaten straight from the container while he scrolled through his phone, television on in the background, his wife folding clothes from the airer, or ironing in the front room. The evening routine never varied. After dinner, Phillips would head off for a brisk walk round the block before his nightly shower at nine.

The killer remained still, pressing deeper into the shadows as a young couple passed by, their footsteps echoing off the pavement. They never glanced towards his hiding spot. People remained blind to threats lurking in plain sight.

Weeks of surveillance had revealed Phillips' secrets.

The falsified safety reports. The corners cut to save money, leading to deaths he'd evaded responsibility through legal manoeuvring. Two workers were dead because of his negligence, yet he'd never faced proper justice. The courts had failed, but that failure ended tonight.

The killer checked his equipment: cable ties, chemicals, spare phone for recording.

The need for justice burned stronger now. Reeves and Morton had faced their punishment and confessed their crimes before death. But there were more he needed to hunt down. His list grew longer as he uncovered fresh targets. Each one vetted, researched, and their guilt confirmed before his brand of sentencing.

A car turned on to the street, headlights sweeping past his position. The killer pressed against the side of the van, becoming one with the shadows until the vehicle passed.

Through the window, Phillips settled into his armchair with a pile of papers. The sight fuelled the killer's rage, but he held it in check. Timing mattered more than emotion. Justice required patience, planning, perfect execution.

Phillips rose from his chair and removed his reading glasses. Right on schedule.

A fox crept along the garden wall, its eyes reflecting the street light. The killer remained motionless as it passed, his presence undetected by even the sharpest senses. Nature's predators recognised one of their own, a fellow hunter stalking prey in the night.

Few suspected the truth that lived behind his careful mask of normality. His colleagues saw only what he allowed them to see, blind to his true purpose.

Phillips' living room light clicked off, plunging the ground floor into darkness, with just the first-floor landing and front bedroom lights on. The killer remained in position, counting the minutes until his target left the house.

Rain fell, fat drops pattering against leaves overhead. The killer ignored the growing dampness. The need for action pulled at him, but the time wasn't right. Phillips opened his front door, held his hand out to gauge the rain, then headed back in again. He'd broken his routine.

Shit.

He wasn't going to take his walk. The killer pursed his lips and clenched his teeth.

Thunder rumbled in the distance as he melted away from his observation post. Another night of surveillance was complete, another piece added to his understanding of his target's patterns. Soon Phillips would face justice for his crimes, but not tonight. The moment had to be perfect, the stage set for his final confession.

The murderer went through the back gardens, avoiding the lit streets. His dark clothing shed water like a second skin as the rain intensified. Each step moved him closer to home. To the ordinary life that served as his cover. Tomorrow he would return to his watching place and continue building his case against Phillips.

Justice demanded patience. But when the moment came, Phillips would burn like those he had condemned through his negligence. The thought brought a smile to the killer's face as he disappeared into the rainy night.

Let Phillips enjoy his comfortable routine for now. Soon enough, he would face true judgement for his crimes. The killer's smile widened as he pictured the scene to come.

20

THE FRONT DOOR closed behind Karen with a soft click. She'd barely taken two steps into the hallway when Zac emerged from the kitchen, crossing the space between them in long strides. His arms encircled her, pulling her close.

"Missed you," he murmured into her hair.

Karen melted into his embrace, tension seeping from her shoulders. These moments meant everything. Proof of his recovery and of their growing strength as a couple. A few months ago, such casual affection had been unthinkable.

"How was your day?" she asked, reluctant to break the contact.

"Good. Made dinner with Summer. She's upstairs doing homework."

Karen pulled back and studied his face. His eyes held a spark. "You seem better today."

"I am." He kissed her forehead. "Go see Summer. She asked about you earlier."

Karen climbed the stairs, her footsteps muffled by the thick carpet. Summer's bedroom door stood ajar, music drifting into the hallway. She knocked gently on the door frame.

Summer sat cross-legged on her bed, textbooks spread around her. She glanced up, a smile lighting her face. "Karen! Dad said you might be late tonight."

"Wrapped up earlier than expected. Wanted to come home and see my favourite lady." Karen winked and sat on the bed. "How's the homework going?"

"Almost done." Summer closed her biology textbook. "Can I talk to you about something?"

"Of course."

Summer twisted a strand of hair around her finger. "There's this boy in sixth form. Tom. He's in my chemistry class."

Karen kept her expression neutral despite the flutter of protective concern in her chest. "Tell me about him."

"He's nice. Smart. Makes me laugh." Summer's cheeks flushed pink. "He asked if I wanted to go for a milkshake this weekend."

"And do you want to?"

"Yes. No. I don't know." Summer flopped back against her pillows and scrunched her eyes. "I've never had a boyfriend before."

Karen shifted closer. "That's nothing to be embarrassed about."

"But everyone else has. Lucy's been with her boyfriend for six months. Sarah's had three different ones." Summer's voice dropped to a whisper. "They've all... you know."

"Had sex?"

Summer nodded, not meeting Karen's eyes.

"Listen to me." Karen waited until Summer looked up. "What other people do doesn't matter. Those decisions are yours to make, when you're ready. No one else gets a say."

"But what if Tom expects..."

"Then he's not the right person," Karen said. "Anyone worth your time will respect your boundaries and wishes."

Summer pulled her knees to her chest. "Lucy said boys lose interest if you make them wait."

"That's rubbish. The right person will care about you, not just what you can give them." Karen paused, choosing her next words. "Your body belongs to you. Don't let anyone pressure you into something you're not comfortable with."

"But everyone's talking about it. In the common room and at lunch. It's like that's all anyone cares about." Summer rested her chin on her knees. "Sarah keeps going on about how amazing it is, and Lucy posts all these couple photos. I feel like I'm falling behind."

Karen shifted to face her stepdaughter and stroked her hair. "Can I tell you something? When I was your age, I felt the same pressure. My best friend started dating early, and it felt like a race I was losing."

"What did you do?"

"To keep up, I rushed into a relationship I wasn't prepared for. Hardly a relationship, if you ask me. I was so scared. It was a mistake." Karen's voice softened. "Looking back, I wish I'd trusted my instincts instead of listening to everyone else."

Summer lifted her head. "Did it end badly?"

"Not badly, just... empty. We had nothing in common

except wanting to say we had a boyfriend or girlfriend. That's not enough to build anything real on."

"I really like Tom," Summer admitted. "But the thought of doing anything physical makes my stomach knot up."

"That's your body telling you you're not ready. It's okay to like someone and still want to take things slow." Karen smiled. "Real relationships aren't like social media posts or common room gossip. They're about connection, trust, feeling safe with each other."

"But what do I say if he brings it up?"

"Be honest. Tell him you want to get to know him better first. If you'd like to go for a milkshake or to see a film, go, but set your boundaries early. A decent person will respect that."

Summer picked at a loose thread on her jumper. "What if he tells everyone I'm frigid or something?"

"Then he shows his true character and he's someone who doesn't deserve your time or trust." Karen reached out to still Summer's fidgeting hands. "Anyone who tries to shame you for knowing your own mind isn't worth a second thought."

"I don't want to be the only virgin in year twelve."

"I promise that you're not. Those who talk the most about sex are often the ones with the least experience. And there's nothing wrong with waiting until you're ready. Whether that's next month, next year, or years from now."

Summer's shoulders relaxed. "How will I know when I am ready?"

"You'll feel excited rather than anxious. Those butterflies in your stomach will feel nice, not scary. You'll trust the person. Most importantly, you'll want to do it for yourself, not because anyone else expects it." Karen squeezed her hand. "There's no rush, Summer. I made some

A Matter Of Justice

horrible mistakes growing up, and they left me confused about love and relationships as an adult. Then your dad came along, and I knew he was the right one for me. These years aren't a race to tick off experiences. They're for figuring out who you are and what you want."

"Dad would die if he knew we were talking about this."

Karen laughed. "Your dad wants you to be safe and happy. But I understand some things are easier to discuss with me. I'm always here if you need to talk."

"Even about embarrassing stuff?"

"Especially about embarrassing stuff. Better to ask questions than stumble around in the dark." Karen's tone turned serious. "Promise me something? If you decide to have sex, whenever that might be, come talk to me first. Not because I'll judge, but because I want you to have the information you need to stay safe."

Summer nodded, her face flushed but relieved. "Thanks, Karen. For not treating me like a kid."

"You're growing up. Part of my job is helping you navigate that." Karen stood, stretching. "For now, focus on getting to know Tom. See if you enjoy spending time together. Everything else can wait until you're ready."

"What if I'm never ready?"

"Then that's fine too. There's no rulebook for this stuff, Summer. Just be true to yourself."

They talked for another hour about relationships, pressure from peers, and the importance of self-respect. By the time Karen headed downstairs, Summer seemed more settled, and more confident in her right to move at her own pace.

LATER THAT NIGHT, Karen propped herself against the headboard, cradling a mug of camomile tea. Zac climbed in beside her, his warmth a comfort after the long day.

"Summer okay?" he asked.

"She will be. Just needed some reassurance."

Zac nodded, understanding in his eyes. "Thank you for being there for her."

Karen set her mug on the bedside table. "What do you think of her dating?"

"Terrified," he admitted. "She'll always be my little girl. And being a dad, in my mind, no boy is good enough for her. But I trust her judgement. And she has you to talk to about things she might not want to discuss with her dad."

Karen squeezed his hand, then reached for the case file she'd brought up. "Speaking of trust issues, help me work through something?"

"The vigilante case?"

She opened the file, spreading photos across the duvet. "Two victims. Violence increasing with each victim."

Zac studied the images. "Reeves killed someone while high, so the killer used gas. Morton drugged and raped women, and groomed children, so he suffered a painful death by chemicals."

Karen nodded. "But why these two in particular? There must be dozens of similar cases."

"What connects them?"

"At the same prison for a short while. They both went through York Crown Court. They received lenient sentences."

Zac's brow furrowed. "Someone with intimate knowledge of the cases, then. Access to records, understanding of evidence procedures."

"My thoughts too." Karen gathered the photos. "The killer's methodical, leaves no trace evidence. He knows what we look for at crime scenes."

"Could be police, legal staff, court employee..." Zac trailed off, mind working through possibilities.

They bounced theories back and forth until Karen's eyes grew heavy. As she filed away the photos, Zac's arm slipped around her waist.

"I've missed this," he murmured. "Working cases together."

Karen turned into his embrace, hoping he'd say that. As much as it was great to chew over the case, she wanted to ignite something in Zac, hoping it would reassure him about returning to work. "Soon. Kelly's setting up your return-to-work meeting."

His arms tightened. "I know. Just need to prove I can handle it."

"You can. You just did," she said, pointing at the file. "You're stronger than you think."

They settled into comfortable silence, the case file forgotten on the floor. Karen felt Zac's breathing even out as he drifted towards sleep. These quiet moments meant everything. Proof that despite trauma, despite fear, they were getting closer to how Karen remembered them.

21

A FLOCK of birds drifted across the sky and past Kelly's office windows. Karen noticed the cup of coffee on her boss's desk sat untouched, steam no longer rising from its surface. She sensed Kelly's tension as her superior reviewed the case notes in front of her.

"Two murders in under a week," Kelly said, each word measured. "I need to know where we are with this."

Karen shifted in her chair. "The lab confirms it's the same killer based on voice analysis from the phones. Slight Manc twang. Nothing in terms of DNA evidence or witnesses. Partial boot print from scene two."

Kelly's eyes narrowed. "The press will be all over this. What else do we have?"

"Still checking CCTV for both locations. Nothing yet."

"And the second victim?"

"James Morton. Convicted sex offender. Plenty of allegations. Only one conviction because of technicalities." Karen paused. "There's a pattern emerging. Both victims escaped proper justice because of legal loopholes."

Kelly's phone rang. She glanced at the screen and held

up a finger for Karen to wait. "Yes, sir... I understand... No, I appreciate the sensitivity..." Kelly sighed. "DCI Heath is handling the investigation... Yes, I'll keep you informed."

The call ended and Kelly's shoulders dropped. "That was the chief constable. The press has picked up on the vigilante angle. He wants this wrapped up fast."

"We're making progress," Karen said. "The killer's knowledge of approach points to someone with inside knowledge of the system. We've officers reviewing court records, looking for connections between the cases."

"What about the dogging site where you found Reeves?"

"Regulars identified him as a frequent visitor. DNA analysis from his car shows multiple sexual partners, both male and female. But none match any profiles in the system."

Kelly drummed her fingers on the desk. "The chief's worried about the fallout. These victims might deserve punishment, but we can't allow a vigilante to execute people on our streets."

Karen thought of the crime scenes, the second more brutal than the first. "The killer's not finished. He's got a mission, a sense of righteous purpose. He wants confessions before he punishes them."

"Then find him before he strikes again." Kelly glanced at Karen. "What's your next move?"

"I'm going to call HMP Bullingdon. Both Morton and Reeves served time there. Their sentences had a five-month overlap. Might give us a connection we've missed."

"Give me regular updates. Senior management pressure will only increase the longer this goes on."

Karen stood and gathered her notes. At the door, she paused. "The killer's methodical, patient. He studies his victims before striking. That level of planning takes time."

"Then use it against him," Kelly said. "Find out how he's choosing his targets. Break his pattern before he claims another victim."

Karen returned to her office and settled behind her desk. She pulled up the prison's contact details on her computer screen. Time to find out if anyone at Bullingdon could shed light on the connection between her victims.

Karen dialled the governor's direct line, drumming her fingers on her desk while she waited. The line clicked after three rings.

"Governor Sharma speaking."

"Morning. DCI Karen Heath, York Police. Thank you for taking my call. I'm heading up a double murder investigation. I need to discuss our victims, two former inmates. Mark Reeves and James Morton."

A pause on the line. "Ah. Yes. I heard about their deaths on the news. Nasty business."

"We're trying to establish any connections between them during their time at Bullingdon. Their sentences overlapped by five months."

Papers rustled in the background. "Give me a moment to pull up their files... Right. Reeves kept his head down, stuck to the rules. Model prisoner in fact. Worked in the kitchen, attended rehabilitation programmes, never caused trouble."

"And Morton?"

"Different story altogether. Multiple disciplinary reports. We caught him with a mobile phone hidden in his cell. The phone contained pornographic images, some involving minors. Lost all his privileges for three months after that."

Karen made notes as Sharma spoke. "Did they interact? Share any common associates?"

"Nothing in the records suggests direct contact. They were housed in different wings. Morton stayed in D wing with the sex offenders. Reeves was in B wing with general population."

"Any staff members who worked with both of them?"

"I've worked hard to improve access to education and support services," Sharma said. "Each wing has dedicated officers and support workers. There's minimal crossover for security reasons."

"Could someone have arranged hits on them from inside?"

"Possible. Prison gangs are an ongoing issue, though we've made progress in breaking them up. Rivalry between wings happens, but..." Sharma broke off mid-sentence as she answered her phone. "Hold on, there's an incident..." she whispered. "What? When?"

Karen heard muffled voices in the background.

"I'm sorry, DCI Heath. I need to deal with this. One of our inmates just threw a bowl of urine and faeces over Officer Morley."

Karen pulled a face. "Sounds delightful."

"All part of the job," Sharma replied, her tone grim. "Though I doubt Morley sees it that way right now. Look, I'll get my staff to compile detailed reports on both Reeves and Morton. Any contact, shared activities, visitors, and everything we have. I hope it helps. Where should I send it?"

Karen provided her email. "One more thing. Did either of them experience problems with other inmates? Threats, fights, anything that stood out?"

"Reeves kept to himself. Morton was a target for obvious reasons, but we managed any threats. The segregation unit protected him when needed." A commotion erupted in the background. "I must go. Morley is raging."

"Of course. Thank you."

The line went dead. Karen sat back, processing the conversation. The contrast between the victims' prison behaviour matched their histories. Reeves playing the model prisoner while hiding his true nature, Morton unable to control his deviant impulses even behind bars.

She opened a new case note on her computer and typed up the key points. The lack of direct connection during their incarceration suggested the killer's motivation went beyond prison grudges. Someone was selecting targets based on their crimes and sentences, not their behaviour inside.

Her phone vibrated. A text from Jade: *Court records show both cases went through York Crown Court. Checking dates now.*

Karen replied: *Good work. Look for anyone involved in both trials. Court staff, lawyers, and press. Then check public attendees.*

With just an hour to spare until she needed to attend the PM on Morton, she returned to her notes, adding questions that needed answers. How did the killer choose these specific victims from all the criminals who'd escaped proper justice? What made Reeves and Morton special? And most importantly, who would be next?

22

The killer crouched in the shadows beside Phillips' car, positioned at the end of the narrow driveway that ran along the side of the semi-detached house. The location offered perfect concealment. Hidden from street view by the building's bulk, yet mere feet from the side door Phillips used each evening for his walk.

Through the living room windows, Phillips moved between rooms, following his usual evening routine. The past weeks had revealed his habits. Tonight, the killer would break that pattern forever.

A fox darted across the garden, sniffing the air before disappearing through a gap in the fence. Until it passed, the killer remained still.

Right on schedule, the living room light clicked off. As footsteps approached the side door, the killer's muscles tensed. Phillips emerged, pulling the door closed behind him. The moment his key turned in the lock, the killer struck.

"Make a sound and your wife dies first." The killer

pressed the knife against Phillips' kidney. "Then your daughters."

Phillips froze.

"Your car keys. Where are they?"

"In... in my coat pocket."

"Get them. Any noise, any signal to the neighbours, and your family suffers. Understand?"

Phillips nodded, sweat beading on his neck despite the evening chill. He retrieved the keys with shaking hands, metal jingling in the darkness.

"Get in. I'll tell you where to go."

The killer guided Phillips to the car with small prods of the knife. Hidden from the street and neighbouring windows, the driveway's position provided perfect cover as he forced Phillips into the vehicle and slid in behind.

"Head to the old printing factory on the industrial estate. Drive. No sudden moves."

Phillips pulled away from the house, his knuckles white clutching the steering wheel. "Please. I have money. Whatever you want."

"Shut up and drive."

The streets grew darker as they left the residential area behind. The killer had chosen the location with care. The abandoned factory where Phillips' negligence had killed two workers. Poetic justice in making it the scene of his own death.

The factory loomed ahead, its broken windows gaping like empty eye sockets. Phillips parked where instructed, in the loading bay hidden from the road.

"Out. Inside."

The killer marched Phillips through the derelict building to a room he'd prepared earlier. A metal chair surrounded by drums of industrial chemicals. The acrid smell filled the space.

"Sit."

Phillips sank into the chair. The killer bound him at speed with cable ties securing wrists to the arms, ankles to the legs. No chance of escape.

"Alan Phillips. Former health and safety manager. Your negligence killed Thomas Reid and Michael Cooper." The killer held up his phone, recording light blinking. "Confess."

"I don't know what you're talking about..."

The first punch snapped Phillips' head back. Blood sprayed from his nose, speckling his shirt.

"The falsified inspection reports. Cutting corners to save money. Because of your greed, you destroyed lives. Confess."

"It wasn't my fault! The company had targets."

Another punch silenced him. The killer continued the beating, landing one blow after another, targeting areas of largest pain with minimum risk of unconsciousness. Phillips needed to remain awake for his confession.

"The truth. Now."

Phillips spat blood. "Yes. I falsified the reports. The filters in the ventilation system needed replacing, but it would have cost too much. I marked it as satisfactory."

"And the workers?"

"The chemical fumes built up. They didn't have proper breathing equipment because I signed off on substandard masks." Blood streaked Phillips' face. "They died because of me. Because I cared more about bonuses than safety."

The killer nodded, satisfaction burning in his chest. "Final justice arrives."

He moved to the chemical drums, opening the valves he'd prepared. The liquid splashed across Phillips' legs, soaking into his clothes. The smell of industrial solvents filled the air.

"Please... my family..."

"Will learn the truth about your crimes." The killer stepped back, retrieving a lighter from his pocket. "Like the families of those you killed learned the truth about their loved ones' deaths."

The flame caught. Phillips screamed as fire engulfed him, the chemicals speeding up the blaze. He thrashed for a mere few seconds before his body stilled. The smell of burning flesh filled the air, a sickly sweet, acrid, and nauseating smell.

The confession phone clattered to the floor as the killer retreated, leaving his third act of justice to burn itself out.

Outside, the killer took in a deep lungful of clean night air. His first wave of targets was complete. Three criminals who had escaped proper punishment now faced true justice. But he wasn't finished with his work.

He pulled out a notebook, reviewing the names he'd compiled through his research. More corrupt scum awaited judgement. Further confessions needed recording. More justice demanded delivery.

As his latest victim died in a ball of flames, the factory's windows glowed orange. Smiling, the killer walked away. The fire would destroy evidence, but Phillips' confession would survive on the phone.

The next phase would begin soon. But first, there was one late addition to this round that needed to be dealt with.

23

As Karen entered, a chill cut through her clothes. Izzy stood to one side of the cadaver, her red hair tucked beneath a surgical cap.

Morton lay on the steel table, his torso split open in a Y incision. His internal organs sat in steel trays, each removed and weighed as part of Izzy's examination. The pathologist's gloved hands prodded and poked as she documented her findings.

"Hi, Izzy, sorry I'm late. I got distracted while reviewing case notes. Looks like you're well advanced in the examination," Karen said, joining her at the table and peering over the cadaver before taking a step back to scan the body from head to toe. Morton's body bore the marks of his attack, both inside and out. The sight made her grimace.

"You're always late, Karen. I'm not sure why you bother. Easier to send one of the others and let them go through the torture of watching my masterful work." Izzy raised a brow and laughed.

"The chemical burns are extensive," Izzy said,

gesturing Karen closer. "The bleach caused severe damage to his mouth and upper respiratory tract."

Karen pulled on a paper mask and stepped forward. The brutality of Morton's final moments became clear as Izzy pointed out the injuries. His tongue appeared swollen and discoloured, the tissue damaged beyond recognition.

"The burns extend down his oesophagus into his stomach." Izzy lifted a section of tissue. "See this discolouration? The bleach stripped away the protective lining, exposing raw flesh beneath. The mucosal membrane is destroyed."

She pointed to areas where the tissue was black. "These darker regions show full thickness burns. The chemicals ate through multiple layers of tissue. Each swallow would have caused excruciating pain."

Karen's stomach tightened as Izzy continued her examination. The pathologist picked up a clipboard and made additional notes.

"His lungs tell the worst story." Izzy moved to the organ tray. "The chemical fumes triggered an intense inflammatory response. His airways closed up while the bleach burned through the tissue. Look at the bronchi."

She indicated the damaged lung tissue. "These dark patches show where the chemicals ate into the membrane. The alveoli, these tiny air sacs, are destroyed. His lungs filled with fluid as the tissue broke down."

Izzy separated sections of lung tissue. "The haemorrhaging here suggests he fought for every breath. Each inhalation drew more chemical fumes deeper into his respiratory system. The damage was catastrophic."

"Time frame?" Karen asked.

"Minutes, not seconds. The bleach caused immediate burning upon contact, but death came from oxygen deprivation as his airways swelled shut." Izzy set down her clipboard. "He remained conscious through most of it. The pain would have been unimaginable."

She moved to examine Morton's throat. "The larynx shows severe chemical burns. Damage to his vocal cords, caused by the burns, explains the distorted voice in the confession video. Speaking would have caused intense pain."

The examination continued as Izzy documented each injury. Bruising patterns across Morton's torso revealed the beating he'd received before the chemical attack. His bound wrists showed deep ligature marks where he'd fought against the restraints.

"Defensive wounds on his forearms." Izzy pointed to dark bruises. "The killer subdued him before administering the bleach."

She lifted Morton's arm. "The ligature marks tell us he struggled violently. See these deeper cuts? Went through skin and muscle, right down to the fascia."

Karen studied the injuries, her mind recoiling from the implications. Each detail painted a picture of prolonged suffering.

"The beating came first?" she asked.

"Yes. Blunt force trauma to his torso, but nothing fatal. The killer wanted him alive and aware for the chemical burns." Izzy picked up a fresh pair of gloves. "The tissue damage tells us he swallowed multiple mouthfuls of bleach. At least three distinct waves of chemical exposure."

"Forced to drink it?"

"The pattern of burns suggests the killer poured it into his mouth. Some spilled down his chin. See these external burns on his neck and chest? But most went down his throat. The oesophageal burns show distinct layers of damage."

Izzy raised a part of Morton's stomach tissue. "His stomach lining shows severe compromise. The bleach resulted in internal bleeding. These perforations show places where the chemicals damaged the stomach wall."

She shifted to inspect Morton's face. The chemical burns had transformed his features into a grotesque mask. His lips appeared black and cracked, while his tongue protruded between damaged teeth.

"The fumes damaged his nasal passages." Izzy showed the extent of the injury. "When he fought for breath, he inhaled more chemicals. Each breath brought fresh agony until his airways closed. The tissue damage extends into his nasal cavity and sinuses."

Karen forced herself to focus on the technical details rather than the horror of such a death. "Christ. This is savage. Cause of death was oxygen starvation you say?"

"Yes. Caused by asphyxiation because of acute chemical burns and subsequent inflammatory response." Izzy began closing the Y incision. "The bleach caused massive tissue damage, but the lack of oxygen killed him. His lungs couldn't process air through the swelling and damage."

She pointed to Morton's fingernails. "He broke several nails trying to escape the restraints. The pain must have been severe enough to make him fight past the point of self-injury."

Izzy stayed focused as she worked, but Karen noted the tension in her shoulders.

Izzy continued. "The bleach concentration was high enough to cause a huge amount of pain without immediate death. They wanted him to suffer. The chemical burns to his mouth prevented him from spitting out the bleach, forcing him to swallow or inhale it."

Karen nodded, processing the revelations. Their killer

had evolved from Reeves' swift execution to this prolonged torture.

"I'll send over a full report later today," Izzy said, finishing her sutures. "Including detailed analysis of the chemical composition and tissue damage. The toxicology results might tell us more about the specific type of bleach used."

"Thanks." Karen took a step back. The technical examination had revealed the savage nature of Morton's final moments. As she left the mortuary, the doors swung shut behind her, but the image of Morton's chemical burns remained. Their killer's appetite for justice had evolved into a hunger for pain.

24

Karen tapped her fingers on the counter at Costa Coffee, the queue in front of her moving at a glacial pace. After what she'd witnessed that morning, the normality of people ordering their flat whites and discussing weekend plans felt surreal. She needed caffeine to push through the rest of this day.

The shop buzzed with the hiss of the coffee machine, clatter of cups, and the chatter of customers. A barista called out customers' names with the enthusiasm of a sloth commentating at a snail racing championship, while another arranged pastries in the glass case. Karen shifted her weight, checking her phone. No updates from the team yet.

"Cappuccino, please," she said when she reached the front. The barista nodded as Karen stepped to the side, scanning the packed tables. A young couple shared a pastry, heads bent close together. Two women in business suits typed on laptops. A mother tried to clean her toddler's sticky hands. An elderly man sat alone by the window, completing a crossword puzzle in between sips of his drink.

None of them knew about the horrors she'd seen, the evil that walked among them. Any of them could be next. The thought made her stomach clench.

Her phone buzzed in her pocket, Dan's name lighting up the screen.

"Karen, I think we have another one," he said with a sigh. "Industrial estate off Huntington Road. Fire service is already here."

Karen's stomach dropped. "Fuck. No." Her tone drew looks of surprise from other customers.

"Looks like our guy."

"I'm on my way." She caught the barista's eye. "Sorry, but I need that coffee now. Emergency." She held up her warrant card, guilt mixing with urgency as she tapped her credit card on the reader. The young barista's eyes widened as she hurried to finish preparing Karen's order.

THE STREETS BLURRED past as she followed Waze's directions, her coffee cooling in the cupholder. Not another one. Not so soon. She pulled up to the industrial estate ten minutes later, greeted by a wall of blue lights. Two fire engines, multiple police cars, and an ambulance created a cordon around a derelict warehouse. A crowd had gathered at the edges, phones held high to capture whatever glimpse they could.

Ed and Preet waited for her at the tape line. Their expressions confirmed her worst fears.

"What have we got?" she asked, ducking under the cordon.

"Male victim inside," Ed said. "Fire service responded

to reports of smoke about an hour ago. They found..." He shook his head. "It's bad, Karen. Black as a lump of coal."

"Chemical agents present," Preet added. "Some kind of industrial cleaner or solvent. Fire service says we can't go in until they clear it."

"ID?"

"Nothing yet," Ed replied.

Karen paced the perimeter, frustration building with each step. The crowd of onlookers had doubled, cars slowing as they passed. Their killer wanted this. Attention, spectacle, and fear. A news van pulled up at the edge of the cordon, a reporter already speaking into a microphone.

"Get uniform to push that lot back," Karen said, nodding at the growing audience. "And someone needs to control this traffic before we have an accident."

The next hour dragged by in a haze of tension as emergency vehicles came and went. With daylight fading fast, and the possibility they could be here for hours, Karen stood with Ed and Preet as the hazmat team made repeated trips in and out of the building.

"Any witnesses?" she asked.

Ed shook his head. "Security guard spotted smoke coming from the building during his rounds. Called it in straight away. Place has been empty for months, scheduled for demolition next year."

"Perfect spot for our killer," Preet said. "Isolated, abandoned. No CCTV coverage."

"He's planned this," Karen said. "Like all the others. Nothing left to chance."

Finally, after what felt like days, the fire service gave them clearance to enter. Karen pulled on a Tyvek protective suit and mask, the material crinkling with each movement. The mask pressed tight against her face, limiting her peripheral vision. Ed and Preet suited up beside her, their normal features rendered alien by the protective gear.

"Remember," the station commander warned, "the air's still toxic in there. Keep your masks on. If you feel light-headed or nauseous, get out at once. We've set up a decontamination station by the entrance."

They entered through a side door, boots crunching on broken glass. The warehouse was a vast space filled with shadows and decay. Graffiti in garish colours covered the walls, the only brightness in the gloom. Their torch beams cut through the darkness, revealing remnants of the building's industrial past. Rusted machinery, empty pallets, and debris scattered across the floor. Water dripped somewhere in the darkness, the sound echoing off concrete walls.

The odour hit Karen first, even through the mask. A burning, chemical stench that made her eyes water. Under it lay something worse, the unmistakable smell of burnt flesh. Her empty stomach clenched. The air hung heavy with particles she didn't want to think about.

Their footsteps echoed as they moved deeper into the building. Paint peeled from the walls in long strips.

They rounded a corner and Karen stopped short. The body lay sprawled in the centre of a cleared space, surrounded by empty chemical containers. The victim's clothes had melted into his skin, his features unrecognisable. A phone on the floor nearby. The killer had arranged the scene, a theatre of death for them to find.

"He's escalating," Ed said. "Getting bolder."

Karen nodded, unable to look away from the scene. Their killer had taken his time here, drawn out the suffering. He wanted them to see his work, to understand his message.

"Full scene documentation," she ordered. "Every detail, every container, every mark on these walls. Did he choose this location for a reason?"

The forensic team moved in and set up arc lights in the darkness. Each burst of light revealed fresh horrors. The way the chemicals and fire had eaten through clothing and flesh. The victim's last position of agony, and deliberate arrangement of evidence.

"The fire service used foam to neutralise the chemicals," Preet said. "It's compromised the scene."

Karen bit back a curse. Their killer would have known this would happen. Known the emergency response would disturb his stage-managing. Perhaps that was part of his plan too. Hide all traces of him.

She moved closer to the bucket containing the phone, careful not to disturb anything. Like the others, it would contain a confession. It would show their killer's twisted sense of justice at work. The phone's screen reflected their torch beams, a dark mirror in the gloom.

Three victims in less than a week. Each death more brutal than the one before it. The killer was speeding up, growing more confident with each success.

She looked at the body one last time before stepping back. They needed to stop him before he struck again. But first, they had to wait for the evidence. Wait for the phone to be processed. Wait for forensics to complete their sweep.

The waiting was always the hardest part. But today, standing in this tomb of concrete and chemicals, Karen feared they were running out of time.

25

Karen left home at five, the streets dark and empty. She'd written a note for Zac and Summer before creeping downstairs in the predawn silence. The investigation pulled at her, drawing her back to the factory before the rest of her team arrived.

She stopped at an all-night café near the industrial estate. The fluorescent lights cast harsh shadows across vacant tables while a tired server poured coffee into a paper cup. Karen squinted as she ordered toast, though her appetite had vanished. The café radio played old hits to an empty room.

Wrapping her hands around the coffee, Karen let the warmth seep into her fingers as she stared at the untouched toast. It sat on a chipped plate, butter pooling in the ridges, curling at the edges where the heat had already faded. She took a single bite, chewing without tasting, her mind already pulling ahead to what waited at the factory.

By the time she left, the sun was creeping above the horizon. Police tape fluttered in the morning breeze, marking off the crumbling building from the world of ordinary commerce. Delivery vans rumbled past on their morning rounds, drivers averting their eyes from the crime scene.

Officers remained at the scene, keeping the curious at bay. The whole building was an active crime scene and SOCO would be back today. Karen ducked under the cordon. The sound of her steps resounded through the deserted halls as she made her way to the kill room. The chair remained fixed to the concrete floor, surrounded by scorched circles where chemical drums had stood. Daylight filtered through broken windows, illuminating patches of soot and melted plastic.

The smell lingered, but not as potently as last night. The stench combined a mix of melted plastics, chemicals, and burnt flesh. Not pleasant, but tolerable. Karen pinched her nose as her brow furrowed.

The killer had staged everything. But for whose benefit? Did it give him a kick?

Karen circled the chair, reconstructing the scene. His victim would have seen the chemical drums. Known what they meant. The killer had forced him to face the consequences of his actions before death. The thought of his terror, his final moments of agony, pressed against her mind.

Her phone buzzed, shattering the morgue-like quiet.

"Karen, it's Jade. We have a name. The victim's Alan Phillips, former health and safety manager. SOCO retrieved a name from a partially burned Lloyd's debit card recovered from the victim's clothing. His wife reported him missing last night when he didn't return from his evening walk. But then she realised his car was missing too. We found it three streets away from the scene. Ed and Bel are heading there now. I've put a FLO on standby."

Karen thought it through before replying. "Did he agree to meet the killer here? Or was he driven here under duress? We need his phone records to see if the killer contacted him, and full forensics on the car. Let's check for CCTV on the routes he may have followed to get here."

"I'll get the ball rolling right away."

Karen pressed the phone closer. "What else?"

"Here's where things get interesting. I ran his name through the system. He was charged with negligence in a previous role. Two workers died from chemical exposure after he falsified safety reports at his former place of employment. Want to know what's even more interesting?"

"Go on, before I wet myself. The suspense is killing me, pardon the pun," Karen teased.

"He worked for a printing firm based at the same location where he was murdered."

Karen's eyes widened as she turned on the spot and looked at her surroundings.

"You're kidding. Shit. So the killer brought him back to where it all began for Phillips."

"Sounds about right," Jade replied. "And there's more. All three of our cases were heard at York Crown Court. Phillips avoided prison. Prosecution fell apart when a key witness changed their testimony."

"Made Phillips die where his actions killed others."

"Ed and Bel are heading to speak with his wife now." Papers rustled on Jade's end. "There's more. The witness who changed their story? Killed himself six months after the trial. Left a note saying he couldn't live with the guilt of letting Phillips escape justice."

Karen absorbed this new information. "He's doing

what the courts couldn't. This was always his plan. Reeves, Morton, Phillips. He studied them all. Knew their routines, their vulnerabilities. When to get them."

The morning light strengthened, revealing more details. Scuff marks on the floor showed where Phillips had fought against his restraints.

"The court connection's significant," Karen said. "Check employee records. Someone who worked there during all three cases. Someone with access to files, transcripts, witness statements. It might not be a member of the public as I first thought, as they wouldn't have access to all the details including where the victims lived."

"Already started. Going back five years, cross-referencing anyone with police or military training."

Karen finished the call and stood in the empty factory. The killer had turned this abandoned space into a death chamber. She took a final look at the chair before leaving. Three victims connected through the same court. Three confessions extracted through escalating violence.

The next victim was out there somewhere. Karen had to find them before it was too late.

She walked the perimeter of the factory, noting the broken fence panels and overgrown loading bays that had allowed the killer private access. The building's neglect had served his purpose, providing isolation for his work.

A uniformed officer approached, notebook in hand. "Ma'am, found something round the back. Tyre tracks in the mud, fresh ones."

Karen followed him to a narrow access road behind the factory. Two distinct sets of tracks cut through wet earth. One entering, one leaving. The killer had driven here, or left, or both.

"Can you put in a call to forensics? We need impressions made of these tracks," she instructed.

Her phone vibrated with a message from Kelly: *Press conference at eleven. Need update on investigation.*

The media would descend soon, hungry for details about the vigilante killer stalking York's streets. They'd spin stories of justice and vengeance, turn victims into villains, paint the killer as some dark hero.

Karen checked her watch. Time to head back, brief her team, prepare for the circus ahead. But first, she needed another coffee. The morning's discoveries had drained the effectiveness of her earlier cup.

As she walked to her car, a news van pulled into the estate. More would follow. The killer's audience grew with each death, his message spreading through headlines and broadcasts.

26

ED STOPPED OUTSIDE THE PHILLIPS' home. Neither detective moved to get out of the car.

"This part never gets easier," Bel said, staring at the neat front garden and splash of green grass.

"Good. The day it does get easier is the day we need new jobs." Ed clutched his warrant card. "Her whole world's about to change."

They walked up the drive in silence, their footsteps heavy with the burden of the news they carried. A milk bottle sat by the front door, untouched since morning delivery. Ed rang the bell.

Adrienne Phillips opened on the second knock, her eyes red rimmed from a sleepless night of worry.

"Mrs Phillips? I'm Detective Constable Ed Hyde, and this is Detective Constable Belinda Webb." Ed held up his warrant card. "May we come in?"

Adrienne gripped the door frame. "Have you found Alan?"

"Is there somewhere we can sit down?"

The woman nodded as her concerned gaze darted between the officers.

She led them into a living room filled with family photos. Ed noted the pictures spanning decades. Holidays, graduations, and celebrations frozen in time. Adrienne dropped into an armchair, twisting her wedding ring.

"Mrs Phillips." Ed kept his voice gentle. "We found your husband's car near the old industrial estate off Huntington Road."

"But he's okay?" Her voice cracked. "He just broke down or…"

"I'm very sorry." Ed paused, allowing the weight of his words to settle. "We discovered a body at the old printing factory. Items in his possession, including his wallet, suggest it was Alan."

"No." Adrienne shook her head. "No, there's a mistake," her voice rose with each word. "You need to check again. It can't be him. He's probably in hospital or something?"

Bel moved to sit beside her, maintaining a respectful distance. "We understand this is difficult, Mrs Phillips. We do believe it's Alan."

"But… how?" The colour drained from Adrienne's face as reality crashed in. Her hands shook, and she pressed them against her mouth to stifle a sob. "Oh, God. Oh, God, no."

"I know this is overwhelming," Ed said. "We'll assign a family liaison officer to support you. They'll help guide you through everything that needs to happen next."

Tears spilled down Adrienne's cheeks. Her shoulders shook with suppressed grief. "I knew something was wrong when he didn't come home. But then the car was gone too. I wasn't sure why. He never breaks his routine. Never."

Bel offered her a tissue box from the coffee table. "Take your time, Mrs Phillips. We're in no rush."

Several minutes passed as Adrienne struggled to compose herself. Her fingers shredded the tissue in her hands. "The police came last night when I reported him and the car missing. They said to wait, that he might have gone to the pub, but Alan doesn't drink. He hasn't touched alcohol since the trial."

"Can you tell us about yesterday evening?" Ed asked. "Did Alan seem different? Worried about anything?"

"He was normal. Watched television after dinner, said he needed fresh air." She pressed her hands against her eyes. "His walk helps him think, he said. Every night at eight, the same route. So I'm not sure why he took the car. I tried his mobile when he didn't come back, but it went straight to voicemail."

"Had he mentioned any concerns of late?" Bel's tone remained soft. "Problems at work or with anyone?"

Adrienne lowered her hands, revealing eyes filled with fresh tears. "Two weeks ago, I saw someone watching our house. A man in dark clothes, standing across the street. I thought he was trying to break into cars."

"Did you report this?" Ed pulled out his notebook.

"No. When I looked again, he disappeared. But I saw him three more times that week." Her voice caught. "I should have called the police. Should have done something."

"This man," Bel pressed gently. "Did Alan know about him?"

"I told him, but he said I was being paranoid." Fresh tears fell. "After the trial, Alan changed. Those deaths at the factory haunted him, but he kept saying the company forced him to cut corners. Corporate pressure made him do it."

Ed exchanged a glance with Bel. "Did anyone threaten him? Hold grudges about the trial?"

"The victims' families were angry, but that was years ago." Adrienne grabbed another tissue. "Alan insisted he wasn't responsible. Said the system made him follow procedures that put profit over safety. He carried that guilt, even if he wouldn't admit it."

"Did he mention anyone following him? Any strange phone calls or messages?"

"No, nothing." Adrienne's hands trembled as she reached for a framed photo on the side table. She and Alan on holiday, both smiling at the camera. "This was last summer in Cornwall. Our last proper holiday together."

They continued questioning her, balancing their need for information against her growing distress. Each answer built a picture of Alan Phillips. A man who deflected blame while guilt ate at him.

"We'll need to take a formal statement," Bel said. "But that can wait. The family liaison officer will contact you today. They'll help you through the formal identification and other arrangements."

"Do you have family nearby?" Ed asked. "Someone who can stay with you?"

"My sister lives in Acomb. I'll call her. My daughters live further away." Adrienne clutched the photo frame to her chest. "How did he die? Did he suffer?"

"The investigation is ongoing, but he was murdered," Ed said, avoiding details of the brutal death. "We'll keep you informed through the liaison officer. They'll be your contact with us."

"I should have gone with him." Her voice broke. "He

asked me to walk with him, but I wanted to finish the ironing."

"Mrs Phillips, it's not your fault," Bel said as she stood and handed her a business card. "Here are my details. Call if you can think of anything else. Once again, I'm sorry. I know it's difficult, but can we have his toothbrush and comb if he uses one?"

"Why?"

"To run DNA analysis to formally confirm his identity," Ed replied.

"But I can do that if I see him, please," the woman pleaded.

Bel and Ed exchanged a glance.

Ed cleared his throat. "Unfortunately, you won't be able to see the body. He suffered extensive injuries which will make formal identification in person impossible."

Adrienne's eyes widened in shock as her hand shot up to her mouth, and fresh tears fell. She tried to talk, but a piercing wail escaped her lips.

It was another hour before Bel and Ed could leave as they waited for Adrienne's sister to arrive.

Outside, Ed and Bel walked to their car in silence.

"That never gets easier," Bel said as they reached the vehicle.

"It shouldn't." Ed stared at his notebook.

"The surveillance matches Reeves' case. Our killer studied them all."

"Learning their routines, choosing his moment." Ed started the engine. "Phillips kept to strict patterns. Made himself an easy target."

They drove back towards the station, the traffic building around them. The radio crackled with updates about road closures near the factory, reminders of the horror they'd seen.

"She'll find out eventually," Bel said. "About how he died. The press will run with it."

"That's what the FLOs are for. To prepare her, support her through it." Ed turned on to the ring road. "Though how do you prepare someone for news like that?"

The car fell silent as they processed the morning's interview.

27

Karen watched her team sift through court records; their faces lit by computer screens. Papers covered every surface of the SCU as officers created lists of attendees, press contacts, and court staff from hundreds of cases. Empty coffee cups littered the desks, evidence of their long search through dusty files.

The stack of papers on Ed's desk threatened to topple as he added another folder. "Three more cases with similar outcomes. Defence used identical arguments each time."

"Cross-reference everyone present," Karen said. "Look for names that appear multiple times."

Preet rubbed her eyes. "The records go back five years. That's hundreds of people to check."

Ty lifted another box on to his desk. "Court reporters, legal staff, and members of the public. The lists go on."

"Check them all," Karen said. "Every name matters."

Dan yawned as he entered another set of details into his spreadsheet. "The filing system's prehistoric. Half these records need translation from ancient hieroglyphics."

"Keep at it." Karen noted her team's flagging energy. Time for reinforcements.

She picked up her phone and ordered pizzas. Her team needed fuel for the long night ahead. Twenty minutes later, the smell of fresh pizza filled the room as an officer from the front desk arrived with six large boxes. Karen cleared space on the central table, spreading out the feast—pepperoni, margherita, BBQ chicken, plus boxes of wedges and wings.

"Food break," she called.

A cheer broke out as her team abandoned their desks, gathering around the table. The tension lifted as they reached for slices and traded observations about the case. Paper plates appeared from desk drawers as officers claimed their preferred toppings.

"Three murders in a week," Dan said, grabbing a handful of wedges. "He's on a mission."

Ty picked up a slice of pepperoni. "Or desperate. Each death's more violent than the last."

"Focus on the evidence," Karen said. "We'll find the connection."

Claire wiped the sauce from her chin. "The court archives lack organisation. Half the attendance records need updating into an easier to read format."

"Keep pushing," Ed said between bites. "There's a pattern here somewhere."

The team relaxed as they ate, sharing theories between bites. Even Jade managed a smile as she reached for the chicken wings. These moments mattered. Brief respites from the darkness they faced.

"The victim profiles match the killer's sense of justice," Preet said.

Dan grabbed another slice. "But why these three?"

"That's what we need to find out," Karen replied. "What makes these victims special? They may not be in all fairness. They may have been randomly selected from a long list."

Officers passed napkins and shared packets of chilli sauce. The communal meal brought a moment of normality to their grim task. Karen watched her team recharge, knowing they needed this break before diving back into the mountain of files.

Detective Superintendent Kelly strode in. A hush fell over the room.

"The press has the vigilante angle," Kelly said. "The chief constable's office fielded calls all afternoon. We need results."

Karen nodded. "We're reviewing every case file, building lists of..."

"Work faster." Kelly's tone left no room for argument. "Three bodies in public places. The media's calling him the 'Justice Killer'."

After Kelly left, the team returned to their desks. The pizza boxes sat forgotten as they dived back into court records. The moment of levity evaporated under renewed pressure.

Karen stepped into the corridor and called Zac.

"Perfect timing," he said. "Just had visitors from the station. Thompson and Davies stopped by."

"That's great. How did it feel?"

"Good. Normal. We talked shop, caught up on gossip." His voice carried fresh energy. "The evaluation. I think I'm ready."

"I know you are." A reassuring sigh rushed through Karen's chest.

"Summer's been asking about joining the police cadets again."

"What did you say?"

"That we'll discuss it. She's persistent, like her dad."

"She'll make a great copper one day."

"Don't encourage her," Zac laughed. "I'm not ready for that conversation."

"Neither is Michelle," she replied.

Footsteps approached. Karen turned to see Bel rushing towards her, papers clutched in her hand.

"Found something," Bel said. "Robert Shaw. His name appears at nine different trials in the past year. Runs a website about lenient sentences and injustices."

"Zac, I have to go."

"No worries. I'll see you later."

Karen slid her phone into her back pocket. "Tell me more."

"Former military. Vocal critic of the justice system. Posts videos about cases where criminals escape proper punishment. His YouTube channel has over a hundred thousand subscribers."

"Background?"

"Royal Military Police. Multiple tours in Iraq and Afghanistan. Lives in York now. His site documented all three of our victims' cases."

Karen's pulse quickened. "Get me everything. Speak to the MOD and get a copy of his military record, then his current activities and known associates."

"There's more." Bel flipped through her notes. "He attends court often and documents proceedings. Posts detailed breakdowns after concluded cases where defendants received reduced sentences."

"His military training may have helped with the

murders," Karen said. "The surveillance and evidence procedures, the crime scene clean-up."

"He knows the finer details of cases. Knows the system's weak points."

"What about his current location?"

"Lives in a flat near the city centre. We have him on the system. He's received death threats for his activism and reported it to the police. No further action was taken."

Karen considered this new information.

"Want me to have a chat with him?"

"Not yet."

"I'll keep digging into his background."

"Good work." Karen checked her watch. "I want to visit the courts tonight after we finish here. Fresh eyes might spot something we've missed."

Karen watched Bel return to the incident room. Shaw's activities made him a person of interest.

She rejoined her officers. The pizza boxes lay empty, their job done. Her team was recharged and ready to press on.

Files covered every available surface as the team worked through dozens of court records. The task seemed endless, as the evening stretched ahead with officers cross-referencing names, dates, and case details.

Karen moved between desks, checking progress, offering guidance where needed. The pressure from above added urgency to their search, but she wouldn't let it rush their process. Thoroughness mattered more than speed.

The killer had chosen three victims for whatever reason. Understanding his selection process could lead them to his next target if they found the pattern in time.

28

Karen pushed through the heavy glass doors of York Crown Court. Her footsteps echoed off marble floors in the empty entrance hall. The brass wall clock above reception showed seven thirty p.m., long past the departure time for judges, barristers, and clerks.

A security guard perked up at his desk as she approached. She held up her warrant card. "DCI Heath. Here to see Clive Mott."

The guard checked his list. "He's in his office. Third floor. Through the scanner please."

Karen placed her bag on the counter for it to be scanned and walked through the metal detector.

The guard checked the monitor beside him and nodded. "You're good to go. Do you need me to show you the way?"

"Thanks, but I'll find it." She smiled and retrieved her belongings before heading off.

Karen took the stairs, her mind mapping the building's layout. Corridors branched off each landing, leading to courtrooms and administrative spaces. The courthouse operated through a maze of restricted zones, each secured by key card access points.

She found Clive's office tucked away in a back corner. The door stood open, revealing him hunched over paperwork at his desk.

"Mr Mott?"

He glanced up, running a hand through thinning grey hair. "DCI Heath. Your office said you were coming."

"Thanks for staying late." Karen settled into the visitor's chair. "I need employee records for the past five years."

Clive's expression tightened. "That's sensitive information. I can't just hand it over."

"Three people are dead. Each case went through this court." Karen took a seat beside his desk. "We need to check everyone who had access to case details."

"Our staff undergo background checks and security clearance."

"Which is why we need those records." Karen stressed. "Times of employment, roles, access levels, everything. It's part of a wider investigation of the court. We're looking at public and press attendees too."

Clive drummed his fingers on his desk. Through his window, Karen watched a cleaner move between offices emptying bins.

"The staff won't like it," he said.

"Neither will the families of our victims."

He sighed and turned to his computer. "It'll take time to print everything."

"I'll wait and stretch my legs in the corridor. Been sitting all day and my sciatica is playing havoc with my right leg," she lied and stood, wincing for effect.

While Clive worked, Karen wandered the corridors. Key card readers marked doorways to record storage and

IT sections. A standard security system, but one that logged every entry.

She paused at a window overlooking the car park. Court staff came and went each day, carrying files and laptops. Who noticed which cases they accessed? Who tracked what information left the building?

The printer whirred behind her as Clive gathered the records. "Each role has specific access rights," he said as Karen returned. "Clerks can't view restricted files. Admin staff stick to their assigned cases."

"What about supervisors?"

"Limited oversight. Need-to-know basis." He straightened a pile of papers. "But determined people find ways around security."

Karen turned to face him. "Such as?"

"Shoulder surfing while someone enters passwords. Copying files when no one's watching." He shrugged. "We track breaches, but we can't spot everyone."

"Do you keep logs of access attempts? Failed logins, unauthorised entry tries?"

"IT handles that." Clive gathered the printouts. "Forty-seven current employees, plus those who've left since 2019. Contact details, employment dates, assigned duties."

Karen accepted the stack. "I need building entry logs, too. Who comes in early, stays late, works odd hours."

"That's…" Clive hesitated. "That's more complicated. Multiple systems track different areas."

Karen tucked the papers into her bag. "And email me a list of anyone disciplined for security breaches."

Clive nodded but studied her through narrowed eyes. "The staff are good people. Hard workers."

"I'm sure they are." Karen shook Clive's hand and moved towards the door. "But someone's targeting people who passed through these courts."

She left Clive at his desk and retraced her steps through the building. Empty corridors stretched into shadow. Behind locked doors lay thousands of files. Evidence, transcripts, and witness statements. A treasure trove of information for anyone with the right access.

The security guard glanced up as she passed his desk. How many people slipped past each day, badges displayed, access granted? The killer walked these halls, gathered intelligence, chose targets.

The street lights cast pools of light across the courthouse steps as Karen walked to her car. She paused at the top, looking back at the building's solid bulk against the darkening sky. The windows glowed from security lighting within, creating the illusion of life in the empty structure.

Three victims connected through these halls. Public galleries offered perfect vantage points to observe defendants. Court listings provided addresses. Transcripts revealed the failures of justice that marked targets for death.

Karen unlocked her car, sliding into her seat. Her mind circled through possibilities as she started the engine. A member of the public, dedicated to documenting cases? Someone with legitimate access to court records? Both paths led to potential suspects.

She turned on to the main road, the evening traffic thinning as she headed home. The employee records sat on her passenger seat, names waiting to be checked. Each one a potential link.

The radio murmured updates about roadworks and weather forecasts. Karen switched it off, focusing on the case details. Their killer chose victims through the court system but moved like a ghost through crime scenes. The level of planning pointed to someone who was smart and in no hurry to be found.

But that knowledge spread beyond court employees. Police officers, lawyers, and forensic staff. Countless people understood how evidence worked. The court connection narrowed their search yet opened fresh questions.

She pulled into their driveway, smiling at the sight of lights glowing in the windows. Zac waited inside on the eve of his evaluation.

Karen gathered her things. Work could wait until morning. She unlocked the front door, breathing in the scent of cooking that filled the hall.

"Hey," Zac called out.

She found him at the stove, stirring a pan of pasta sauce. The kitchen counter held chopped vegetables and garlic bread warming in the oven.

"You cooked." Karen set her bag down, moving to kiss his cheek.

"Needed to keep busy." Zac's shoulders tensed as he stirred. "The evaluation…"

"Will go fine." Karen squeezed his arm. "You're ready."

"Am I?" He turned to face her.

"Stop, you pussy." Karen took the spoon from his hand and winked. "You've done the work. Built yourself back up. The evaluation's a formality."

Zac nodded but worry creased his features as he chewed on his lip. "Summer asked to come. For support. Bless her."

"What did you tell her?"

"That she's too young, and this is police business." He checked the garlic bread. "She understood. Said she's proud of me."

"We both are." Karen reached past him to reduce the

heat under the sauce. "You've fought through every step of recovery. Faced your fears. That's real strength."

The tension eased from Zac's shoulders as he plated the pasta. They carried their dinner to the table, the case files forgotten in Karen's bag. Tonight was about Zac.

"Tell me about your day," he said, breaking off a piece of garlic bread. "The courthouse visit?"

Karen shook her head. "Not tonight. Tonight's yours."

They ate in silence, knees touching beneath the table. Zac's breathing steadied as the evening passed, his anxiety about the evaluation fading into background noise.

Karen watched him clear their plates, noting the sureness in his movements. The man who'd struggled to leave the house now cooked dinner, cracked jokes, and planned his return to work. Each small victory built towards this moment.

Tomorrow she'd dive back into the investigation. Tonight she'd focus on Zac, on supporting his final steps towards rejoining the force.

29

In Dr Morales' office, Jade sat back in the leather chair, her fingers twisting the tissue in her lap.

"Tell me about your first week back," she asked.

"Three bodies in five days." Jade's voice cracked. "I thought I could handle it. The scenes, the violence. But..." She pressed the tissue to her lips.

"What happened at the scenes?"

"The first one... I had to leave. Couldn't breathe. Then Karen found me being sick in the ladies." Jade's shoulders hunched. "Some detective I turned out to be."

"You returned to work after significant trauma. No one expects immediate recovery."

"The team does. They need me functional, not falling apart at crime scenes." Tears spilled down Jade's cheeks. "I used to process evidence, examine bodies, chase leads. Now I can't look at a corpse without my chest seizing up."

"Your reaction is natural. The body remembers trauma even when the mind tries to push forward."

"But I'm letting everyone down. Karen's carrying my weight, protecting me from the worst parts." Jade's voice rose. "What if I never get past this? What if I can't do my job any more?"

"Your skills haven't vanished," Dr Morales said. "They're buried beneath layers of protective responses. Think about the second scene. You stayed longer and pushed through the initial panic."

"Until the photos triggered another attack."

"Yet you recognised the signs, removed yourself before it escalated. That shows progress in managing your responses."

Jade wiped her eyes. "I want to be useful again. The team's drowning in evidence, court records, witness statements. But I keep freezing up and second-guessing every decision."

"Let's examine that. What specific aspects of the job feel overwhelming?"

"Everything." Fresh tears fell. "The responsibility. The pressure to spot crucial details. One missed clue could mean another death." Her breath hitched. "If I mess up..."

"Stop." The doctor held up her hand. "You're catastrophising. Breaking down complex tasks into unbearable burdens. Let's focus on what you have accomplished since returning."

"I managed a few witness interviews. Helped sort court records." Jade's voice strengthened. "Found a connection between cases that might help find the killer."

"Those achievements matter. They prove your investigative instincts remain intact."

"But a sergeant should handle more. Karen needs her second in command, not a broken..."

"You're not broken," Dr Morales cut in. "You're healing. There's a critical difference." She paused. "Close your eyes. Picture yourself at a scene before your trauma. What do you notice first?"

Jade closed her eyes and fell silent for a few moments. "Evidence patterns. Spatial relationships. How things connect." The words came easier now. "My mind would map possibilities, build sequences of events."

"That analytical ability still exists. The trauma hasn't erased your training or experience. It's created barriers we need to work through."

Jade opened her eyes. "How? I can't keep hiding behind Karen while bodies pile up."

"By acknowledging your progress without demanding instant recovery. By trusting that each small step forward rebuilds your confidence." Dr Morales picked up her pen. "Walk me through your process when examining evidence. What worked before these murders?"

Jade adjusted her posture in her chair. "I kept distance. Treated the files like a puzzle. Names, dates, evidence, and relying on science and technology. Pieces that needed connecting."

"That approach served you well. What changed at the scene?"

"The reality crashed in. This wasn't paperwork any more. It was a body. Char marks. Chemical burns." Jade's hands trembled. "I pictured him suffering. Pictured myself..." She broke off, pressing her palms against her thighs.

"Notice what's happening now," Dr Morales said. "Your body tenses. Your breathing quickens. These are warning signs we can use."

"So I can run away?"

"To regulate. To maintain control while processing difficult scenes." Dr Morales set aside her notepad. "What drives you to continue this investigation?"

Jade considered the question. "The victims and the people they hurt. Escaped proper justice. Part of me thinks they deserved punishment, but not like this. Not torture."

"You empathise with their victims while recognising the killer's actions cross a line."

"Yes." Jade's voice strengthened. "The law exists for a reason. Without it, we're no better than the criminals."

"That clarity of purpose matters. How might catching this killer help your recovery?"

"I..." Jade paused. "I need to prove I can face darkness without breaking. Show myself I'm still a detective."

"The killer transforms crime scenes into theatres of punishment. Yet you process evidence, find connections, push through fear to seek justice."

"When I can stay in the room." Jade's shoulders slumped. "Half the time I end up hyperventilating in the corridor."

"Yet you return. Each time you step back into a scene, you reclaim power over your trauma."

Fresh tears welled in Jade's eyes. "But what if I can't handle it when it matters? What if we find another body and I can't function?"

"You're catastrophising again. Let's focus on evidence, not fear. What's your role in the current investigation?"

"Court records. Witness statements. Building profiles of potential suspects." Jade wiped her cheeks. "Karen keeps me away from the worst parts."

"Because she understands recovery takes time. But you're still contributing crucial elements to the case."

"This killer..." Jade sighed throwing up her hands. "They plan everything. Study victims for weeks. Turn their crimes into their punishment. It's calculated, cold."

"You're analysing patterns. Applying your training. The detective in you remains sharp."

"I want to help stop them. Not just for the victims or

their families." Jade's voice dropped. "For myself. To prove I can."

"That motivation can fuel recovery, but it needs balance. Push too hard, too fast and..."

"I shatter again?"

"You risk overwhelming your coping mechanisms. Small steps and controlled exposure is how we rebuild confidence."

Jade nodded, her breathing steady now. "Yesterday I reviewed crime scene photos. Made it through half before the panic hit."

"That's progress. Next time you might manage more. Each exposure builds resilience."

"The killer won't wait for me to heal. They're getting worse, becoming more dangerous."

"Focus on what you can control. Your responses. Your contributions to the investigation. Let Karen handle the aspects you're not ready for."

"But I need to be ready. The team needs me."

"You're already proving your worth through analysis and insight. The physical scenes will become easier with time."

Jade stood and paced to the window. "I keep thinking about the families. Phillips' wife, Reeves' ex. Their lives shattered because someone appointed themselves judge and executioner."

"Your empathy drives you to seek justice. Channel that energy into the aspects of investigation you can manage now."

"The killer believes they're delivering justice. But true justice needs limits, accountability." Jade paced around the room.

"That distinction matters." Dr Morales checked her

watch. "We need to wrap up as I have another client soon. What's your focus for the coming week?"

"Build on what works I guess." Jade returned to her chair. "Trust that Karen knows my limits better than I do right now."

"And remember—healing takes time. Some days will feel like regression. That's normal."

Jade gathered her coat. "Thank you. For helping me see I'm not completely useless."

"You're a long way from useless. Keep building on your strengths. The rest will follow."

30

Zac pulled into the parking space outside the medical centre and cut the engine. His phone buzzed. A text from Karen lit up the screen: *You've got this. Ready for you to come back. So proud of you x*

He read the message twice, letting the words sink in. Karen's belief in him had been unwavering through his darkest moments. He pocketed the phone and headed through the main doors.

The medical centre's reception area smelled of disinfectant and coffee. A clock ticked on the wall as Zac gave his name to the receptionist. She directed him to the second floor.

Dr Helen Foster's office door stood open. She rose from behind her desk as he entered, offering her hand. "Lovely to see you DCI Walker. Please take a seat."

"Thank you. It's good to see you too, but I admit, I'm a tad nervous."

She smiled. "Nothing to worry about. It's only a chat. You wouldn't be the first, and I doubt you will be the last to feel a little anxious about coming to see me."

Zac smiled, though her attempt to play down the seriousness of the meeting did little to affect the turmoil now raging in his stomach.

Zac settled into the chair opposite her desk. Dr Foster had kind eyes behind black-rimmed glasses, her grey hair cut in a practical bob.

"How are you feeling about returning to work?" she asked, opening his file.

"Better than I expected." Zac sat up straighter. "The panic attacks have stopped. I'm sleeping through most nights now."

Dr Foster made a note. "And the flashbacks?"

"Less frequent. The therapy techniques help when they happen."

"Good." She looked up from her notes. "Tell me about your support network."

"My daughter Summer stays with us most of the time. We cook together, hang out, and watch films." A smile tugged at his lips. "And Karen, she's been there through all of it."

Dr Foster's pen paused. "You mentioned Karen in our last session. You expressed concern for her safety?"

Zac's shoulders tensed. "The job puts her at risk. Every day."

"That bothers you?"

"How could it not?" The words came out sharper than he intended. He took a breath. "Sorry. It's just I've seen what happens when things go wrong. When you lose someone."

"Is that affecting your judgement about returning to work?"

Zac considered this as he narrowed his eyes. "No. If anything, it makes me more determined. Karen needs someone watching her back. The whole team does."

"But Karen?"

Heat crept up Zac's neck. "We're close. She helped me when I couldn't help myself."

She set down her pen. "Zac, I need to be certain you can separate your personal feelings from your professional duties. Your concern for DCI Heath is understandable, but it can't compromise your decision making."

"I understand that." Zac met her gaze. "Karen's one of the best officers I know. She doesn't need me hovering over her. She needs me doing my job."

She nodded, making another note. "How do you feel about leading investigations again?"

"Ready." The answer came without hesitation. "I know my triggers now. I've got strategies in place."

"And if you feel overwhelmed?"

"I'll talk to someone. Karen, my therapist, you. I won't let it build up again."

She leaned back in her chair. "Tell me about the nightmares. Are they still occurring?"

Zac looked down, playing with his nails and finding a bit of dirt beneath one of them. "Not often. Maybe once a month... if that."

"What happens in them?"

"Different scenarios. Sometimes I'm back at the scene. At times..." He paused, his jaw tightening. "I'm too late to save someone."

"Karen?"

"Among others." Zac's fingers drummed against his thigh. "The team. Summer."

She wrote something in her file. "That's a natural response to trauma, Zac. But I need to know how do these fears manifest in your daily life? Do they affect your decision making?"

"I'm more cautious now. More aware of risks." Zac

stopped drumming his fingers. "But I also know I can't control everything. That was part of what broke me before, trying to protect everyone all the time."

"That's good insight." The doctor adjusted her glasses. "What about your relationship with Michelle? How are things with Summer's mother?"

The change of subject caught him off guard. His expression darkened. "She's... difficult. Uses Summer to get at me sometimes."

"How do you handle that?"

"Focus on Summer. She shouldn't have to deal with adult problems." Zac's voice softened. "Karen helps there too. Reminds me to stay calm, think things through."

She raised an eyebrow. "Karen seems to be a significant source of support. That's great."

"She is," Zac said. "Karen and I balance our personal and professional lives. We both understand the demands of the job."

The psychologist adjusted her glasses. "How do you manage that balance, especially in high-risk situations?"

"We established clear boundaries early on. At work, she's DCI Heath, my colleague. The engagement doesn't change that."

"And in dangerous situations?"

"Our training takes over. We trust each other's judgement." Zac's voice held steady. "If anything, our relationship has made us better officers. We understand each other's strengths and weaknesses."

The older woman made a note. "What about the strain of you both being in dangerous situations? How do you cope with that?"

"It's difficult." Zac ran a hand over his jaw. "But we knew what we were signing up for. We talk about our fears and support each other through the tough days."

"You mentioned nightmares earlier. Do they involve Karen?"

"Sometimes." His expression darkened. "But they're less frequent now. I've learned to process things instead of burying them."

Grey hair caught the morning light as she nodded. "Tell me about your support systems outside of Karen."

"Summer's my anchor. Seeing her keeps me grounded." Pride crept into his voice. "She's accepted Karen into her life. They've built their own fantastic relationship. In fact, I think she gets on better with Karen than she does with Michelle at the moment. It might be a phase that she is going through, but she seems to be more willing to confide in Karen these days. I see that as a positive step."

"That must help, having that family unit."

"It does. Summer knows we both face risks at work. She worries, but she understands." Zac straightened in his chair. "We're honest with her, age appropriate of course."

Behind her glasses, keen eyes studied him. "What strategies have you developed for managing stress?"

"Regular exercise. Meditation." A slight smile crossed his face. "Karen joins me for morning runs now and then. It helps clear our heads before work."

"And professionally? How will you handle the transition back?"

"One day at a time. I know my triggers, my limits." Zac's hands remained steady on the armrests. "Karen and I agreed at work, the job comes first. We leave our personal life at home."

She closed his file, opening a fresh notebook page. "Walk me through a high-stress scenario. How would you respond?"

"I focus on protocol. Trust the team. Trust Karen's abilities as an officer." His voice carried conviction. "Our relationship doesn't compromise our judgement, it strengthens our communication."

"Good. And afterwards?"

"We decompress together. Talk things through." Zac's expression softened. "Having someone who understands the job and the pressure helps."

"What about your ex-wife? How does Michelle feel about your engagement?"

Zac's jaw tightened. "She's... accepted it. For Summer's sake."

"And the custody arrangements?"

"They're working better now. Karen helps me stay calm when Michelle tries to provoke a reaction." He paused. "Summer spends more time with us. She likes the stability."

The psychologist wrote another note. "Let's talk about your coping mechanisms when you're separated during operations. How do you maintain focus?"

"I remind myself of our training. Trust in our teams." Zac leaned forward. "The job taught us both that we can't control everything. We accept the risks, focus on what we can control."

"Have you discussed contingency plans? As a couple?"

"Yes. We've updated our wills, sorted out guardianship for Summer if..." His voice trailed off. "We face reality head-on. No point pretending the risks don't exist."

The wall clock ticked in the silence. Outside, footsteps passed in the corridor, voices murmured. She studied his face, considering.

"We'll need one more session before I make my final recommendation." She consulted her calendar. "Can you come back Tuesday?"

The words hung in the air. Zac felt his stomach tighten

but kept his expression neutral. Progress, not perfection. His therapist's mantra echoed in his mind.

"Tuesday works." He reached for his phone to mark the date. Karen's message still lit up the screen, reminding him of everything he had to fight for.

31

Karen stared at the stack of files on her desk, the words blurring as she checked her phone for the tenth time that hour. No messages from Zac. Her impatience grew. The evaluation dragged into its second hour.

A coffee cup sat cold and untouched beside her keyboard. The clock on the PC screen rolled on past eleven as she pulled another case file closer, hoping work might distract her from thoughts of Zac facing Dr Foster's questions.

Her mobile lit up. She grabbed it, but Dan's name flashed on the screen instead of Zac's.

"Karen, you need to take a look at this." Dan's voice crackled with excitement. "Ty found something in the CCTV."

Karen pushed back from her desk. "On my way."

She strode on to the main floor where her team huddled around Ty's computer. The screen showed grainy footage from a street camera near Morton's flat.

"Watch this," Ty said, pointing to the corner of the

frame. A white Toyota Prius cruised past Morton's building. "Same car appears three times that night."

"It's the same vehicle?" Karen leaned closer.

"The number plate." Ty zoomed in on the image. "But here's where it gets interesting." He switched to footage from Reeves' street. "Look familiar?"

The same white Prius rolled past Reeves' house two days before his murder. Though the image quality obscured the driver's features, Karen caught a glimpse of a white male behind the wheel.

"The plates are fake," Dan said. "We ran them through the system. They belong to a Ford Focus in Newcastle."

Ty pulled up a third video. "This one's from the industrial estate, the night before Phillips died." The Prius appeared again, headlights cutting through the darkness as it circled the area.

"As we thought." Karen straightened. "Keeping tabs on them before striking."

"Multiple passes by each location in the days leading up to the murders." Ty clicked through more footage. "Morton's place received special attention. The car showed up six times in twenty-four hours."

Karen's phone buzzed in her pocket. She ignored it, focused on the breakthrough unfolding before her.

"Can we enhance the driver's image?"

"Tech team's working on it." Dan handed her a printout. "The best shot we have shows a white male, medium build. Nothing distinct enough for facial recognition."

"Bollocks. What about traffic cameras? He must have driven between locations."

"Working on it." Ty typed commands, bringing up a map of York. "If we track the Prius's movements, we might find where he lives, or the direction he travelled from."

Ed joined them, clutching fresh printouts. "I checked

vehicle licensing records. No white Prius registered in York matches our time frame."

"He's smart enough to use fake plates," Karen said. "The car could be stolen, borrowed, or registered elsewhere."

"Or bought privately," Bel added from her desk. "Cash deal, no paperwork."

Karen studied the footage again. The driver was in no hurry. If this was their killer, then he chose viewing spots, positioned himself in a way that didn't draw attention, and so far had done very well in evading being captured on CCTV... until now.

"Get this to every officer in York." Karen grabbed a marker and added details to the incident board. "I want that car found. Check garages, mechanic shops, and any other place where it could be hidden."

Her phone buzzed again. Zac's name lit up the screen.

The team fell quiet as she answered. "How did it go?"

Zac's voice carried a mix of relief and tension. "One more session next Tuesday. Then she'll decide."

"That's good news." Karen kept her tone steady despite her racing pulse. "We'll talk tonight?"

"Yeah. Got to run. Meeting with personnel."

Karen cut the call and looked back to her team who were all nervous for her and Zac. "No news yet. More hoops to jump through."

A collective groan rippled around the room.

"Right." She cleared her throat. "Dan, coordinate with traffic division. I want every camera in York looking for that Prius. Ty, keep working backwards through the footage. Find out where else this car has popped up."

Preet raised her hand. "What about Robert Shaw? His website mentioned all three victims."

"Good point." Karen nodded. "Check if he drives a

Prius. And pull his phone records, check the cell site data for where his phone was during the surveillance periods caught on CCTV."

Claire presented a new stack of papers. "Court records show Shaw attended nine trials in the past year. Three involved our victims."

"He's looking more interesting by the minute," Karen said. "But we need evidence, not coincidences. Ed, take Bel and visit local car dealers. Someone might remember selling a white Prius. Long shot I know, but I need every angle covered. This isn't a triple murder investigation. We're hunting a serial killer and they're as dangerous as can be."

The investigation room hummed with renewed energy as officers attacked their tasks. Keyboards clicked as searches expanded. Phones buzzed with the hum of conversations.

Karen moved between desks, reviewing findings, directing searches. The Prius gave them their first solid lead. Proof their killer studied targets before striking.

Her phone stayed silent in her pocket as she worked, but thoughts of Zac's evaluation lingered. One more session stood between him and returning to duty. For now, she had a killer to catch.

The CCTV footage played on a loop on Ty's screen, the white Prius ghosting through York's streets. Each pass marked another step in the killer's preparation. Each sighting brought them closer to understanding his methods.

"Claire, I need ANPR coverage across York. Set up alerts for those plates but check registrations of every white Prius too. He might switch them again."

Claire nodded and turned to her computer. "I'll pull camera locations from the council."

"The public might recognise this car," Dan said. "We could put out an appeal."

"Not yet." Karen replied. "If we spook him, he'll ditch the Prius, and we'll lose our best lead. I need to run it past Detective Superintendent Kelly first."

Jade approached. "Found something in the digital records. Someone accessed each victim's case file on several occasions before their deaths."

"Court system or police database?" Karen asked.

"Court. Someone checked Reeves' file eight times in the week before he died. Morton's records show similar patterns."

Karen's pulse quickened. "What about Phillips?"

"Five viewings in three days." Jade swiped through her data. "The timestamps cluster around early morning and late evening."

"Outside normal court hours," Karen said. "Who has that level of access?"

"Working on it. The system logs users, but someone this careful may have borrowed credentials."

Ty called from his desk. "Got another sighting of the Prius. Two streets from Phillips' house, four days before he died."

"Track its movements," Karen instructed. "Build a map of everywhere it stopped."

A text from Kelly popped up on her phone: *In meetings all morning. Urgent?*

Karen typed back: *Significant breakthrough. Need to discuss public appeal soon.*

"The digital access bothers me," Jade said. "Our killer knows procedure, understands evidence. Now we find they've got court system access?"

"Narrows the pool," Karen replied. "Check employee records against Toyota owners."

Ed returned clutching printouts. "Local dealers drew a blank on recent Prius sales. But Leeds police reported three stolen last month."

"Get the details," Karen said. "If one matches our car..."

"Already checked." Ed spread photos across the desk. "Different colours."

Claire raised her hand. "ANPR network's active. First alert just came in. A white Prius spotted on Fulford Road twenty minutes ago."

"Direction?" Karen demanded.

"Heading out of York. But the image quality's poor. We can't confirm if it's our car, but we have a part plate match."

Karen grabbed her coat. "Dan, with me. Claire, get a few unmarked cars out to sweep the streets. This car is right on our doorstep. The rest of you keep digging. Jade, focus on those system access times. Either court employees researched victims after hours, or someone hacked their system."

They rushed to Karen's car, the morning traffic parting as she hit the lights. No siren, if their killer was nearby, they didn't want to announce their presence.

"Think he's still watching potential victims?" Dan asked as they turned on to Fulford Road.

"He picked targets through the courts," Karen said. "The Prius let him study their routines. Question is: who's next?"

Her phone rang. Kelly's name lit up the display. Dan answered, putting it on speaker.

"What's this about a breakthrough?" Kelly asked.

Karen outlined their discoveries: the Prius, the digital access, the surveillance pattern.

"Public appeal's risky," Kelly said. "If we show our hand…"

"He'll abandon the car," Karen finished. "But if someone recognises it…"

"Give me an hour. I'll speak with the chief constable."

The call ended as they came back along Fulford Road. No sign of the white Prius.

"We'll circle back," Karen said. "Check side streets. He has to park somewhere."

Her phone buzzed with a message from Jade: *Court system access came from three different accounts. All belong to admin staff who work normal hours.*

Karen's grip tightened on the steering wheel. Someone borrowed legitimate logins to hide their tracks. The question was: who had that kind of access and knowledge?

They spent another hour searching streets and car parks, but the white Prius remained elusive.

32

Bel strode into Karen's office an hour later, files clutched against her chest. "You need to see this."

Karen glanced up from her computer screen. "The court employee checks?"

"Two things." Bel dropped the files on Karen's desk. "First, a court clerk named Stephen Matthews. His wife died two years ago. A drink driver ploughed into her at a junction. The driver got eighteen months."

"Another grievance against the system," Karen said. "Like our website crusader Robert Shaw."

"But here's the interesting part." Bel opened the second file. "Richard Ashworth, KC. He defended all three of our victims."

Karen sat forward. "What?"

"Mark Reeves got eight years, out in five, after Ashworth argued his remorse would lead to rehabilitation. James Morton escaped major charges through legal technicalities, ending up with just eighteen months for possessing indecent images. And Alan Phillips," Bel tapped the paper. "Ashworth got him off when his key witness changed testimony."

Karen grabbed the file, scanning the details. "The witness who killed himself?"

Bel nodded. "The case collapsed after his testimony changed."

"These were Ashworth's last major cases before retirement?"

"His grand finale. Three defendants who should have faced serious time walked away with token sentences or nothing at all." Bel pulled out more papers. "The press called him 'The Miracle Worker'. Known for getting acquittals in impossible cases."

Karen spread the court documents across her desk. "Matthews processed paperwork for these trials?"

"As court clerk, he handled all the administrative tasks. Scheduled hearings, managed exhibits, recorded proceedings." Bel pointed to a signature. "His name appears on every document."

"He watched Ashworth dismantle each case." Karen stood and paced around her room. "Saw justice fail three times. Have we found any connection between Matthews and Shaw? Friends? Same pub? Anything?"

"Not yet. But I'll work on that angle. There's more. Matthews changed after his wife's death. Took on extra shifts, stayed late to catch up on paperwork."

Karen turned. "And his wife was killed by a drink driver... is the driver still alive?"

"We assume so. There are no records involving him on our systems. I'll run a check to find his last location." Bel checked her notes. "According to Matthews' supervisor, Matthews threw himself into work. Never took sick days, volunteered for overtime."

"Perfect cover for studying cases," Karen added. "What about the Prius?"

"No vehicle registered in his name." Bel handed over another printout. "But several court employees mentioned he started using different cars after his wife died. Said he couldn't bear to keep driving their old one."

Karen grabbed her phone. "Check local rental agencies. He'd need something untraceable for surveillance."

"Already did." Bel gave a tight smile. "He has keys to the building. Security logs show his pass being used during early mornings and late evenings."

"The same hours someone accessed our victims' files." Karen dialled Ed's number. "We need surveillance on Matthews. Track his movements but keep a distance. I don't want to pull him in yet. If he spots us..."

"He'll know we're closing in," Bel finished.

Ed answered on the second ring. Karen outlined their discoveries. "We need eyes on Matthews, but nothing too close. He knows procedure and will spot a standard tail."

She ended the call and studied her notes. Three photos stared back at her: Reeves, Morton, Phillips. Each man escaped justice through Ashworth's legal expertise. Each died confessing their guilt.

"Ashworth retired two years ago," Bel said. "Still lives in York."

Karen traced the connections between victims. "Did Matthews handle all of Ashworth's cases?"

"For the last five years of his legal career. Every file, every hearing, every ruling." Bel checked her notes. "His supervisor says Matthews kept detailed records of Ashworth's courtroom tactics. Apparently, he found the man obnoxious."

Karen's eyes narrowed. "Studied his methods. Watched him twist evidence, manipulate juries."

"The supervisor mentioned something else." Bel pulled out another page. "Matthews kept newspaper clippings about Ashworth's cases."

Karen paced the office. "These three victims weren't random. They represented everything Matthews hated about the system thanks to Ashworth."

Bel shook her head. "The grief and rage must have consumed him."

Karen stopped at the window. "Check his home address. Ashworth lives in York. Where exactly?"

"Millionaires' Row." Bel tapped her tablet. "Bought the house with his retirement package."

"Living in luxury. Nice." Karen turned back to Bel. "Matthews could have left the courts and worked elsewhere. Why would he stay and face criminals day after day. Surely, the pain of seeing people pass through the system, some ending up with lenient sentences, would be... torture."

Bel locked eyes with Karen and raised a brow as she lingered on the last word.

"His supervisor says the job changed him. After his wife died, Matthews became obsessed with detail. Worked longer hours, triple-checked every document."

"The perfect clerk." Karen picked up her coat. "No one questioned his dedication because grief explained everything."

Preet appeared in the doorway. "The security company sent over more logs. Matthews accessed the building forty-seven times outside normal hours in the past month."

"Cross-reference those times with our victims' movements," Karen ordered. "I'm interested in knowing if he used court computers to plan his surveillance."

The investigation room buzzed with activity as Karen briefed her team. Officers tracked digital footprints while others coordinated surveillance. Their killer had hidden behind court procedures and legal expertise, but his mask cracked.

"Dan, check Matthews' personnel records. I want everything. Performance reviews, complaints, and disciplinary actions. Ty, focus on his building access. Every time he used his pass after hours, I want to know what files he viewed."

"What about Ashworth?" Claire asked. "Should we warn him?"

Karen shook her head. "Not yet. Matthews might have him under surveillance. One wrong move could push him to strike."

Ed returned, clutching fresh printouts. "Matthews' workstation accessed case files for six other defendants. All Ashworth clients, all avoided serious sentences."

"More targets." Karen grabbed the papers. "Get uniform to each address. Tell them to go in plain clothes. Discreet welfare checks only. We can't tip our hand."

Matthews sat at the centre of their web: court clerk, grieving widower, witness to justice's failures. Each death stripped away another layer of his façade. The question remained, would he recognise the net closing around him before they could stop his mission?

Karen scribbled on her pad, the connections multiplying. Three victims dead. One retired barrister living in comfort. And between them, a court clerk whose pain had twisted into righteous fury. If Matthews was following his pattern, he was studying more targets right now. The time between kills shortened with each execution. They needed to move fast.

"Get me everything on his wife's death," Karen told Bel. "Inquest transcripts, police reports, witness statements. The driver who killed her started this. I want to know exactly what Matthews saw in that courtroom."

Karen settled by Bel's desk with a fresh coffee as Bel spread military records across the surface.

"Robert Shaw's service history raises questions," Bel said. "Twenty-two years in the RMP, Special Investigation Branch. Several overseas tours. Commendation for bravery."

"Criminal investigation experience?" Karen pulled a file closer.

"He specialised in military corruption cases. His commanding officer noted his talent for surveillance and evidence gathering."

Karen studied Shaw's service photo. The military short grey hair and rigid posture marked him as career forces. "His expertise would be useful. He'd be the type of person Matthews could use to do his dirty work?"

"Technical knowledge, combat training, understanding of evidence procedures." Bel tapped Shaw's discharge papers. "Left the army in 2019 after disagreements with senior command over case handling."

"His website chronicles legal failures." Karen opened her laptop and searched for the site in Google. "Each post breaks down how defendants escaped justice through technicalities."

Bel handed over a printout. "Detailed analysis of our victims' trials, criticism of Ashworth's tactics, calls for tougher sentencing."

Ed knocked on the open door. "Shaw's bank records show cash withdrawals near each murder site."

"Dates?" Karen asked.

"Two days before Reeves, morning of Morton's death, and the night Phillips died."

"Could be a coincidence," Bel said. "His flat's in that area."

Karen nodded in deep reflection. "What else do we know about his current activities?"

"Runs his website full-time. Posts daily updates on court cases." Bel checked her notes. "Lives alone in a fortress of an apartment. Multiple security cameras, reinforced doors."

"Paranoid?"

"His blog's attracted death threats. He's reported several to local police, which is why we know about Fortress Shaw!"

Karen rocked back in her chair. "Both suspects make sense," she said. "Matthews lost his wife to a broken system. Shaw built a career exposing corruption."

"Matthews worked inside the courts," Bel replied. "But Shaw has the tactical training and has attended cases as a member of the public. Did they form a sense of kinship?"

"The murders show both planning and rage." Karen turned from the window. "Matthews witnessed Ashworth distort justice. Shaw documented the failures."

Ty appeared with fresh printouts. "Shaw's phone records place him close to the industrial estate when Phillips died."

"He follows cases," Bel said. "Could be research for his website."

"Or surveillance." Karen added the phone data to her notepad. "What about his movements during the other murders?"

"Working on cell tower data," Ty said. "But his phone often goes dark for hours."

"Counter-surveillance training." Karen studied her notes. "He knows how to avoid detection. Might leave his phone at home."

Claire entered. "Shaw's YouTube channel posted breakdowns of each victim's trial. The videos went up days before their deaths."

"Selecting targets?" Bel asked.

"Or documenting cases for his followers." Karen scrolled through Shaw's website. "His audience expects coverage of controversial verdicts."

The evidence pulled in multiple directions. Matthews knew the court system inside out, understood how Ashworth operated. Shaw brought military expertise and a platform for tracking legal failures.

"They had access to cases," Karen said. "Both understood how it all worked... and sometimes failed."

"Shaw's military record explains the technical kills," Bel said. "Matthews' court position gave him inside knowledge."

Dan approached with his laptop. "Shaw's social media shows he attended all three trials. Posted live updates from outside the court."

"Like Matthews, he witnessed Ashworth's victories first-hand." Karen rubbed her temples. "The rage could belong to either man."

The investigation files and printouts displayed their suspects' lives in parallel.

"Keep digging into both," Karen told her team. "Bank records, phone data, and CCTV. I want everything. One of them will make a mistake."

"The next victim's out there," Karen said. "Whether it's Matthews or Shaw, they won't stop until we catch them, and in the meantime, I need a chat with Shaw."

33

The killer parked his Prius three streets from the abandoned chemical plant, switched off the engine, and checked his watch. From his position, he noted two entry points. A loading bay with rusted shutters and a fire exit with broken hinges. Perfect.

He opened his notebook, marking times and locations with the same detail he brought to court records and observations. Each page chronicled potential targets, their movements, the evidence of their crimes. The skills he'd learned over years of court processes served him now. Detail mattered. Errors brought consequences.

The air carried the smell of motor oil and damp concrete as he walked the perimeter. The building's shell rose against gloomy skies, its windows dark hollows in brick walls. His footsteps crunched on broken glass. Nature reclaimed the grounds through cracks in the tarmac, but the structure remained solid. Private. Contained.

Inside, he traced pathways between machinery. The torchlight caught dust particles floating in the air. Chemical tanks lined the walls, their warning labels faded but legible. He touched the cold metal, thoughts turning to the workers who'd died here. More victims of corporate greed, of profits over safety.

A rat skittered past his feet. The beam followed its path to a drainage channel that bisected the floor. The killer knelt, tested the grating. Loose. He marked it in his notes. Another detail to consider when planning the scene.

The upper level offered clear sight lines to both exits. Rusted catwalks creaked under his weight as he paced the distance. Eight steps to the stairs. Twelve to the door. He recorded each measurement, each potential risk or advantage. The court system taught him the importance of preparation. Evidence. Process. The difference between justice served and justice denied.

His next target deserved special consideration. Richard Ashworth, KC lived in comfort while families grieved. The barrister's retirement marked the end of a career built on technicalities and legal sleight of hand. But retirement wouldn't shield him from true judgement.

The killer checked his previous notes. Ashworth kept regular habits. Breakfast at the same café, afternoon walks in the park, evenings at his computer. The observation phase neared completion. Time to prepare the stage for his last performance.

He photographed the chemical storage area. The labels told him what he needed. Corrosives, solvents, and industrial cleaners. Tools to extract a confession.

The factory floor stretched into darkness. He pictured Ashworth bound to a chair. The barrister's legal brilliance meant nothing here. No technicalities existed in this court. No deals. No reduced sentences. Only truth and consequence.

The world continued while he planned his own brand of justice.

He made final measurements, noting the distance between support columns. The space needed preparation, cleaning, lighting, and the proper arrangement of tools. Each death refined his technique. Each confession brought him closer to balance.

The killer closed his notebook and tucked it away in a jacket pocket.

He checked his watch and pulled out his phone, searching for the files in his folders. Court transcripts filled the screen. Case after case of Ashworth's legal victories. A photo caught his eye. A young woman's face on a newspaper website. Emma Taylor, twenty-six, killed at a pedestrian crossing. The driver tested positive for cocaine.

The news article burned into his mind. Emma's mother collapsed in court as Ashworth presented character witnesses, painted pictures of the driver's reformed nature, his commitment to rehabilitation. Eight months in prison. Eight months for stealing a life.

Blood rushed in his ears. The factory's darkness pressed around him as faces flashed through his thoughts. A child left without a mother. Parents burying their daughter. A husband's empty bed. Lives shattered while Ashworth collected his fee.

His fingers struck the keys. More cases emerged. Drivers impaired by drugs, alcohol, or exhaustion. Each time, Ashworth twisted evidence, found loopholes, reduced sentences. The barrister's retirement speech praised his dedication to justice. The words rang hollow against the graves of victims.

The screen illuminated his notes. Emma's killer expressed remorse, promised change, walked free in months. Now he lived in Spain and posted beach photos on social media. Her family's suffering meant nothing to men who valued profit over morality.

His phone lit up with a court notification. Tomorrow's cases, tomorrow's parade of technicalities and deals. The system ground on, producing paperwork instead of justice.

The chemical tanks stood silent, waiting. They would need filling to extract truth from lies, force acknowledgement of guilt. Ashworth's legal brilliance held no power against industrial cleaners, against the pain he would suffer.

Cold air brushed his face as he climbed the upper walkways. Through the broken windows, light pollution painted the sky orange. Below, shadows marked where he would position lights, cameras, tools of documentation. The court taught him to record everything. Evidence created truth.

He remembered Emma's father in the witness box. The man's hands had shaken as he'd described finding his daughter's body. Ashworth's cross-examination had stripped away dignity, reducing grief to theatre. The barrister's questions had suggested Emma's own negligence. Her death had become a technicality, a legal argument instead of human loss. More faces crowded his thoughts. A teenage boy killed by a drink driver. The driver's wealthy parents had hired Ashworth. Three months suspended sentence. A mother of three struck down in a hit and run. The driver had claimed temporary insanity. Ashworth had won him treatment instead of prison.

The killer's jaw tightened.

He paced the walkway, measuring steps between columns before returning to his car. The space below waited for his design. Not long to go.

34

Karen and Bel stood at the entrance to Shaw's apartment block, studying the security camera mounted above the door. The device tracked their movements, a red light blinking as the lens adjusted.

Karen pressed the intercom. A crackle of static burst through the speaker.

"Yes?" A man's voice carried an edge of suspicion.

"DCI Karen Heath and DC Webb, York Police." Karen held her warrant card towards the camera. "Robert Shaw?"

"Who's asking?"

"The police. We need to speak with you."

Silence stretched for several seconds. "Your credentials again, please. Closer to the lens."

Karen exhaled through gritted teeth. "Mr Shaw, they're clearly visible."

"The angle's wrong. Two steps back, hold them higher."

"You can't be serious."

"I need to verify your identity. People can fake police warrant cards."

Karen's knuckles whitened around her ID. "Mr Shaw, we can do this the easy way, or I'll return with a tactical entry team and take in your bloody door. Your choice." Karen looked at Bel and shook her head.

"Turn the cards sideways," Shaw instructed. "Show both sides."

"For God's sake," Karen shouted. "I'm calling the station. Have them send..."

"No need for threats." Shaw cut in. "But security protocols exist for a reason. Rotate the cards."

Karen complied, jaw clenched as she displayed each angle. "Satisfied?"

"Your colleague's card now. Same procedure."

"Right." Karen stepped back. "I'm done playing games. You've got ten seconds to buzz us in, or I'm requesting an emergency warrant. Your choice."

The intercom remained quiet. Karen's finger moved towards the button again when a buzz signalled the door release. They stepped into a stark hallway that reeked of bleach.

Four floors up, Shaw's door dominated the landing. Steel reinforced hinges flanked a frame wrapped in metal. A camera peered down from the corner.

The sound of multiple locks disengaging echoed through the corridor. Karen counted six distinct clicks before the door opened.

Robert Shaw filled the entrance, his military bearing clear in his rigid posture. A fresh scar marked his right hand, the skin pink and puckered.

"Come in." He stepped back, gesturing them through. "Shoes off, please. The floor's been cleaned."

"Not happening. We either come in or I take you in. Your choice," Karen snapped.

Shaw scowled at them before a flick of his head.

The apartment stretched before them, walls transformed into a heady collage of newspaper clippings, court documents, and crime scene photos. Red string connected related cases, creating a web of investigation across the space.

"Quite the collection," Bel said, studying a section devoted to drink-driving cases.

Shaw moved to his desk, a metal military surplus piece positioned to face the door. The computer and six monitors sat on the desk, arranged more like a trading floor in an investment bank than a small apartment in York. "Research for the website. Each case is a failure of justice."

"Your documentation's extensive." Karen indicated the wall of clippings. "Must take considerable time to compile."

"The truth requires attention to detail." Shaw settled into his chair, spine straight. "But you're not here about my website."

"Three murders in five days. Each victim connected to cases you've written about."

Shaw's expression remained neutral. "Unfortunate coincidence. My work focuses on exposing systemic failures, not encouraging violence."

"Your military record shows expertise in surveillance and evidence collection," Bel said. "Skills our killer possesses."

"Along with thousands of others." Shaw's fingers drummed once against his desk. "Former police, security services, and forensic staff. The knowledge isn't unique.

You're clutching at straws. The door is behind you, come back when you have something more concrete."

Karen threw back a sarcastic grin as she stepped closer to the wall, examining a cluster of articles about Mark Reeves. "You attended his trial. Posted detailed breakdowns of the proceedings."

"Public record and the viewing gallery. Anyone could access the same information."

"But not everyone maintains such thorough surveillance of legal proceedings." Karen turned to face him. "Your website documented all three victims before their deaths."

Shaw's eyes narrowed. "Are you suggesting I'm responsible?"

"Should I be?"

"I expose corruption through legal channels. Through truth." He gestured to his walls of evidence. "My methods involve keyboards and cameras, not violence."

"Yet you only track cases that ended in reduced sentences," Bel said. "Record the details of defendants who escaped proper punishment. Perhaps you reached the stage where enough was enough?"

"Knowledge is power." Shaw stood, his movements rigid. "The system protects the wealthy, the connected. Someone must document its failures."

Karen studied his face, noting the tension in his jaw. "Your posts about Richard Ashworth criticise his methods. Calling him a 'perversion of justice' if I remember correctly."

"A barrister who twisted truth into lies. Who turned victims into statistics." Shaw's voice hardened. "But criticism isn't confession, DCI Heath. You're hunting a killer while I hunt corruption."

The room fell silent save for the hum of computer

fans. Shaw's evidence wall loomed behind them, years of investigation compressed into paper and string. A section near his desk caught Karen's attention. Fresh articles about chemical plants and industrial accidents.

"Your recent posts focus on workplace safety violations," Karen said. "Cases where negligence caused deaths."

"Public interest stories." Shaw moved to block her view. "Corporate manslaughter deserves exposure."

"Like Alan Phillips?" Bel asked. "You wrote about his case last week."

"A man whose cowardice led to the deaths of two workers. Who walked free while families grieved." Shaw's mask slipped, revealing a flash of rage. "The courts failed them. The system failed them."

"And now Phillips is dead," Karen said. "Killed at the same factory where his negligence caused those deaths."

Shaw's expression closed. "A detail I included in my coverage of his murder. Along with Reeves and Morton. The public deserves to know when justice finds a way."

Karen watched Shaw adjust a newspaper clipping that hung crooked on his wall. His fingers smoothed the paper with military exactness, aligning it with the surrounding articles.

"Tell me about your security measures," she said.

Shaw turned from the wall. "Death threats come with exposing corruption. People prefer their dirty secrets to stay buried."

"The cameras and reinforced door. That's beyond standard protection."

"Four break-in attempts this year." Shaw moved to his computer, tapping a key to wake the screen. "Two men tried forcing entry last month. The cameras caught them testing my locks at three a.m."

Bel stepped closer to his desk. "Did you report it?"

"Called 101. Filed incident reports." His mouth twisted. "Your colleagues suggested better locks. As if I hadn't considered that."

The flat resembled a fortress, but one designed to keep threats out rather than secrets in.

"These threats," she said. "They relate to specific cases?"

"Corrupt officials. Defence lawyers. OCGs. Anyone I expose." Shaw pulled up a folder on his screen. "I document each incident. Date, time, method of threat. Evidence matters."

"Do you know Stephen Matthews?" Karen asked. "A court clerk connected to several cases."

Shaw's brow furrowed. "No. Should I?"

"He processed paperwork for trials you covered."

"I deal with hundreds of cases." Shaw shook his head. "Court staff blur together unless they're involved in corruption."

Karen caught Bel's eye, exchanging a silent acknowledgement. Shaw's denial carried no trace of deception.

"Your military background," Bel said. "It gave you insight into evidence collection."

"The RMP taught me to build cases through documentation." Shaw gestured to his walls. "Each article, each connection, reveals patterns of injustice."

"But you never acted on those patterns?"

"My website reaches thousands. Change comes through exposure, and I don't encourage violence. Seen enough blood and guts to last a lifetime." He straightened papers. "The public deserves truth."

Karen studied his movements. Sharp, controlled, but underlaid with tension. Not the tension of guilt, but of constant vigilance.

"Your cameras record everyone who approaches the door?"

"Twenty-four-hour coverage. Multiple angles." Pride crept into Shaw's voice. "The system alerts me to unusual activity."

"That level of surveillance suggests serious concerns for your safety."

Shaw's shoulders tightened. "My work creates enemies. Certain sections of society would like me to stay silent."

"These enemies," Karen pressed. "They include anyone connected to our victims?"

"No direct threats." Shaw touched the scar on his hand. "But experience taught me preparation matters. Better cameras than casualties."

Karen moved towards the door.

He began disengaging his locks. "Your killer understood that too. Clever."

Karen paused at the doorway. "You sound like you admire their methods."

"I admire attention to detail. Not murder. Happy hunting, officers."

Outside, Karen called Ty as Bel called the lift.

"Ty. I need a deeper background trawl on Shaw. Everything since discharge." She waited for the lift doors to open. "Focus on threat reports. Check if any connect to our victims or the courts."

"You think he's involved?" Bel asked as they descended.

"No. His security suggests fear, not guilt. He's protecting himself from something." Karen ended the call. "Or someone."

"But his expertise matches our killer." Bel added.

"Surface similarities. Shaw documents corruption

through official channels. Our killer delivers personal justice." The lift reached ground level. "Shaw fears violence. Our killer embraces it."

"His denial about Matthews felt genuine," Bel said.

"Agreed. Two separate men fighting the same system through different methods." Karen started the engine. "Shaw exposes corruption. Matthews punishes it."

35

Jade hunched over her keyboard, scrolling through endless lines of digital access logs. Her neck ached from hours of scrutinising user IDs and timestamps, but something in the data caught her attention. She sat up straight, pulling the screen closer.

"Hold on," she muttered, tracing the pattern with her finger. The same partial user ID appeared across multiple searches. All focused on Ashworth's cases.

Her pulse quickened as she dug deeper into the logs. The ID surfaced repeatedly, accessing files for Reeves, Morton, and Phillips. But the searches went beyond basic case details. Someone had examined Ashworth's defence strategies, witness statements, and procedural challenges. Was this Matthews?

She opened a fresh document and began mapping the timeline. The searches clustered around specific periods. Late nights, early mornings, and times when the courthouse stood empty. Each victim's file had been pulled multiple times before their death.

The pattern grew clearer as she collated the data.

Jade reached for her coffee, but the cup sat empty.

This wasn't random research. It showed purpose and a focus on Ashworth only. There were no similar patterns she located for other legal representatives.

She clicked through to the system log files, hoping to identify the user, but hit an issue when the log showed an error recorded:

"DATA UNAVAILABLE — SYSTEM CRASH RECOVERY INCOMPLETE"

Jade rubbed her eyes. Not what she hoped for.

She accessed the IT maintenance records. During the period in question, the court's digital archive had suffered a catastrophic failure. User logs, access records, and authentication data were all erased and then needed to be reinstalled from server backups.

The timing struck her as too convenient. A system crash that destroyed evidence of who accessed these specific files? The odds seemed remote, but the attempt had backfired when the backups restored everything.

She dialled the court supervisor's number, drumming her fingers as it rang.

"Administration, Clive speaking."

"DS Whiting, York Police. I need information about system access during March and April."

Papers rustled in the background. "That period's problematic. We lost data in the crash."

"I've got a partial user ID which starts with CT. Any way to narrow that down?"

"CT?" Keys clicked as he checked his records. "That's our standard prefix for court staff. Clerks, typists, and admin all use CT followed by numbers."

Jade's stomach sank. "How many users are we talking about?"

"Current staff? Around half of them. Plus any past employees who left in the past year."

She pressed her forehead against her desk. "No way to identify specific users from that period?"

"Sorry. The crash corrupted most of our authentication logs. IT claimed it was a power surge, but..." He paused. "Well, timing seemed odd."

"Odd how?"

"System had been stable for years. Then crashes, wiping specific data?" He lowered his voice.

Jade straightened. "Could someone have caused it deliberately?"

"You'd need serious technical knowledge. Access to the server room." Keys clicked again. "But in theory? Yes."

She noted this in her file. "Who had that level of access?"

"IT staff, senior administrators, some court officers." He sighed. "Look, I shouldn't say more without proper channels. Send an official request?"

"Of course. Thanks for your help, but time isn't on our side. There's enough evidence for me to have valid concerns that the murders are linked to the court and its staff. As a result, we need to question them as part of our enquiries. Can you arrange for a private room to be made available for me as I'll be there tomorrow?"

"Is that necessary?"

"Yes," Jade replied firmly.

"Very well. I'll have a room ready for you."

Jade hung up and stared at her notes. The partial ID taunted her. So close to a breakthrough, yet still out of reach. Dozens of potential users, and their prime suspect worked in the courts.

She pulled up the staff directory. Pages of names scrolled past, each a potential match for the CT prefix.

Without the full ID, she had no way to narrow it down, but a name jumped out from the list. Stephen Matthews.

She was about to call Karen but stopped. What could she report? A partial ID used by half the courthouse? A convenient system crash that might or might not be sabotage?

The evidence sat before her in fragments, but nothing she could prove until she started interviews tomorrow.

Jade gathered her notes and stood. She needed coffee, fresh air, space to think. Someone had covered their tracks, but they couldn't erase everything.

36

Karen pushed through the SCU doors with Bel close behind. The investigation room buzzed with activity as officers hunched over computers and case files. Ty waved them over to his desk, his screen filled with screenshots from Shaw's website, online discussion forums, and blogs.

"He has a lot of threats online, but as many who praise what he does," Ty said, turning his monitor. "Most hate stuff targets his coverage of corruption cases."

Karen leaned closer to read the messages. The language turned her stomach. "Nature of the threats?"

"Death threats, warnings to stop investigating, promises of violence." Ty scrolled through the evidence. "One person threatened to burn down his flat after he exposed their lenient drink-driving conviction."

Bel sat on the edge of the desk. "Any connection to our victims?"

"Nothing direct. But Shaw documented their cases in detail." Ty pulled up archived blog posts. "His analysis reads like a prosecutor's brief. Technical, factual, and focused on legal failures."

Jade approached. "I checked his posting history. Shaw sticks to proper channels. Court records, witness statements, and trial transcripts. But that seems to piss off plenty who comment, telling him to mind his own business or else."

"He's a gobby shite," Karen said.

"But that points away from him as our killer." Jade spread printouts across Ty's desk. "Shaw exposes corruption and is vocal about it. He wouldn't then go on to kill because he'd be screwing himself over. Our killer, who we believe could be Matthews, stays out of the limelight and delivers personal justice through violence."

"His security measures are extreme, but going on what we have here, I'm not surprised," Bel added.

Preet entered the room with a fresh set of documents. "Found something in Shaw's financial records. Regular donations from a legal reform group. They fund his quest."

"Legitimate backing," Karen noted. "His work serves a broader cause."

Karen paced between desks. "Shaw's research could help narrow our evidence gathering, but there's still nothing connecting him with Matthews. I don't want to question Matthews until we have more evidence. We'll spook him and I don't want that."

Claire approached with a transcript. "Just got off the phone with Shaw's former commanding officer. Says Shaw's dedication to proper procedure bordered on obsession. He documented everything."

"That tracks with his current methods," Jade said. "Every article backed by evidence. Every claim supported."

"His website and YouTube traffic spiked after each

murder," Ty reported. "He posted detailed breakdowns within hours."

"Professional interest," Preet suggested. "The cases fit his criteria."

"Or he knew details we haven't released," Karen countered.

Karen gathered her team's attention. "Shaw could prove valuable. He remains a person of interest, but we proceed with caution."

"I'll monitor his posts," Ty offered. "Track any recent cases he covered."

"And I'll dig deeper into those threats," Jade added. "See if any connect to our investigation."

A front desk officer strode into the SCU, his face tight with concern. "DCI Heath, this arrived five minutes ago. Courier on a bike. Made off before I could take his details. We've scanned it. No threat."

He thrust a padded envelope towards Karen. The team fell silent as she pulled on latex gloves and examined the package. No address. No postmark. Just "DCI Heath" written in block capitals.

The envelope's weight felt familiar.

Bel retrieved an evidence bag from her drawer while Karen opened the package. A mobile phone identical to those left at the murder scenes slid on to her desk.

"Secure the front desk CCTV," Karen said. "Find out who delivered this. There'll be a reg plate we can trace if they came by bike or car."

Ty rushed to check security footage. Karen placed the phone in the evidence bag, her hands steady despite her racing pulse.

"Two video files," she noted, examining the screen through the plastic. "Both recorded today."

The team crowded round as Karen played the first

clip. The police station's entrance filled the frame, officers coming and going during shift change.

"He's watching us," Bel whispered.

The second video sparked greater concern. Richard Ashworth stepped out of his house, briefcase in hand. The camera followed his progress to his car, capturing his number plate and regular morning routine.

"Timestamp shows this was recorded three hours ago," Jade said.

"He's chosen his next target." Karen's voice hardened. "And wants us to know. He's taunting us."

Ty returned, breathless. "Front desk cameras show a courier service delivery. Standard uniform, but the company logo's blurred. The courier parked his bike on the street, away from the cameras."

"He planned every detail." Karen grabbed her coat. "Jade, with me. The rest of you find that courier. Check every company in York."

"I'll coordinate with forensics," Ed said. "See if we can pull prints from the envelope."

"And I'll put surveillance on Ashworth's house," Bel added.

Karen pulled a face. "No. The killer's watching. He'll spot a standard team."

"Then what's the plan?" Jade asked, following Karen towards the door.

"We warn Ashworth ourselves. No marked cars, no uniforms." Karen's keys jingled as she retrieved them. "The killer wants an audience. We don't give him one."

The team scattered to their tasks as Karen and Jade rushed to the car park. The videos replayed in Karen's mind.

"He's got some balls," Jade said as they reached Karen's car.

"Yep. And I want to cut them off with a pair of garden shears!" Karen started the engine. "The other victims were practice. Ashworth's his endgame."

As she drove away, Karen floored the accelerator, taking Jade by surprise.

"Steady, I've only returned to work. I'm a bit fragile!"

"My bad. Didn't see the 'Handle With Care' sticker slapped on your forehead!" Karen laughed.

Karen swung the car towards Millionaires' Row, overtaking slow traffic where possible.

"Slow down, Karen. I'm going to throw up."

"Oh, shut up, granny."

"He's mapped Ashworth's routine." Jade remarked in between being thrown from side to side.

"Like the others." Karen navigated through traffic. "But this time he wants us to watch. But why the heads-up?"

"Yes. This is out of character for our suspect. Maybe it's not Ashworth. Could this be his attempt to push us in the wrong direction while he targets a different victim? Check in with Ed and get an update of the surveillance on Matthews and have him call Shaw too. I need to know where they both are."

Jade nodded as she reached for her phone.

The streets of York's most exclusive neighbourhood stretched before them. Victorian mansions sat back from the road behind iron gates and mature trees. Karen spotted the house number from Ashworth's file and pulled up across the street. A black Mercedes sat in the curved driveway.

"Let's hope he's home," Jade said.

37

Karen pressed the intercom beside Ashworth's wrought-iron gates. The brass plate beneath bore his name and KC title in prominent letters. Behind the gates, pristine gardens framed a Victorian mansion with tall bay windows.

The speaker crackled. "Yes?"

"DCI Heath and DS Whiting, York Police. We'd like to talk to you."

A pause. "Regarding?"

"Your safety, Mr Ashworth. It's urgent."

The gates swung open with an electric hum. Karen and Jade walked up the gravel drive, past sculpted hedges and stone planters bursting with winter colour.

Ashworth waited in his doorway, a silk dressing gown belted over cotton pyjamas. His grey hair stuck up in tufts, but his bearing held the same authority it commanded in court.

"To what do I owe this intrusion?" His gaze swept over their casual clothing with evident distaste.

"May we come in?" Karen asked. "This requires privacy."

He stepped back, gesturing towards a study that breathed wealth. Persian rugs, antique furniture, oil paintings in gilt frames.

"Three men connected to your cases died this week," Karen said, declining his offer of a seat. "Mark Reeves, James Morton, Alan Phillips. Each killed after recording confessions about their crimes."

Ashworth settled into a wing chair, crossing his legs. "Tragic, but hardly my concern. My role ended when they left court."

"The killer filmed you this morning." Jade's voice carried an edge. "Documented your schedule, your movements."

"A reasonable concern." He waved his hand. "I'll increase my security."

Karen's jaw tightened. "You obtained reduced sentences for each victim through legal manipulation. The killer views you as responsible for justice failing."

"Justice?" Ashworth barked out a laugh. "I upheld the law. Every defendant deserves proper representation."

"Even when you knew they were guilty?"

His expression hardened. "Guilt requires proof beyond reasonable doubt. I created that doubt through legitimate means. It was the twelve members of the jury that had the final say. Not me."

"While families grieved," Jade said.

"Emotion has no place in law." Ashworth stood and poured himself a measure of whisky from a crystal decanter. He held up the bottle in the officers' direction. "Drink?"

"No thanks," Karen replied.

"My duty was to my clients, not their victims."

"That duty let killers and predators walk free with little or no punishment." Karen stepped closer. "Now someone's correcting those verdicts."

He sipped his drink. "Through murder? That's not justice, it's barbarism."

"The killer sees you as the enabler. You may be his next victim. We can arrange protection..."

"Unnecessary." Ashworth cut her off. "My security system cost more than your annual salary. The grounds have motion sensors, cameras, and the security company have mobile response units."

"Technology won't stop him," Jade warned.

Ashworth's lip curled. "Common criminals with basic precautions. My measures are rather more sophisticated."

"Your arrogance blinds you to the danger," Karen said. "This killer studies his targets, learns their routines. He won't strike until he's ready."

Ashworth rolled his eyes as if thoroughly bored with the conversation.

"The protection detail is non-negotiable," Karen said, standing firm in Ashworth's book-lined study. Leather-bound law volumes lined oak shelves from floor to ceiling, interrupted only by framed certificates and awards.

He poured a second whisky, ice cubes clinking against crystal. "I've explained my position. My security measures suffice."

"No system is perfect," Karen said.

Ashworth settled into his leather chair, authority radiating from his posture. "I don't require your help or protection. I've received threats throughout my career, and as you see, I'm still here. It's the nature of the job."

Karen produced her card. "Take my number. Any suspicious activity, you call day or night."

He glanced at the card without taking it. "My panic

button connects straight to a private security firm. Their response time averages three minutes."

"Who'll arrive too late." Karen placed the card on his desk. "Reeves died in his car. Bound Morton in his flat. Burned Phillips alive. Your cameras won't stop someone that determined."

"Is that a threat, DCI Heath?"

"A warning. He'll find a way past your defences."

"Your concern borders on harassment." Ashworth drummed his fingers against his glass. "Focus on catching this vigilante instead of pestering me with predictions of doom."

"Uniform officers will drive past every hour," Jade cut in from her position near the door. "Consider it public service."

"I consider it a waste of resources." Ashworth checked his gold watch. "As I said, my legal career exposed me to threats before. None materialised."

"Take the card." Karen pushed it closer. "Ignore our warnings if you want but keep this number."

He accepted it with obvious reluctance, tucking it beneath a crystal paperweight. "Will that satisfy your duty of care?"

"No." Karen met his gaze. "But it's all we can legally do without your cooperation."

"How noble." His lips twisted. "Protecting even those you disapprove of."

"Unlike you, I don't pick who deserves justice."

Ashworth's face darkened. He stood, moving to the window overlooking his manicured gardens. "Justice? I operated within the law. Every acquittal, every reduced sentence came through proper channels. The system works because we don't rely on emotional whims."

"You twisted the law," Jade said. "Used technicalities to free guilty men."

"I provided the defence my clients paid for." He turned back and sighed. "The system worked as intended. Each verdict came from proper procedure."

"Tell that to Rachel Fenway's parents," Karen said. "Or the children and women James Morton hurt. Your procedures destroyed lives."

"Emotional manipulation has no place in law." Ashworth gripped the back of his chair. "Evidence alone determines guilt. The rest is irrelevant."

"Evidence you buried under procedural challenges." Karen moved towards the door. "The killer won't care about your procedures."

"Are you expressing approval of his methods, DCI Heath?"

"No." She faced him again. "But I understand his motivation. Every person you freed through legal tricks left victims behind. Now those choices have consequences."

"Consequences?" He barked out a laugh. "I retired with full honours. My reputation remains intact."

"Your reputation won't stop him. I'm posting officers nearby whether or not you approve."

"Do what you must, DCI." He waved towards his door. "Station an army outside if it pleases you. But keep them beyond my gates."

"When he comes for you..." Jade began.

"If." Ashworth raised one finger. "If he comes. Your dire predictions assume I'm helpless. I've faced threats before."

"The others thought that too." Karen reached the doorway. "Check your doors. Watch for suspicious vehicles. Trust no one who arrives unannounced."

"Yes, yes." He returned to his desk. "Good day, officers. I trust you can see yourselves out."

They walked through his marble hallway and out into the evening.

"Stuck-up prick," Jade muttered as they reached their car.

Karen started the engine and pulled away. "He thinks he's safe. Call the station. I want the first patrol car here within fifteen minutes. And get everything on his security company. Staff records, shift patterns, response protocols."

"You think the killer might infiltrate them?"

"He studies his targets." She checked her mirror. "Every defence has a weak point." Karen grabbed her radio. "Control, put me through to Detective Superintendent Kelly."

38

Karen padded through the kitchen in her flannel pyjamas, grateful for the quiet morning. No urgent calls meant Ashworth remained safe, protected by patrols that circled his street through the night. She poured coffee into her favourite mug, inhaling the rich aroma as steam curled towards the ceiling.

The kitchen clock ticked past six. Papers spread across the table detailed Matthews' court records and Shaw's military service. She'd spent a few hours last night reviewing them.

The front door clicked as Summer left for her morning run. Karen smiled at the girl's dedication. The house settled into peaceful silence, broken only by the central heating's gentle hum.

Footsteps creaked overhead as Zac woke. Karen cracked eggs into a bowl, whisking them before adding milk, salt, and pepper. She poured the mix into a frying pan. The simple task cleared her mind after nights of chasing shadows.

"Something smells good." Zac appeared in the doorway; his hair mussed from sleep.

"Scrambled eggs. Want some?"

He crossed the kitchen and wrapped his arms around her waist. "I'd rather have *you*. Summer's out..."

Karen smiled. This is what she needed. The old Zac, the one who couldn't keep his hands off her. "Later, I promise. Food first."

He pinched her waist. "Kelly called a moment ago."

Karen set down the whisk. "And?"

"Meeting's arranged for next week. About my return." His voice carried fresh confidence despite the undertone of anxiety. "Foster sent her report."

Karen turned in his embrace. "That's brilliant news."

"Mind-numbing desk work at first." His fingers traced patterns on her back. "But it's a start."

"You're ready." She touched his cheek, noting the steadiness in his gaze. "The old Zac's coming back."

"Different version maybe." He released her and leaned against the counter. "But stronger in some ways. I understand things now that I didn't before."

"Such as?"

"How to face fear instead of fighting it. When to push forward and when to step back." He picked up her coffee mug and took a sip. "That asking for help takes more courage than pretending everything's fine."

Karen rescued her mug with mock outrage. "Make your own."

"Too comfortable watching you cook." His smiled. A sight that grew more frequent as recovery progressed.

She returned to the eggs, adding butter to the pan. "Summer will be pleased. She's missed having you at work."

"Michelle less so." Zac's expression tightened. "She called yesterday, said returning too soon risks relapse."

"Ignore her. The doctors cleared you. Kelly trusts their judgement."

He nodded and shrugged. "Part of me knows I'm ready. But another part..."

"Fears letting people down? No one expects perfection. Take each day as it comes."

"The team's changed since I left. New faces, different dynamics."

"They respect you. Value your experience." She plated the eggs and passed him cutlery. "Besides, someone needs to keep your crew in line."

Zac's laugh carried genuine warmth. "Poor sods have been stuck with your temperate management style when you've helped."

"Cheeky git." She swatted his arm. "Eat your breakfast before it gets cold."

They settled at the table. Karen watched Zac tackle his food with renewed appetite, another sign of progress that brought quiet joy.

"I've missed this," he said between bites. "Normal mornings. No pressure to pretend I'm coping."

"You never had to pretend." She squeezed his hand. "Not with me."

His fingers interlaced with hers. "I know. You saw through the act anyway."

"When do you start?"

"Next week I guess. Kelly wants me to sit on my arse. Get back into the rhythm before taking on cases."

Karen nodded. "Smart approach. Gives you time to adjust."

"Time to prove myself too." Zac pushed his empty plate away. "Show everyone I can handle it."

"The only person you need to prove anything to is yourself." Karen stood to clear the dishes. "The rest will follow."

"The counselling helped with that. Made me see how much energy I wasted trying to meet impossible standards."

Summer burst through the front door, face flushed from her run. "Morning! Oh, eggs, yum, any left?"

"In the pan." Karen gestured with her chin. "Your dad's got news."

Summer grabbed a plate, scooping up the remaining eggs. "Yeah? Good news or weird news?"

"Back to work next week." Zac's voice held pride beneath the nerves.

"About time!" Summer dropped into the chair beside him. "Does this mean I can finally join the police cadets?"

"Nice try." Zac ruffled her hair. "But no."

"Worth a shot." She demolished her breakfast with teenage efficiency.

Karen watched Zac's expression soften as he stared at Summer's empty plate.

"She's proud of you," Karen said. "We both are."

Zac stood and pulled her close. "Couldn't have done it alone."

His strength felt solid against her, grounding them both in this moment of ordinary peace before the day's demands intruded. Karen breathed in his familiar scent, grateful for these precious minutes before murder and justice claimed her attention once more.

"Ew, there are children present!" Summer mocked as she pretended to throw up.

"Right." He stepped back. "Time to face the world. Want me to save you some dinner? Might do a shepherd's pie."

"Sounds good."

Zac gave Karen a quick kiss. "I'll go grab a shower while you two chat."

His footsteps faded up the stairs as Summer opened the cupboard and grabbed her favourite cereal bowl. A blue one with white polka dots she'd picked out years ago. The Rice Krispies rattled into the bowl.

"More food?" Karen raised an eyebrow. "After those eggs?"

"Growing girl." Summer poured milk over her cereal. "Besides, I ran three kilometres this morning."

Karen topped up her coffee. "Everything okay? You seem deep in thought."

"Yeah." Summer stirred her breakfast, making the cereal pop and crackle. "Remember our talk? About Tom and... stuff?"

"Of course."

"We went for that milkshake yesterday." Summer's spoon clinked against the bowl. "He tried to hold my hand."

"And?"

"I let him." A small smile played across her face. "But when he suggested going back to his after, I said no."

Karen set down her mug. "Good for you."

"He got a bit mardy at first, but then I explained I wanted to take things slow." Summer looked up. "Like you said, wait until it feels right and when I'm certain and ready."

"How did he take it?"

"Better than I expected. Said he respected my choice. Not sure I believed him." She spooned up more cereal. "We're going to the cinema on Saturday instead. In public, where I feel safe."

Pride swelled in Karen's chest. "You handled that well."

"Lucy keeps saying I'm boring." Summer's voice dropped. "That I should just get it over with."

"Lucy's opinion doesn't matter. Your body, your choice." Karen shifted to sit beside her. "You do it when you're ready."

"What if he loses interest?" Summer pushed her cereal around the bowl. "Sarah says boys need... you know."

"Any decent boy will respect you." Karen touched her arm. "If Tom can't handle waiting, he can bugger off."

"But what if?"

"No what ifs. Trust your instincts." Karen clasped her hand. "You felt uncomfortable with his suggestion, so you said no. That's strength, not weakness."

Summer nodded. "He texted later to apologise. Said he got carried away."

"That's positive. Shows he's thinking about your feelings." Karen sipped her coffee. "How are you feeling about Saturday?"

"Nervous. But excited too." Summer's eyes lit up. "We're seeing that new Marvel film."

"Nice neutral choice." Karen smiled. "What time's he picking you up?"

"Meeting at the cinema. Dad offered to drive me." Summer finished her cereal. "Is that weird? Having my father drop me off for a date?"

"Not at all. Shows you're sensible about safety." Karen took her empty bowl. "Any other concerns?"

Summer rubbed her nose. "What if he tries to kiss me?"

"Only if you want him to." Karen rinsed the bowl. "No pressure, no rush."

"Thanks." Summer stood and hugged her tight. "For listening. Mum just lectures about reputation and proper behaviour. Yet she's the one who reeks of booze most evenings."

"That's what I'm here for." Karen hugged back. "Any time you need to talk."

Summer squeezed tighter. "Love you."

"Love you too, sweetheart." Karen released her. "Now go get ready for school before you're late."

"Yes, boss." Summer headed for the door, then paused. "Oh, and Karen? I'm glad Dad found you."

Karen watched her bound upstairs, marvelling at how their relationship had grown. From awkward first meetings to genuine trust and affection.

The shower called, but Karen paused in the hallway, listening to the ordinary morning sounds of her family preparing for their day. Summer's music drifted from her room while Zac hummed off-key in the bathroom. Normal moments worth protecting. Karen headed for the bathroom, her mind already turning to the promise she'd made Zac earlier. She'd surprise him in the shower.

39

Ed waited outside York Crown Court, a takeaway cup steaming in one hand. His face brightened as Jade approached.

"Coffee?" He held out a second cup.

"You're keen." Jade accepted the drink. "Anyone would think you missed this place."

"Three years reading law at Warwick." Ed gazed up at the building's Victorian façade and let out a contented sigh. "The smell of legal papers and sound of barristers' gowns swishing through corridors brings back memories. Ahh."

"You crack me up, Ed. We're here to investigate, not reminisce."

Clive met them at reception, his shirt collar askew beneath his security pass. "Interview room's ready. Second floor." He led them through empty corridors, their footsteps echoing. "Staff know you're coming. I'll send them up one at a time."

The room held a table, four chairs, and windows overlooking the car park. Jade settled into position while Ed arranged his notebook and pens as if going into battle across a crowded courtroom.

Their first interviewee arrived promptly, a court typist who processed documents for Morton's trial. Jade leaned forward. "Talk me through your interactions with the defendant."

The typist described updating records and managing exhibits. Her answers flowed under Jade's questioning.

More staff followed. A security guard. Two admin assistants. An usher. Each brought fragments of information about the court's inner workings and who had access to what files. Jade drew out details, while Ed documented every word.

The morning went by in a flash. By their fourth interview, Jade's questions had grown sharper, more focused. Her confidence expanded with each response.

"Coffee break?" Ed suggested after their eighth staff member left.

Jade checked her watch. "Quick one. Matthews is next."

They found an empty staff room. Ed poured coffee from a machine while Jade reviewed her notes.

"The admin team's stories match," she said. "Late-night access requires senior approval."

"But no one monitored who stayed after hours." Ed stirred sugar into his cup. "Perfect cover for studying case files."

"But Matthews processed everything. He's senior to all of them." Jade tapped her pen against the table. "The whole system passed through his hands."

"Including Ashworth's cases."

"His supervisor mentioned changes after his wife

died." Jade flipped pages in her notebook. "Longer hours. Extra shifts. Volunteering for complex cases."

"Doing his research." Ed sipped his coffee.

"While maintaining a front of dedication." Jade stood and paced the small room. "Every witness praised his attention to detail."

"The perfect clerk."

"Who watched Ashworth manipulate justice." Jade binned her empty cup. "Ready?"

Ed gathered their notes. "Lead on."

MATTHEWS KNOCKED TWICE. His knuckles rapped against the wood with so little sound that they almost didn't hear him.

"Come in," Jade called.

He entered with slow steps, his posture court perfect. Every detail of his appearance spoke of restraint from his polished shoes to his pressed suit. Nothing flashy. Nothing distinctive. The kind of face that blended into crowds. His eyes shifted between them.

"Thank you for meeting us," Jade said. "Please sit."

Matthews settled into the chair, adjusting his tie. Dark circles shadowed his eyes, yet his gaze remained alert. Ed opened his notebook while Jade studied their witness.

"How long have you worked here?" she asked.

"Fifteen years next month." His voice carried the flat tone of someone reciting facts. "Started in records, moved up to clerk."

"Your colleagues praise your dedication."

A tight smile crossed his face. "The work demands care. And I want the best outcome for every case that comes through the courts."

Jade nodded and cut to the chase. "I understand your wife passed away. I'm sorry for your loss."

Matthews stiffened. His fingers curled against his thighs. "Two years, three months."

"Would you like to tell us about her?"

His gaze dropped to the table. "Pamela worked as a teaching assistant. Primary school. The children made cards after..." His voice cracked. "I keep them in a box. Can't look at them."

"That must be difficult."

"Each day brings challenges." He straightened his already straight tie. "Some mornings the bed feels like quicksand. The house..." He paused. "Every room holds memories."

"Is that why you spend so much time here?"

"Work helps. Keeps my mind occupied." He pulled at his collar. "The silence at home... it echoes."

"Your supervisor mentioned you took on extra responsibilities."

"The courts need dedicated staff. Budget cuts left gaps." Matthews straightened a pen on the table. "I fill them."

"Even at six in the morning?"

"Sleep proves difficult. Might as well make use of those hours." His hand trembled as he reached for the water glass. "Pamela used to joke about my workaholic tendencies. Now work keeps me sane."

"We noticed increased access to case files during late nights or early mornings, often before most staff were in." Jade watched his reaction. "Particularly those involving Richard Ashworth, KC."

Matthews' expression closed. "Many people view senior counsel records."

"Using court IDs beginning with CT."

"Standard prefix. Many of us share that designation." He shrugged, but tension threaded through his shoulders.

"But few work past midnight."

"I process paperwork. Update files. Nothing unusual about administrative tasks."

"Which files drew your attention?"

"Whatever needed doing. Court procedures generate endless documentation."

"Ashworth's cases in particular?"

"High-profile counsel attracts interest." Matthews' fingers drummed once against his thigh. "Nature of the profession."

"Even after retirement?"

"His methods created precedent. People study his techniques." A muscle ticked in his jaw. "Legal education requires understanding past cases."

"Including cases where defendants escaped proper justice?"

His eyes snapped to Jade's face. "Justice follows procedure. The courts ensure fair process."

"Like the driver who killed your wife?"

Matthews went still. "That case concluded. Nothing to discuss."

"Eighteen months for taking a life." Jade leaned forward. "Seems light."

"The system..." His voice croaked. "The system works as designed."

"Does it?"

"We're done." Matthews stood, shoulders rigid. "Unless you're suggesting something?"

"I appreciate your time." Jade held his gaze. "We may have more questions."

"My door stays open. The courts value transparency."

He left with slow steps again, but his hands had curled into fists.

The room fell silent. Jade met Ed's gaze.

"His control cracked when you mentioned his wife," Ed said.

"The grief felt real." Jade stood and stretched her arms overhead. "But something felt off."

"Agreed. His eyes never settled. Kept scanning the room."

She stopped by the window. "How to appear cooperative while revealing nothing."

"He knew we were coming,"

"The whole building knew." Jade watched Matthews cross the car park below. "His answers protected the court's reputation while telling us nothing useful."

"Classic deflection." Ed closed his notebook. "What triggered you?"

"The shift when I mentioned Ashworth. His tone changed. Like personal anger leaked through professional control."

"Worth digging deeper?"

"We push harder. Check his records and files." Jade gathered her notes. "Find what that perfect clerk facade hides."

"If it hides anything."

"My gut says it does, and it's game on. I've poked the bear. Let's see what he does now. We have him under surveillance." Jade tapped her notebook against her palm.

Ed stood. "Want to grab lunch while we plan our next move? It might get hairy in the coming hours, so we may as well fuel up now."

Jade nodded, her mind processing Matthews' performance. His grief for Pamela rang true, but something darker lurked beneath that pain. After months of doubting herself, her instincts had sparked clear warnings throughout the interview. That certainty felt like recovering a lost weapon.

"His wife's death broke him," she said. "And I think it broke him enough to kill."

"Only one way to find out." Ed held the door.

40

He took multiple diversions and dipped in and out of car parks before arriving. After his conversation with the police, he needed to beef up his surveillance and counter-surveillance tactics. This method was tried and tested in the field and after he pulled up in the leisure centre car park and swiped in, he left through the Costa Coffee shop situated at the back of the complex in a different car.

After arriving at his destination, he moved through the abandoned factory, footsteps sure in the darkness. Each item required placement—chemicals arranged how he wanted, and tools positioned for most effect. No detail escaped his consideration.

Light from his torch caught the metal chair bolted to the concrete floor. He'd selected it for durability, tested its strength against resistance. The surrounding platform provided space for his equipment while keeping escape routes clear.

Industrial drums sat in the gloom, their warning labels stark under his beam. He touched each container, confirming their contents matched his requirements.

Hydrochloric acid. Sodium hydroxide. Potassium permanganate.

His phone buzzed. Another notification. He disregarded it, concentrating on preparing Ashworth's judgement. The barrister's comfortable retirement would end soon. No more manipulation of justice. No more families destroyed by legal trickery.

The memory struck without warning. Pamela's broken body on the mortuary slab. The driver's cocaine-fuelled journey through a red light. Her shopping scattered across the tarmac while blood pooled beneath her head.

Then Ashworth's voice in court, smooth and calming: "My client expresses profound remorse. His contribution to local charities, his work with youth groups, these paint a picture of redemption."

Matthews' grip tightened on his torch. Eighteen months. The driver served twelve before early release. Now he posted photos from Spanish beaches while Pamela's grave gathered leaves.

He checked the chemical seals, ensuring proper pressure. The court's evidence procedures had taught him patience. Each step required verification. Documentation. The proper forms submitted through the right channels.

A rat skittered past, drawn by smelling his presence. Its eyes reflected red in the torchlight before it vanished into shadow. Nature claimed this space, but tonight it served a higher purpose.

The platform's metal groaned as he tested its strength. Eight steps to the observation point. Twelve to the emergency exit. He'd measured each distance, mapped every route.

His notebook held two years' planning. Ashworth's schedule. The barrister's arrogance blinded him to surveillance. Each dog walk, morning and afternoon, followed the same path. Each café visit occurred at preset times.

Matthews positioned his recording device on a tripod bought for that specific purpose.

Pamela's voice echoed in his mind: "You work too hard, love. The paperwork will wait." But she'd never seen how the system twisted truth into lies.

He arranged his tools on a steel table. Cable ties. Pliers. Duct tape. Mobile phone. Each item selected for purpose rather than pain. Ashworth's suffering meant nothing compared to the truth he'd reveal.

The observation platform provided clear sight lines for both exits. He'd reinforced weak sections, tested load limits. Nothing could interfere with tonight's judgement.

His phone displayed court listings for the next day. Cases waiting for processing. Files requiring updates. The ordinary world continued while he prepared extraordinary justice.

He touched Pamela's photo in his wallet. The image showed her last Christmas, before a cocaine-addled driver had shattered their future. Her smile was burned into his memory, driving him towards this moment.

The chemicals waited in darkness. Their labels promised cleansing fire, purifying truth. Ashworth would face final judgement in this room, forced to acknowledge every life his legal expertise had destroyed.

Matthews checked his watch as he moved towards the exit. Time pressed forward. Shortly, Ashworth's afternoon walk would follow its usual route.

Everything stood ready.

THE PARK WAS empty after lunch as Matthews watched Richard Ashworth approach. Right on schedule. The barrister's black Labrador strained against its lead, nose pressed to long grass.

From his position behind an oak tree, he tracked their progress. His camera clicked in silence, documenting each step of Ashworth's ritual. The path wound through rhododendron bushes towards the duck pond. No deviation from routine.

Ashworth paused to check his phone; his free hand buried in an overcoat pocket. No joggers. No other dog walkers. The isolation suited Matthews' purpose.

His own phone displayed the message, crafted over weeks of planning: "Evidence of misconduct in Regina v Hopkins. Payment records show defence counsel received undisclosed funds. Meet to discuss implications."

One press would start everything. Matthews' thumb hovered over "Send" as he watched Ashworth bend to unleash his dog. The animal bounded towards the water, splashing through shallow edges while its owner scrolled through emails.

The message transmitted with a soft chime. Through his camera lens, Matthews observed Ashworth's reaction. The barrister's shoulders stiffened as he read. His head turned, scanning the empty park.

Perfect. Matthews captured each micro expression, confusion, concern, and fear. Legal reputations crumbled under corruption allegations. Even retired KCs feared exposure of past misdeeds.

Ashworth called his dog back and put it on the lead, cutting short its water play. The animal resisted, shaking droplets from its coat. Its owner's voice carried across the grass: "Come on, boy. Home."

Matthews' second message pinged: *Factory off Hunt-*

ington Road. Three p.m. Bring no one. Your reputation ends today unless we talk.*

More photos documented Ashworth's response. The barrister's pace quickened, his free hand clenched around his phone. The threat struck deep, piercing the armour of wealth and status.

Through the camera, Matthews watched his target retreat towards the park gates. Ashworth's usual measured stride dissolved into urgent steps. The dog sensed its owner's distress, pressing close to his legs.

Matthews allowed himself a moment of satisfaction.

His phone buzzed with Ashworth's reply: *Who are you? These allegations lack foundation. I'll contact the police.*

Empty threats. Matthews typed his response: *Evidence goes public at four p.m. Your choice. Private discussion or public destruction.*

The park returned to silence. Ducks paddled across the pond, unaware of justice taking shape.

In his car, he reviewed the photos. Each frame showed Ashworth's confidence crumbling under threat.

Matthews' mind turned to Pamela. How Ashworth had defended her killer. Today balanced those scales. He started his engine, thoughts fixed on the afternoon ahead. He knew the barrister's ego wouldn't risk public exposure. Ashworth would turn up. Matthews allowed himself a small smile.

His phone displayed one last message from his target: *This discussion requires discretion. I'll come alone.*

Matthews didn't reply. No need. He was ready.

41

Karen stepped through the doors of York Crown Court and made her way towards the security desk. A guard looked up from his crossword puzzle.

Karen presented her warrant card. The guard didn't move, but nodded towards the scanners, where a colleague stood. Riled by his rudeness, Karen paused and glared at him. "Quick question. When you went to school, did it teach you the art of communication? By that I mean, did you ever learn to talk?"

The guard looked up from his puzzle. If she was expecting a reaction from him, none was forthcoming. He looked at her with a face that suggested he was thoroughly bored with life before returning to his puzzle book.

"I didn't think so!" she tutted and moved away, not willing to waste her breath on the man any further.

"ID, and please put all your belongings in the tray for me," the other guard asked, pointing to the scanner tray.

Karen placed her belongings in the plastic container. Her phone, warrant card, keys, and notebook clattered against the bottom. The guard studied her ID before nodding towards the metal detector.

This is better, Karen thought. Not only was the second guard more polite, but his request came with a cheeky grin which Karen soon realised was him being more than friendly because he didn't take his eyes off her as she passed through the scanner and retrieved her belongings on the other side.

The machine beeped as she walked through. The guard waved his wand over her outfit, pausing at her belt buckle. Karen waited, arms raised, while he completed his checks.

"Second floor," he said, handing back her belongings. "DS Whiting's expecting you."

"Enjoy the rest of your day, because you've certainly made mine," he said, as Karen made her way into the building.

Still got it, Karen thought as she smiled.

Karen climbed the stone staircase, passing barristers in black gowns who clutched case files to their chests. The corridors branched off each landing, their walls lined with dark wood panels that absorbed the overhead lighting.

She found Jade and Ed in the interview room, papers spread across the table's surface. Empty coffee cups marked the hours they'd spent questioning staff.

"Your turn for a break," Karen told Ed. "Get some fresh air."

Ed gathered his notebook and pen. "Matthews gave us plenty to think about. His grief feels genuine, but something's off."

After Ed left, Karen settled into his vacant chair. "Walk me through the interviews."

"Most staff painted the same picture," Jade said.

"Matthews keeps to himself, works constant overtime, takes pride in his efficiency."

"Any personal relationships at work?"

"None. Eats lunch alone at his desk. Minimal chat with colleagues." Jade pushed a heap of papers across the table. "But look at his work patterns. The man lives here. First to arrive, last to leave."

Karen scanned the documents.

"Complete transformation." Jade tapped her pen against her notepad. "The court records show an obsession with detail."

"Especially Ashworth's cases?"

"The logs show increased activity whenever Ashworth appeared in court. Matthews insisted he had to be the one who documented everything."

A knock interrupted them. Clive entered, his tie askew and shirt collar crumpled. "Thought I'd check how you're getting on."

"Pull up a chair," Jade said. "We need to discuss Matthews."

Clive took a seat. "Good clerk. Keeps everything running smoothly."

"But?" Karen prompted.

"Changed after his wife died. Poured his energy into his work. Started arriving before sunrise, staying past midnight." Clive tugged at his collar. "The dedication worried me."

"In what way?" Jade asked.

"Grief needs processing. He buried himself in paperwork instead." Clive glanced at the door before continuing. "Found him asleep at his desk more than once. Dark circles under his eyes. Weight loss."

"Did you suggest counselling?" Karen asked.

"Required it. Part of his return-to-work assessment."

Clive sighed. "He attended six sessions, got signed off, then doubled his hours."

Jade flipped through her notes. "Tell us about his annual rituals."

"Lays flowers every year on the anniversary. Not just at her grave, but at the primary school where she taught, and an office where she worked before that." Clive shook his head. "Bit odd, marking spots with no connection to her death."

Karen exchanged a glance with Jade.

"We need to check his system access," Karen said. "Login records, file requests, anything that shows his activity patterns."

Clive stood. "Follow me. Everything's logged on to the main database."

They walked through the maze of corridors to his office. The room smelled of coffee and old papers. Clive settled behind his computer and typed in his password.

"Here we go." He scrolled through a listing. "Activity log for the past two years."

Karen studied the screen over his shoulder. Hundreds of entries filled the display. Times, dates, and file references. Matthews' access revealed a particular pattern.

"Can you filter by time?" she asked. "Show only out-of-court hours activity."

Clive adjusted the search parameters. New data filled the screen.

"That's not normal," he said. "No clerk needs to review this many cases."

"Or this many case files," Jade added. "Look at the volume."

Karen received a text from Dan: *Patrol checked Ashworth's house twice in the past hour. No response at door or gates. Car missing from drive. Mobile goes straight to voice-*

mail. Security company confirms alarm system disabled from inside at 2:15 p.m. No signs of forced entry.

She showed the message to Jade. "We need copies of these logs."

"I'll print everything," Clive said.

Karen dialled Dan's number as Clive's printer hummed to life. Matthews laid flowers at the factory each year, marking his wife's memory. Now the building held a darker purpose. The perfect place to deliver his brand of justice.

Clive's printer churned out page after page of Matthews' login records. Karen spread them across his desk while Jade created a timeline on her notepad.

"Look at this pattern," Jade said. "He accessed Ashworth's case files every night for two weeks before each murder."

Karen picked up a sheet dense with timestamps. "The amount of detail he collected."

"Here." Clive pointed to his screen. "He only pulled every case where Ashworth secured reduced sentences. Created digital copies, downloaded evidence files."

"Can you show his badge scans for today?" Karen asked.

Clive typed commands into his terminal. "Strange. He left the building at twelve thirty."

"Right after our interview." Jade straightened in her chair. "Did he give notice?"

"No." Clive picked up his phone. "Let me check with his department."

Karen's stomach tightened as she studied the access logs.

"His desk's empty," Clive said, ending his call. "Computer shut down, papers cleared away."

"That's not his normal routine?" Karen asked.

"Never. He keeps multiple cases open, stays late to process paperwork." Clive rubbed his neck. "Today everything's gone."

Jade stood and paced round the office. "The timing fits. Ashworth disappeared after two. Matthews left at half twelve. And I poked the bear."

Karen threw her a look of confusion.

"Check his computer history," Karen said. "What files did he access this morning?"

Clive's fingers moved across his keyboard. "Everything related to Ashworth."

"He knew we'd investigate." Jade stopped pacing. "The interview spooked him."

Karen called her team to update them. "Do you have the file on the driver who killed his wife?"

More keystrokes filled the screen with data.

"Twelve months served," Jade read. "Early release for good behaviour."

Karen dialled the unit back and got through to Preet. "We need a search warrant for Matthews' house. We think Matthews has done a runner. What's his current location?"

"One sec," Preet replied before coming back to Karen. "He's at the leisure centre. Been there nearly two hours."

Warning bells rang straight away. "Get the officers to check inside. Is he still there?"

"The car is," Preet replied.

"Doesn't mean anything. We need visual confirmation if he's there or not."

"I'll pass that through now."

"Look at this." Clive opened another file. "Matthews reviewed all the paperwork for his wife's case multiple times."

Karen ended her call. "We need to find Matthews now."

"Why wait two years?" Clive asked.

"I'm not sure. A recent trigger that made him snap. Building evidence. It could be anything." Karen gathered the printed logs.

"And Ashworth represents everything he hates." Jade checked her watch.

Karen read a text from Ty: *CCTV shows Matthews' car heading east on Huntington Road at 2:45. Black Corsa confirmed. It's in the direction of his address.*

"Alert armed response," Karen told her. "Full tactical unit. We move fast but quietly, no sirens, and no lights."

Karen and Jade hurried from his office. Their footsteps echoed through the courthouse corridors as they rushed towards the exit.

"He won't kill Ashworth straight away," Jade said. "He'll want his confession first."

"Which gives us time." Karen pushed through the entrance doors. "But not much. His patience is gone. The interview forced his hand."

42

Karen screeched to a halt outside Matthews' terraced house. Armed officers poured from unmarked vehicles, their weapons trained on the building's facade. Jade joined her behind a parked van as Dan briefed the entry team.

"Front and back," Karen ordered. "Quick and clean."

The officers moved into position. The big red key crashed against the front door, splintering wood around the lock. Two further attempts took the door in.

"Police!" officers shouted as they charged through the doorway. Further officers piled in, more shouts reverberating off the walls as they rushed through every room. Karen followed the first team through, baton drawn as she tucked in behind a firearms officer. The house lay dark and still.

"Clear," came the call from the kitchen.

"Clear," echoed from the lounge.

Karen climbed the stairs, with Jade close behind. Light pierced the gloom through the half-drawn curtains. Three doors lined the narrow landing.

"Bedroom one clear," an officer called from the master bedroom.

Karen pushed open the middle door. The spare room struck her cold. She paused mid step, her eyes taking in the scene. Photos of Pamela Matthews covered every wall. Wedding pictures, holiday snaps, and casual moments frozen in time. Candles crowded a small table beneath the largest image, their wicks black with regular use. Dead rose petals scattered across the surface.

Newspaper clippings about her death filled a cork board. Court documents detailing her killer's trial clustered around the edges, their corners curled with frequent handling. Red ink circled key phrases: "reduced sentence", "mitigating circumstances", "rehabilitation potential".

"Karen." Jade's voice carried a note of unease.

Karen crossed to the master bedroom. The air hung thick with disuse. Pamela's dressing gown draped across a chair; its pink fabric dulled with dust. Her book rested on the bedside table, a bookmark still marking her final page.

A pair of slippers waited beneath the bed. Dried flowers filled a vase on the windowsill. The calendar on the wall remained fixed on the month of her death.

"He's turned it into a bloody museum," Jade said.

Karen opened the wardrobe. Women's clothes lined one side, untouched. A collection of perfume bottles crowded the dresser, their contents evaporated to nothing. Her hairbrush lay on the surface, strands of hair tangled in its bristles.

"Look at the bed." Jade pointed to the right side. "The pillow, the covers. No one's slept here."

The left side bore the impression of a single occupant. Matthews had preserved his wife's half of the bed, a hollow space waiting for her return.

On the dresser, a framed photo showed the couple on holiday. Pamela's eyes sparkled as she hugged Matthews on a sunlit beach. The image captured happiness before tragedy struck. A moment Matthews refused to leave behind.

"Ma'am." An officer appeared in the doorway. "Found his computer in the study."

The small room off the landing held Matthews' workspace. Papers filled filing cabinets in rigid order. His laptop sat closed on the desk beside stacks of court transcripts. Each page bore highlights and annotations in his neat hand.

"Bag it," Karen said. "I want everything. Papers, drives, and any storage devices."

She returned to the spare room. The shrine dominated the space, each photo capturing Pamela's smile. Cards from her students yellowed with age. A box beneath the table holding more memories. Cinema tickets, restaurant receipts, and small mementoes of shared moments.

"Jesus," she muttered as she shook her head, feeling overwhelmed by the sheer scale of what she saw.

In the corner, a child's drawing caught Karen's eye. The crayon figures showed Pamela with her class, stick figures holding hands beneath a yellow sun. "Best Teacher Ever" decorated the top in wobbly letters. The paper's creases spoke of frequent handling.

"Grief twisted into obsession." Karen shouted to Jade as she studied a family photo. "He couldn't move forward, so he moved deeper into the past. Until Ashworth freed her killer."

A photo album lay open on a side table. The last entry showed Pamela leaving for work on her last morning. Matthews had written the date and time beneath in careful script. The next page remained blank. A life interrupted mid story.

Two years of planning of studying cases and tracking targets, led to this moment. They had to reach Ashworth before Matthews forced his confession.

"Hold on," Jade called from the study. "His laptop's unlocked."

Karen returned as Jade clicked through Matthews' browser history. YouTube filled the screen with Robert Shaw's channel dominating the recommendations. Karen lifted a stack of papers from Matthews' desk. Legal documents traced her killer's path through the courts. Each stage bore Matthews' notes on times, dates, and names of everyone involved in reducing the sentence.

"He watched these videos for hours," Jade said.

Karen leaned closer. The titles painted a pattern: "Justice System Failures", "Killers Who Walked Free", "When Courts Protect Criminals". Each video bore Matthews' comments beneath, growing darker.

"Shaw's rants didn't help. It incited Matthews," Karen said.

"Here." Jade opened a spreadsheet. "He tracked Shaw's cases, cross-referenced them with court records." She scrolled through rows of data. "He built profiles of potential targets."

The browser history revealed Matthews' descent. Searches for "justice system failures" evolved into "chemical burns effects" and "industrial accident cover-ups". Each query drew him deeper into darkness.

"These locations." Karen pointed at the screen. "The car park where we found Reeves. The streets around Morton's flat." Her finger traced down the list. "He mapped approach routes, escape paths, blind spots in CCTV coverage."

Jade opened another tab. "Check the dates. He studied each site for weeks before the murders."

The map searches painted Matthews' preparation in digital footprints. Street views, satellite images, and planning documents as he examined his killing grounds from every angle.

"Wait." Karen tapped the screen. "These recent searches. The industrial estate off Huntington Road."

"Dozens of hits in the past week." Jade pulled up the location. "He researched the entire area... access roads, abandoned buildings, and underground tunnels."

"Next site?" Karen suggested.

"Look at this." Jade clicked a folder marked "Final". Inside, photographs showed the location from multiple perspectives. Matthews had documented security patrol routes, noted blind spots, mapped the tunnel network beneath the buildings.

"He planned this." Karen straightened. "The other murders taught him what worked. Now he's ready for Ashworth."

Jade switched back to the videos and for the next few minutes, they both watched Shaw become more agitated, his rants becoming more inflammatory.

"Truth exposed at last." "Someone must balance the scales." "Actions speak louder than words."

"Shaw advocated for reform," Karen said. "Matthews twisted that message into justification."

A corkboard behind the desk caught her attention. Photos of Reeves, Morton, and Phillips hung in a row, each marked with a red cross. Below them, Ashworth's image remained unmarked, a final target waiting for judgement.

"His searches focused on one location." Jade zoomed the map. "The old industrial site. Multiple entries."

"Perfect spot for his endgame." Karen studied the layout. "Isolated and plenty of escape routes."

"We need to get there fast," Jade said, rising from the chair.

"Send these coordinates to the tactical team," Karen ordered. "Matthews chose this location and knows every corner."

Jade copied the map data. "He's creating another kill room."

Karen's phone buzzed with a message from Dan requesting an update. She glanced one last time at the cork board, at Ashworth's unmarked photo beneath his earlier victims.

"Matthews watched Shaw's channel," Jade said as Karen headed for the door. "That must have tipped him over the edge."

43

Karen swung the car into the industrial estate entrance, wheels crunching over broken glass. Two police units sat at the perimeter, lights switched off to maintain cover. An officer stepped from the shadows and approached her window.

"The gates have been forced open, ma'am." He pointed towards a rusted side entrance. "Drug users get in that way according to locals."

Karen studied the sprawling complex of abandoned buildings. Fading daylight caught broken windows and crumbling brickwork. A decade of neglect turned industrial pride into urban decay.

"Teams split up," she told the armed officers positioned behind their vehicles. "Check every building. Move quietly."

Units dispersed across the site, engines muted as they rolled between derelict structures. Empty beer cans rattled across cracked concrete. Wind-blown litter collected in corners. Black mould crept up walls covered in spray painted tags. Generations of graffiti artists had marked their territory in neon colours that glowed against grey brick.

Karen's radio crackled. "Sierra One. White Prius and black Mercedes spotted behind unit seven. Both vehicles are cold."

"Control, all units converge on unit seven," Karen responded. She turned to Jade. "Ready?"

"Let's end this."

They rounded the corner to find armed officers covering the rear entrance. She stopped her car behind an ARV and joined them.

"Any movement or noise?" she asked.

"Nothing so far."

Paint peeled from metal double doors that hung open to darkness. As the officers entered, the stench of urine, vomit, and decay hit them. Years of human misery concentrated in one space.

Jade pressed her sleeve against her nose as her eyes watered. Discarded needles glinted in their torch beams. Empty foil wraps and broken bottles marked desperate nights seeking chemical escape.

Karen drew her baton and stepped inside. A stillness surrounded them.

Their lights caught broken windows high above, graffiti marking every surface. Footsteps echoed through the empty halls as the team advanced. Each room revealed remnants of past industry as rusted machinery, rotting pallets, and mountains of debris came into view. Water dripped from exposed pipes, creating dark pools on concrete floors.

A door creaked somewhere ahead. Karen raised her hand, halting the group. Voices carried from the next section. Too faint to make out words.

"Rear clear," an officer whispered through the radio.

"Loading bay clear."

"Storage area one clear."

Room by room, they pressed forward. Karen's torch beam swept abandoned offices filled with mouldering papers. Past a staff canteen where rats scattered from their approach. Through corridors thick with cobwebs and years of grime.

Karen paused at an intersection. "Left team take north section. Right team sweep south. Radio checks every thirty seconds."

The last door opened on to a vast storage space. Their lights revealed Matthews' stage. A metal chair bolted to the floor. Chemical drums in a circle around it. Cameras on tripods pointed towards the scene. An observation platform waited above. Industrial chains hung from exposed beams, swaying in the draft from broken skylights.

But the room stood empty.

"Check the platform," Karen ordered. Officers moved up metal stairs while others secured the perimeter. The platform groaned under their weight.

Jade examined the chair. "Restraints attached. Look at the set-up. Cameras positioned to catch every angle. He planned to record everything."

Karen studied the chemical drums. Warning labels marked their contents. Industrial-grade acids, solvents, and caustic substances. Matthews had gathered tools for a prolonged execution.

A door slammed deeper into the building. Karen spun towards the sound. "All units hold position. They're still here."

"Movement in the east corridor," a voice whispered through her radio.

"Negative on visual contact," another added.

Matthews knew this space. Each corner, each shadow, each escape route. Karen clicked off her radio to prevent feedback. The team needed silence now.

"Jade, with me. Rest of you maintain positions." Karen pressed her back against the cold brick and steadied her breathing.

Footsteps approached from multiple directions, some firm and purposeful, others stumbling. A voice echoed through the darkness, too distant to make out words.

The trap waited. Now they needed to spring it before he completed his mission.

Karen tightened her grip on her baton. Jade moved to cover the opposite approach. Armed officers held defensive positions around the perimeter.

In the distance, another door opened. Footsteps drew closer.

The game of hunter and hunted played out in shadow and echo. But who pursued whom through this maze of industrial ruins? Karen waited, every sense alert for the next move.

Their pursuit had led here to a second killing room Matthews had crafted, but could they reach him before he forced one last confession?

They crept towards the doorway where pale light spilled into the corridor. The stench of chemicals grew stronger with each step. Karen's eyes burned as acrid fumes drifted through the air.

Matthews stood behind an industrial chair, his court clerk posture transformed into rigid tension. An industrial respirator mask covered the lower half of his face, the filter protruding like a grotesque snout. A clear indicator he'd planned for the toxic environment he'd created. His movements were edgy as he paced behind Ashworth.

The barrister slumped forward in his restraints. His

expensive overcoat bore dark stains where chemicals had splashed. His trousers were torn at the knee, evidence of a struggle. The dog lead still dangled from his pocket. His earlier confidence vanished, replaced by raw terror.

A camera faced the scene, its recording light pulsing in the gloom. Chemical drums created a wall around the chair, their warning labels stark against rusted metal. Karen motioned the armed officers back from the toxic fumes.

"Regina versus Hopkins." Matthews' voice carried the practised tone of court proceedings. "July 15th, 2019. The evidence proved guilt beyond doubt."

"I represented my client according to the law and..." Ashworth's words cut off as Matthews grabbed his hair, wrenching his head back.

Ashworth screamed as his face contorted in pain.

"Tell them how you buried witness statements. How you attacked victims' credibility. How you turned truth into reasonable doubt."

"The law requires proper defence." Ashworth's voice cracked. "Every defendant deserves representation."

"Representation?" Matthews' grip tightened. "You sold justice to the highest bidder. Made murder into manslaughter. Turned rape into misconduct. Your fees bought truth. You were as guilty as the bastard who killed my Pamela!"

Karen edged closer, keeping to the shadows. Matthews' deteriorating state concerned her. The chemical fumes made her eyes water even from this distance.

"Where's your dog?" Matthews demanded. "Left him in the car?"

"I left him at home," Ashworth gasped.

"My wife needed justice!" Matthews slammed Ashworth's head forward. "You defended her killer.

Turned his cocaine use into a mental health plea. Made his choices into illness."

"The evidence supported..."

"The evidence?" Matthews released his grip and stepped back. "I know everything." His hands trembled as he reached for a chemical drum. "Now you're going to do the right thing and confess, or I'll melt the skin off your bones. Tell them how you let criminals escape proper punishment."

"I'll cooperate." Ashworth strained against his restraints. "Money, property, anything you want."

"I want truth." Matthews lifted the drum. "See this? What I have here will make you experience pain like you've never imagined."

Karen touched her radio, switching to silent signal. She needed her team in position before Matthews completed his finale. The chemical fumes posed as much danger as the unstable clerk. One wrong move could trigger a disaster.

"Start with Hopkins," Matthews ordered. "Explain how you knew he killed those children. How you used technicalities to set him free. How much his family paid for justice."

"The prosecution failed to..."

"No!" Matthews yelled and kicked the chair. "Tell them what you knew. What evidence you buried. How many lives you destroyed for profit. Your retirement house paid with blood money."

Karen caught Jade's eye, pointing to positions around the room. Armed officers moved into place, invisible in the darkness beyond Matthews' focus. The chemical drums limited their options. One stray shot could spray acid across the room.

"I was only doing my job and working within the law.

I'm sorry about Pamela. I really am. Please, let's talk about this. What would your wife think now if she saw what you're doing? This isn't right," Ashworth pleaded.

"The system failed!" Matthews screamed. "Failed Pamela. Failed every victim whose killer you set free." He tightened his grip on the chemical container. "Your games and courtroom performances all bought and paid for. But I swear to God, you'll speak the truth now. Before the acid burns it from your throat."

Karen signalled to her team to stand by as she assessed the risk. Matthews' stability deteriorated with each passing moment. His hands trembled. He coughed so hard that his throat gurgled with mucus.

The chemical fumes thickened. Karen's throat scratched even from this distance. She needed to end this before Matthews turned his makeshift court into an execution chamber. But one wrong move could trigger the disaster he'd prepared with such care.

Behind her, armed officers waited for her signal, but she urged them to retreat as she backed away to protect their health. The room had become a powder keg of toxic chemicals and raw emotion.

44

Karen moved into the light, keeping her movements slow and non-threatening as she held out her hands at shoulder height. "Stephen."

Matthews jerked at her voice, his grip tightening on the chemical container. "Stay back."

"Let's talk about this." She kept her distance, conscious of the toxic fumes filling the space. "Put down the chemicals."

"No closer." Matthews pressed the drum against Ashworth's shoulder. The barrister flinched as liquid seeped through his shirt. "One step and I'll pour it over him."

Behind her, Jade stood in the corridor and coordinated with control. "We need fire service support. Full chemical incident protocol."

"I know about Pamela," Karen said.

Matthews' face twisted. "Don't say her name."

"The shrine in your spare room. The photos. Her things untouched." Karen inched forward. "I feel your pain. I know what it feels like to lose a loved one."

"Pain?" Matthews barked out a bitter laugh. "Watching her killer get a slap on the wrist is painful. Listening to him thank the court for its mercy is painful."

The container wobbled in Matthews' grip. A drop of liquid splashed on to Ashworth's neck. The barrister screamed as it burned his skin.

"The prosecution failed to establish intent," Ashworth gasped through gritted teeth. "My duty…"

"Shut up." Matthews struck the back of his head. "Your duty was to uphold the truth."

The blow rocked Ashworth forward. Blood trickled from his scalp, staining his collar.

"The whole building is surrounded," Karen said. "Armed officers cover each exit. No one else needs to die tonight."

Matthews shook his head. His finger tapped against the container's surface. "He has to suffer. Like she suffered. Like every victim suffered while he twisted evidence into doubt."

Sweat dripped down Matthews' face. His shirt clung to his body, dark patches spreading across his chest. The chemical fumes turned his skin pale.

"Your wife taught children to read." Karen whispered. "She shaped young lives. What would she think of this?"

"She'd understand." But uncertainty crept into his tone. "The system protected her killer. Like it protected his clients."

Matthews kicked a smaller container. It rolled across the floor, its contents sloshing. The liquid left smoking trails on concrete.

"The law requires proper defence." Ashworth pulled against his restraints. The cable ties cut into his wrists. "Every case deserves…"

"Rich men's justice." Matthews seized Ashworth's throat. Blood vessels bulged in his neck as he squeezed.

Karen's radio crackled.

"The evidence determined outcomes," Ashworth choked out. "Not emotion."

"Evidence?" Matthews released his throat and grabbed his hair. "You buried proof. How much did her killer pay you?"

Ashworth gasped for air. Red marks bloomed across his neck where Matthews' fingers had dug in.

"This won't bring her back," Karen said.

"Back?" The word emerged as a sob. "I wake up reaching for her. The bed stays cold. Her clothes gather dust." His grip loosened on Ashworth's hair. "The house echoes with silence. I'm waiting to join her."

The chemical fumes grew thicker. Karen's eyes stung. Her lungs screamed for clean air. Behind her, officers shifted positions in need of fresh air from the corridor.

"We can end this without more death." Karen gestured to the chemicals. "Put it down. Walk away."

"Walk away?" Ashworth's voice dripped contempt despite his fear. "After this assault? You'll be locked up forever."

"For God's sake, shut up." Karen cut him off. The barrister's arrogance threatened to push Matthews over the edge.

Matthews released Ashworth and paced behind the chair. His movements turned erratic. The chemical container swayed in his grip.

"He turned her death into a legal argument. Made her killer into a victim." His breathing turned ragged. "The judge praised his dedication to justice."

Liquid splashed on to the floor.

"Stephen, stop." Karen blinked back tears from the fumes. "Think of Pamela. The lives she touched."

"I think of nothing else." His voice cracked. "Her last morning. The shopping list on the fridge. The book she never finished." He gripped the container tighter. "While her killer posts beach photos from Spain."

Karen's radio buzzed. Jade's voice cut through static: "Fire service two minutes out. AFO units in position."

Matthews swayed on his feet, the chemical vapours affecting his balance. But rage steadied his hands as he lifted the container higher.

"Tell them the truth." He turned to Ashworth. The container tilted. Liquid sloshed near the rim.

Ashworth strained against his bonds. "Please. I have children."

"So did your clients' victims." Matthews' finger traced the warning label. "How many families begged for justice while you played legal games?"

Karen measured the distance between them. Too far to reach him before he poured.

"Reopen the cases." Matthews shifted his weight. "Every verdict. Every sentence you corrupted."

Karen kept her position. "Put down the chemicals first. Then we'll talk."

"No." Matthews pressed the container closer to Ashworth. "Promise me. Your word as a police officer."

"I—I can tell you things." Ashworth's voice shook. "Names. Dates. Other barristers who took payments in high-profile cases in London. The Old Bailey."

Matthews went rigid. "What payments?"

"Cash. Property deals. Offshore accounts." The words tumbled from Ashworth's lips. "Defence teams coordinated with prosecutors. Fixed outcomes."

"Stephen, focus on me." Karen recognised the spark in

Matthews' eyes. The confirmation of his darkest beliefs. "Don't let him bait you."

"Harrison, KC orchestrated plea bargains." Ashworth twisted against his restraints. "Mackenzie traded reduced charges for percentage fees."

"Shut up." Karen stepped forward, but Matthews yanked the chemical container back.

"Stay there." His chest heaved with each breath. "Let him speak. Let everyone hear the truth."

The fumes thickened. Karen's throat burned as she reached for a disposable mask from her pocket. Through the toxic haze, she watched Matthews' conviction solidify.

"Bishop handled white-collar cases." Ashworth continued. "Corporate clients paid extra to ensure a certain outcome."

"I bloody knew it." Matthews circled the chair. "Verdicts bought and sold."

"That's not what this means." Karen fought to control the situation. "Individual crimes don't poison the entire process."

"No?" Matthews grabbed Ashworth's jaw. "Tell her about Pamela's killer."

"The evidence suggested diminished responsibility." Ashworth choked out the words. "Standard practice in..."

"Standard practice?" Matthews released him with a shove. "Your standard practice killed my wife. Your standard practice lets murderers walk free."

Karen's radio buzzed. Jade's voice emerged through static: "This is too dangerous. We need to move."

Behind her, an officer coughed. The toxic atmosphere had spread. Matthews' skin turned grey, but determination blazed in his eyes. She knew her actions were putting her life in danger, but a bigger threat remained.

"You keep records?" Matthews demanded. "Proof of these deals?"

"Files." Ashworth nodded. "Documents. Recordings of meetings."

"Where?"

"Home office. Hidden safe. I can take you there."

"No more negotiations." Karen cut in. "Stephen, you're dying in here. These fumes will kill you."

"Dead already." Matthews kicked another container. Chemicals splashed across the concrete. "Died the day she did."

"Think of the evidence." Karen pointed to the camera still recording. "His confession. The files he mentioned. Your death ruins everything."

Matthews paused. The container dipped in his grip.

"The cases need review." His voice rasped. "Public inquiry. Full investigation."

"We'll pursue it." Karen edged closer. "My team will dig into every case. But we need you alive."

"She's stalling." Ashworth's words triggered a fresh rage in Matthews' expression. "Once you're arrested, they'll bury everything. Protection of the profession. Reputation of the courts."

"Shut the fuck up." Karen snapped at the barrister. "One more word and I'll gag you myself."

"Listen to him." Matthews raised the container.

Karen gestured to the camera. "Your recording captures everything. His reputation ends today."

"Not enough." Matthews shook his head. "Pamela deserves more."

"Then help us." Karen took another step. The fumes burned her eyes as she buried her mask in the crook of her elbow. "Work with my team. Show us where to dig."

"Like they worked with families?" Matthews' fingers whitened on the container.

"Stephen, please."

"The cases." His arm tensed. "Swear they'll be reopened. All of them. Public inquiry. Full exposure."

Karen met his gaze. "You know I can't do that. I don't have the authority."

"Then what's left?" The container tilted. "Except to finish this? Make him feel what victims felt?"

She saw the change in his eyes. The last thread of reason snapped. His mission consumed him, fed by Ashworth's desperate confessions.

"I chose them." Matthews' voice dropped. "Each target. Each kill site. Made them face their crimes."

"We know." Karen coughed. "But this ends here."

"No." Matthews straightened. Purpose replaced his earlier uncertainty. "This starts here."

Matthews' fingers tightened around the container.

Karen knew that look. The moment a person in agony stepped past the point of no return.

"Stephen, please," she begged, the smell grabbing at her throat as she retreated to the safety of the corridor. "We can make this right."

His eyes flickered. For a second—just a second—she thought he might let go.

Then his jaw set.

"The courts failed us." His voice was eerily calm. "So I'll be the verdict."

He tipped the container. The air burned. The world blurred.

More fumes swallowed the remaining oxygen as time began to run out.

45

Distant sirens pierced the toxic air as Karen struggled to get oxygen into her lungs.

Matthews jerked at the sound. "They'll bury everything," he said, his voice rough. "Like they buried Pamela's case."

"No." Karen kept her tone level. "Look what you've achieved. Three killers faced justice. Ashworth confessed his corruption."

Matthews yanked off his respirator mask, needing Ashworth to hear his words clearly. "The files..." His face, protected until now, suddenly exposed to the toxic fumes. The effect was almost immediate. His eyes glazing, skin turning ashen beneath the harsh lights.

The chemical taste coated her tongue with metal. Through the haze, she noted Matthews' shallow breathing, the tremors in his hands. His skin had turned waxy, lips tinged blue.

"The system protected them all." He stumbled backwards, catching himself against a drum.

More sirens joined the first, their wails echoing

through broken windows. Matthews flinched at each new sound. The container tilted further in his grip.

"You're right about the system," Karen said. "I've watched killers walk free. Watched defence teams twist evidence until truth disappeared."

His bloodshot eyes fixed on her face. "Then you understand."

"I understand your anger. But this…" She gestured at the chemicals, the bound barrister, the toxic soup filling the air. "This destroys your message."

"The evidence matters," Karen pressed. "Your documentation. Your research. The corruption Ashworth revealed. Dead men can't testify."

The sirens grew louder. Matthews blinked hard, his focus wavering. Sweat ran down his face.

"Listen, Stephen." Karen demanded. "You need medical attention. These fumes are toxic."

"Stay back." But the warning lacked force. His words slurred at the edges.

Behind her, an officer feeling light-headed dropped to one knee. Karen signalled for the team to pull back further. The fumes had turned the air bitter and were now reaching them in the doorway.

"Your wife did so much," she said. "Built foundations for young people. What can you build from here?"

The container slipped in Matthews' grip. Liquid splashed his shoes. He showed no reaction.

"The recordings." His voice dropped to a whisper. "The evidence in my house. My computer…"

"We found it all," Karen said. "Every file. Every document. Your investigation exposed the truth."

Matthews staggered again, catching himself on a drum. The toxic atmosphere had worked into his system. His movements turned sluggish, uncoordinated.

"Promise me." He wiped the blood trickling from his nose with the back of his hand. "Promise they'll examine the cases."

"You have my word." Karen shouted across the void. "But I need you alive to guide us."

Matthews' eyes lost focus, pupils blown wide. His chest heaved.

"The cases..." His words faded to a mumble. "Pamela deserved..."

Ashworth sagged in the chair, head lolling forward. The chemical injuries on his neck had turned black.

Matthews swayed on his feet, the container trembling in his grip.

"You've breathed these vapours for too long," Karen said. "Let us help you."

The container tilted in his unsteady hands. Karen tracked the toxic liquid as it sloshed near the rim.

"Look at your hands, Stephen. The tremors. The chemicals are shutting down your body."

He blinked hard, struggling to focus. "Doesn't matter now."

"It matters to the investigation." Karen reminded him. "Your evidence is vital. We could turn the justice system inside out. But I can only do that with your help."

Fresh blood ran from his nostrils.

"The files..." Matthews sniffed hard and shook his head.

"You never planned to walk out," Karen said. "But these chemicals, you underestimated their strength."

Recognition flickered in his glazed eyes.

"The fumes..." Fear crept into his voice. "Too strong..."

"Let us help you. Before the damage becomes permanent."

Matthews shook his head again. The motion sent him

staggering. "No prison," he gasped. "No cells. Better to end it."

"End what? Your chance to expose the truth?" Karen pressed her advantage. "To show how deep the corruption runs?"

His eyes lost focus. The container slipped in his blood-slicked hands.

"Stephen. Your body's shutting down. But we can still save you."

"Pamela... What have I...?"

"Your choice," Karen said. "Die here, letting them bury the evidence. Or live to testify. Make them face real justice."

Matthews looked at the chemicals in his grip. Understanding dawned in his fading eyes—understanding of what the fumes had already done to his body.

46

Matthews lowered the chemical container, his hands trembling as he placed it on the concrete floor. Even with just minutes of exposure since removing his mask, blood had trickled from his nose, staining his shirt collar. The industrial-grade chemicals worked quickly on unprotected flesh.

"We planned to move to the Yorkshire Dales," he said, his voice raw from the chemical fumes. "Pamela wanted a cottage with roses round the door. Space for children to play."

Karen maintained her distance, aware of armed officers shifting positions in the shadows behind her. "Tell me about these plans."

"Three bedrooms. One for us. Two for the kids we never had." Matthews pressed his palm against his chest. "The estate agent showed us places. We picked paint colours. Pamela kept a notebook of ideas."

Spittle flew from his mouth. The toxic vapours had done their work, breaking down his defences along with his body. His next words emerged as a whisper.

"The driver took everything. Our future. Our family. Our dreams." He sank to his knees beside Ashworth's chair. "He crossed that junction at sixty. Cocaine in his system. But this bastard turned it into a mental health plea."

"The system failed you both."

"Failed?" Matthews struck the floor with his fist. "The driver walks and lives the life he stole from us."

His shoulders shook. Whether from emotion or chemical exposure, Karen couldn't tell. Perhaps both.

"She suffered alone. Trapped in the wreckage while he ran. Died before the ambulance arrived." Matthews clutched his throat. "I should have been there. Should have driven her to work that morning."

"The driver bears that guilt," Karen said. "Not you."

Matthews turned towards her, tears cutting tracks through the blood on his face. "We tried for a baby. Five years of tests and treatments. Nothing worked." His voice cracked. "The morning she died, she thought she might be pregnant. We planned to buy a test after work. The post-mortem confirmed she was pregnant as hCG was detected in blood samples."

The revelation hit Karen hard. She fought to keep her expression neutral as Matthews continued.

"The driver should have died that day. Not her. Not our future." He pushed himself to his feet, swaying as he stood. "God spared the wrong person."

Karen recognised the shift in his tone. The raw grief hardened into something darker. She signalled for the armed officers to maintain positions.

"Every morning I hope she's there," Matthews said. "The house echoes with silence. Her clothes hang untouched. That test we never bought..." His voice broke.

His fingers brushed the chemical wounds on his hands.

"Stephen, you need medical attention. Let me help you face this properly."

"Face it?" He spat blood on to the floor. "I face it every morning. Every night. Every time I walk past that scene. Her voice follows me through the rooms. Her perfume lingers on pillows. But she's gone. While that bastard is out there somewhere."

His stance changed. Muscles tensed beneath his sweat-soaked shirt. Karen's instincts screamed warning.

"The doctor said stress affected fertility," Matthews continued. "Five years of trying. The morning she died..." He let out a scream. "She felt different. Said something had changed."

Karen watched his hands curl into fists. The tremors in his limbs increased.

"You're right about one thing," Matthews said. His voice steadied despite the tremors wracking his body. "Dead men can't testify."

He raised his hands in apparent surrender. "No prison. No cells. Just... darkness."

"Stephen, don't..."

Matthews spun and bolted into the shadows. His footsteps echoed off the concrete as he vanished into the maze of abandoned machinery. The darkness swallowed him whole.

"All units, suspect mobile," Karen barked into her radio. "He's compromised by chemical exposure. Consider him dangerous but vulnerable."

"Control, we need paramedics in full protective gear," Karen ordered. "Multiple chemical exposure victims."

She drew her torch and advanced into the darkness where Matthews had disappeared. His laboured breathing carried through the space, but the sound bounced off walls, masking his location.

The factory's shadows held too many hiding places. Too many corners where a desperate man might make his final stand. Karen remained vigilant, knowing Matthews knew this building's layout far better than her team.

Jade stayed back to coordinate the search teams. "First floor clear. Moving to upper levels."

Matthews' footsteps faded into the depths of the abandoned structure. Blood droplets marked his path across the concrete, but the trail disappeared into darkness. Whether he sought escape or a place to die, Karen couldn't tell. But the chemical exposure meant time worked against them all.

Each breath scraped her throat raw. Matthews had breathed these vapours far longer, his body breaking down even as he fled. She pressed forward into the darkness, following the sound of ragged breathing.

47

Karen pushed forward. Her torch beam caught fallen debris and shattered glass, each step requiring care on unstable ground.

Her radio crackled. "Suspect heading towards east stairwell."

"Copy that." She stepped over a fallen ceiling panel, its rusted nails reaching up like claws. Water dripped from exposed pipes, the steady rhythm masking any noise that might betray Matthews' location.

Through gaps in crumbling walls, yellow beams flashed as search teams cleared adjacent rooms. Matthews knew this space. He'd had mapped every corridor during his surveillance. But chemical exposure slowed him now, each breath drawing more poison into his lungs.

A crash rang out ahead, metal striking concrete. Karen advanced towards the noise, testing each step on the decaying flooring. Needles crunched beneath her boots, remnants of the building's unofficial residents. The torch revealed graffiti-covered walls and piles of rotting mattresses.

"Suspect visual lost," her radio buzzed. "Multiple exits from the upper level."

The building's structure echoed as armed officers moved through parallel corridors. Matthews could circle back, find high ground, or descend into the lower levels. Unless the chemicals claimed him first.

Through broken windows, emergency lights pulsed. Fire crews positioned their vehicles, preparing for potential chemical containment. The scene grew more complex with each passing minute.

A figure burst from a darkened doorway. Karen stumbled back against the rough brick, her heart pounding as she raised her baton. The torch beam caught a gaunt face, eyes wide with drug-induced terror.

"Fuck!"

Her scream pierced the darkness. The man lunged forward, movements jerky and unpredictable.

"Don't move!" Karen blocked his path with her baton. "Back away now!"

Boots thundered on concrete as officers converged. Two uniforms tackled the addict, forcing him face down. Cuffs clicked into place while he muttered incoherent pleas.

"Get him out of here," Karen ordered, forcing air into her lungs.

The officers dragged their prisoner towards the exit. Karen pushed off the wall, the interruption burning precious seconds. Matthews gained ground while she dealt with the distraction.

Fresh coughing echoed from above. Wet, choking sounds. A metallic clang suggested Matthews had reached the upper floor. Karen moved towards a rusted staircase, testing each step before committing her weight. The structure shifted beneath her, years of neglect weakening its joints.

"Upper-level search beginning," her radio reported. "Multiple rooms, unstable flooring."

The stairs opened on to a network of elevated walkways. Metal gratings spanned the open space, connecting storage areas and control rooms. Karen edged forward, torch beam revealing gaps where sections had collapsed.

Blood marked Matthews' trail, dark drops stark against galvanised steel. The path led towards a door hanging askew, its frame warped by time and neglect. Beyond stretched darkness pierced by shards of light visible through the damaged roof.

"This is DCI Heath," she broadcast. "All units hold position below. Suspect cornered on the gantry section."

Water leaked through holes overhead, creating treacherous pools on metal surfaces. The walkway swayed with each careful step. But Matthews had chosen this route, perhaps seeking a final confrontation away from the containment teams.

Karen's torch caught movement ahead. A shadow passing behind translucent plastic sheets that hung from the ceiling. She quickened her pace, boots ringing on steel grating. The walkway's mounting bolts creaked in protest.

Matthews' coughing grew louder, wet sounds that echoed his body's chemical breakdown. Blood spatters increased, suggesting internal damage. He couldn't maintain this pace much longer.

"Be advised," she said into her radio. "Suspect heading towards north-west corner. Structure unstable."

The chemical exposure would overwhelm Matthews soon. His options narrowed with each passing moment—surrender, unconsciousness, or a final desperate act. The building's vast space compressed around them, narrowing to this deadly game of pursuit.

Matthews' footsteps rang out ahead, his pace uneven. Karen matched his route, maintaining distance on the fragile grating. The torch beam picked out remnants of the factory's working days scattered across their path.

Water dripped on to her shoulders as she passed beneath a leaking pipe. The air grew thick with moisture, adding fresh hazards to the corroded metal beneath her feet. But Matthews pushed deeper into the darkness, drawn by desperation or delirium.

Her radio stayed silent as she advanced. Armed officers maintained their containment below. Each step brought them closer to the inevitable confrontation, with only the building's decay as witness.

The gantry ended at a control room, its windows dark and broken. Blood marked the door frame where Matthews had stumbled. Karen paused, listening. She edged towards the coughing sounds echoing ahead.

"No visual on suspect," she whispered into her radio. "North-east section is unclear."

Footsteps crunched behind her. An AFO appeared, MP5 raised. "Ma'am. Permission to assist?"

Karen nodded. "Watch your footing. This place could collapse."

They pushed through a broken doorway. The walkway beyond creaked under their weight, gaps in the grating revealing a twenty-foot drop.

"The chemical exposure will drop him soon," the AFO said.

A crash echoed through the darkness. Karen's torch caught falling debris as a section of the ceiling gave way.

"All units, maintain distance," she broadcast. "Building integrity compromised."

Matthews' boots rang out on steel, his path taking him towards the factory's heart.

The AFO tested a section of walkway. "Ma'am, this won't hold much longer."

"Suspect moving west," the AFO reported. "Request units seal external exits."

Karen's torch revealed a junction ahead. Three walkways branched off, each showing severe corrosion.

A support beam crashed through the grating behind them. The entire section swayed, threatening to tear free. Karen grabbed a railing as the structure stabilised.

"He's trying to bring it down," she said. "Get back to solid ground."

"Ma'am, with respect..."

"That's an order. I know where he's headed."

The AFO retreated, metal groaning beneath his boots. Karen studied the blood trails, noting subtle differences in the pattern.

Her torch caught movement through broken windows —a shadow passing in the gloom. Matthews stumbled forward; one hand pressed against his chest.

48

Karen edged across the rusted grating, each step chancing her luck. The distant shadow of Matthews disappeared behind a partition wall. His blood marked a stark path through the darkness.

A sharp crack pierced the silence. Metal screeched as a section of walkway buckled beneath the retreating AFO's weight. The officer lurched backwards, arms windmilling as the grating gave way.

"Ma'am!" Karen spun towards the sound. The AFO's leg dangled through a hole. His weapon clattered to the floor below.

"Keep going. I'm fine." The officer gripped both handrails to steady himself. Blood trickled down his leg where jagged metal pierced his flesh. "Don't lose him."

Karen balanced on a stable section, torn between pursuit and rescue. Matthews' coughing grew fainter with each moment. Three deaths already marked his mission of twisted justice. How many more would have followed if this final act had been delayed? Now, with chemical exposure, his reign of vigilante justice was over. It would be a miracle if he survived.

The AFO pulled himself higher, but the beam creaked under his weight.

More metalwork groaned. The entire section swayed as rust surrendered to gravity. The AFO's grip slipped, fresh blood coating the beam. His radio crackled with static as it knocked against the metal strut.

"Backup's on the way." The officer's voice strained with effort. "Go. I'm fine, it's just a scratch."

Karen keyed her radio. "Officer down and injured. North-east section, upper level. Immediate assistance required." She mapped the officer's position against the building layout. "Access through loading bay stairs. Medical support needed."

"Copy that," Control responded through static. "Officers making their way now. Five minutes."

The AFO braced himself and leaned back to take the weight off his leg. "Move it, ma'am. I've got this covered."

Karen pushed forward into the darkness. Matthews' path led deeper into the building's core. The choice burned in her chest—an injured officer or a killer who'd struck three times. Protocol demanded she stay, but she needed Matthews to face justice rather than die here.

Metal shrieked as Karen pressed against a wall, taking a moment to assess her position. The AFO's shout echoed through the space, directing incoming units to his position.

She kept moving, tracking Matthews with his wet coughing. The AFO's voice grew distant as Karen advanced, baton ready. Each step took her further from her injured colleague, the choice between duty and pursuit weighing heavier than her stab vest.

Karen's torch caught Matthews' hunched figure at the

walkway's end. He gripped a metal railing, blood dripping from his nose on to his shirt. He gasped with each breath.

"Step back from the edge," Karen called. "This has to stop now. Medical support's waiting below."

Matthews turned. His face bore the chemical exposure's toll—skin grey, lips cracked and bleeding. Sweat plastered his shirt to his body despite the cold. "No cells," he rasped. "No prison."

"It's finished." Karen kept her distance.

Matthews released the railing. Blood oozed from the corner of his mouth as he faced her. His eyes wide from toxicity. "Pamela deserved better."

"She deserved justice. Not this." Karen shifted her stance, noting his tensed muscles. "Let the medical team help you."

Matthews lunged forward. His fist struck Karen's jaw, snapping her head back. She stumbled but kept her footing as he pressed his attack. His next punch glanced off her shoulder.

Karen blocked his third strike, decades of training taking over. She deflected his momentum, using his deteriorating balance against him. Matthews staggered but came at her again.

His boot caught her ribs. Karen screamed in pain twisting to reduce the force. Matthews overextended, leaving his guard open. She struck his solar plexus.

Matthews doubled over, coughing blood that spattered her face. Karen circled left. His next attack carried desperation rather than skill.

She redirected his charge. Matthews crashed into the railing. The structure groaned beneath them as he pushed off the barrier, his face bloodied.

"Your body's shutting down," Karen said. "The chemicals…"

Matthews cut her off with a wild swing. Karen ducked under his arm and drove her knee into his side. He gasped but kept coming, blind rage overriding the toxins in his system.

When his punch connected with her temple, Karen's vision blurred. She caught his next strike and slammed him against the wall. Matthews' head cracked against concrete.

He slumped to his knees, chest heaving. Karen pressed her advantage, pinning his arm behind his back. Matthews bucked against her grip but lacked the strength to break free.

"Stephen Matthews." Karen secured the handcuffs around his wrists. "I'm arresting you for the murders of Mark Reeves, James Morton, and Alan Phillips." She recited his rights as blood dripped from his mouth.

Matthews sagged in her grip.

"Medical team's two minutes out." Karen kept pressure on his shoulders. "Stay with me."

Matthews convulsed. Blood sprayed from his mouth as seizures wracked his frame. Karen held him steady, preventing further injury as the toxins claimed their toll.

"Multiple chemical exposure," she broadcast. "Matthews is critical."

He shuddered in her grip, each breath a battle against the poisons he'd prepared for others. The justice he'd sought turned back on its architect.

49

The sodium lamps cast an eerie orange glow over the industrial estate as waves of emergency vehicles flooded the area. Karen sat in an ambulance, an oxygen mask pressed to her face as she watched the organised chaos unfold before her. Chemical response teams in white hazmat suits moved between their trucks and the factory entrance. The rhythmic flash of blue lights painted the scene in stuttering shadows.

"Deep breaths," the paramedic instructed, checking the pulse oximeter clipped to her finger. "Your oxygen levels are improving but I want you on this for at least another fifteen minutes."

Jade climbed into the ambulance beside her, her own oxygen mask dangling around her neck. "Matthews is en route to York Hospital. They've sedated him. His airways were severely compromised by the chemical exposure."

Karen nodded, pulling the mask away. "Ashworth?"

"Critical but stable. Second-degree chemical burns to his neck and chest. They're transferring him to the burns unit at Pinderfields." Jade's voice carried exhaustion. "The

AFO's being treated for that leg wound. Needs stitches, but no major damage. He's more annoyed about losing his weapon than anything else. He'll be the butt of jokes for weeks to come."

Jade put on her best manly gruff voice as she rattled off a few snarky comments: "Well, at least your aim is better than your grip." "Looks like you've been disarmed... literally." "Brings a whole new meaning to gun control."

They both laughed, though it set off a coughing fit in Karen.

A fire engine reversed past them, its warning beeper cutting through the cacophony of radio chatter and shouted instructions. Teams of firefighters coordinated with hazmat specialists, planning their approach to neutralising the chemical hazard.

"The whole building's being treated as a hot zone," Jade continued. "They found over thirty containers of industrial-grade chemicals up there. Some had been damaged to increase the toxic fumes. Matthews knew what he was doing."

Karen lowered the mask again. "He wanted to die in there. Had it all planned out."

"But you stopped him." Jade squeezed her arm. "Though I could kill you myself for going in after him alone."

"Wasn't alone. Had the AFO with me until..."

"Until he nearly fell through that deathtrap of a walkway." Jade shook her head. "The structural engineer's having kittens about the entire building's stability now."

The paramedic returned to check Karen's vitals again. "Blood pressure is still elevated. How's the headache?"

"Manageable." Karen winced as she took another deep breath. The chemical fumes had left her throat feeling raw, each inhalation scratching like sandpaper.

"We should get you to A & E for proper..."

"No." Karen cut him off. "I'm fine. A couple more minutes on the oxygen will be fine."

Jade shot her a look. "You took a punch to the head, breathed God knows what chemicals, and you're covered in Matthews' blood. You're getting checked out."

Before Karen could argue, Kelly's voice carried across the car park. Their superintendent picked her way between emergency vehicles, face grim as she approached the ambulance.

"How bad?" Kelly asked, taking in Karen's dishevelled appearance.

"I'm fine, ma'am. Just..."

"She needs proper medical attention," the paramedic interrupted. "Potential chemical exposure, injuries from the assault, and elevated vital signs."

Kelly nodded. "Then hospital it is. No arguments, Karen. Jade, go with her. Make sure she gets seen." She turned to survey the scene. "The press are already gathering. This will be all over the morning news."

As if to emphasise her point, camera flashes sparked from beyond the police cordon. Uniformed officers held back a growing crowd of journalists and curious onlookers.

"The evidence from Matthews' house?" Karen asked, remembering the shrine to his wife.

"Being processed now. Along with everything we recovered from the factory. The confession videos, the documentation of his surveillance. It's comprehensive." Kelly's expression hardened. "And Ashworth's admission about corruption in the courts... that's opened a whole new can of worms."

A commotion near the factory entrance drew their attention. A hazmat team emerged supporting a stretcher.

The AFO officer lay strapped down as they rushed him towards a waiting ambulance.

"Right." Kelly straightened. "Hospital. Now. Both of you. I want full medical clearance before either of you set foot back in the station."

Karen knew better than to argue. Her head throbbed where Matthews had landed his punch, and the burning in her throat had only intensified.

"The scene's contained," Kelly assured her. "Fire service says it will take days to clear all the chemicals. But it's over. You got him."

Karen nodded, settling on to a gurney as the paramedics prepared to transport her. Through the ambulance's rear windows, she watched the emergency response continue.

Jade sat beside her as they pulled away, lights flashing but sirens silent in the predawn darkness. "Some breakfast would be good after we get checked out. I know a place that does great eggs Benedict."

Despite her throat's protest, Karen managed a smile. The adrenaline crash was hitting hard now, leaving exhaustion in its wake. But they'd stopped Matthews before his list of victims could grow longer.

The ambulance turned on to the main road, leaving the industrial estate behind. In her mind, Karen could still see Matthews convulsing as the toxins overwhelmed him. She closed her eyes, letting the oxygen ease her burning lungs. The morning would bring paperwork, statements, and questions.

50

Karen stared at her untouched coffee, her throat raw from chemical exposure. The kitchen clock showed six a.m. Four hours since her hospital discharge. The house sat quiet except for the boiler's hum.

The case played on her mind. Despite a good outcome, Matthews had already been sentenced—to years of grief, loss, and the slow, corrosive poison of obsession. He'd been a dead man before he'd even stepped into that factory. And that was what unsettled her the most.

Zac placed a plate of buttered toast in front of her. "You need to eat."

"Not hungry." The words scratched her throat. The hospital had warned about potential irritation for several days.

"Try." He settled opposite her, his own breakfast forgotten as he studied her face. "The bruising looks worse."

Karen touched her jaw where Matthews' punch had landed. The skin felt tender beneath her fingers—a souvenir from a night that had gone to hell. "Doctor said it'll fade in a week."

"When I heard about the factory..." Zac's fingers tightened around his mug. "The chemicals, the unstable walkways... what the fuck were you thinking?"

The question struck a nerve. She'd asked herself the same thing during those quiet moments in the hospital. Karen clenched her jaw, resisting the urge to snap back. If she started second-guessing herself, she'd never do the job right. There hadn't been time to hesitate. There never was.

"But I'm here." Karen forced herself to take a bite of toast. The bread hurt going down.

"This time." Zac pushed back from the table and paced to the window. Dawn painted the garden in grey light. "Next time..."

"Don't."

"I can't help it." He pressed his forehead against the glass. "Every call could be the last. Every scene could turn deadly."

Karen set down her toast. "You knew this when we met. The job doesn't change." The words felt hollow even as she spoke them. Because the job had changed her, changed them both. Each case carved away another piece of innocence, replaced it with wariness, with the knowledge that ordinary people could commit extraordinary horrors.

"I know. But after everything..." He looked at her. "Watching you leave for work becomes harder each day."

She swallowed. She knew the weight of that sentence. Knew he was living with a sick fear every time she left the house. But what was she supposed to say? She couldn't fix that for him. All she could do was love and support him through it.

"And now you're going back too."

Zac's shoulders tensed.

"Having doubts?"

"No. Yes." He returned to the table but remained standing. "Yesterday proved how fast things escalate. One moment you're interviewing witnesses, the next you're fighting for breath in toxic fumes."

She exhaled slowly. He wasn't wrong. The line between routine and catastrophe was razor-thin. And yet... what was the alternative? Walk away? Pretend the world didn't need them?

Karen reached for his hand. His skin felt cold against hers. "The risks make us careful and trust our training."

"Training doesn't stop bullets. Or chemicals. Or..." His voice cracked. "I want to return. Need to. But the thought of either of us facing danger..."

"So, we protect each other. Watch each other's backs and deal with shit along the way."

Zac sank into his chair. "The doctor who treated you called. Asked about ongoing symptoms."

"Standard procedure."

"No. He warned about potential long-term damage from chemical exposure." Zac's voice hardened. "Your throat. Your lungs. They can't predict the effects."

Karen forced down another bite of toast. What else could she do? Panic wouldn't change anything. Worry wouldn't undo the damage. "I'm fine."

"This time." He pushed his plate away. "But Matthews planned to die in there. The chemicals were meant to kill."

"And we stopped him."

"At what cost?" Zac stood again, his breakfast untouched. "Each case risks everything. Each suspect could be the one who..." He stopped, unable to finish.

Karen watched him resume his pacing. The morning light caught the grey at his temples—stress adding years to his features. She had no answer to that. She wanted to say it was worth it. That saving lives would always be worth it. But last night had proved just how much it could take from them.

"I can't quit," she said. "The job matters too much."

"I know. That's what terrifies me. You'll always choose duty over safety. Always push forward no matter the risk."

She swallowed against the tightness in her throat. Was that what he saw when he looked at her? Someone willing to die for the job? Because she didn't feel fearless. She just didn't know how to do anything else.

"Like you did before the attack."

He flinched at the memory. "Perhaps that's why I understand the danger now. Why watching you leave becomes harder."

Karen ignored the protest from her bruised ribs. She wrapped her arms around his waist, feeling the tension in his muscles. "We face it together. Your strength helps me push forward. My determination helps you return."

Zac turned in her embrace. "Promise me something?"

"If I can."

"No more solo pursuits through chemical deathtraps."

Despite her raw throat, Karen managed a small laugh. "Deal. Now eat your breakfast."

He pressed a kiss to her forehead, careful to avoid her bruises. They settled back at the table. Each bite of toast hurt, but she forced herself to eat.

Zac gathered their plates, his movements betraying lingering tension. "You should rest today. Kelly won't expect you in."

"Reports need writing." Karen winced as she swallowed the last of her coffee. "Matthews' evidence needs processing."

"The team can handle it."

"My case. My responsibility." She stood, steadying herself against the counter. "Like yours will be when you return."

His reaction was instant—a flicker of resistance, a muscle tightening in his jaw. He wasn't just worried about her returning. He was terrified about stepping back into it himself.

Zac stilled at the sink, plates forgotten. "That's different."

"No." Karen moved beside him.

"But after yesterday..."

"Yesterday proved why we do this." She touched his arm.

Zac turned to face her. "By risking ourselves?"

"By standing between danger and those who need protection." Karen held his gaze. "You taught me that, remember? Back when I doubted myself after London."

His expression softened at the memory. "You were ready to quit."

"Until you reminded me why the job matters." She squeezed his arm. "Now I'm reminding you."

Zac dried his hands. "Summer asked about my return date."

Karen felt the conversation shift, grateful for the change. "What did you tell her?"

"That I'm nervous but ready." A smile crossed his face. "She said that's what courage means. Being afraid but doing it anyway."

"Smart girl."

"Takes after her dad. Though don't tell her I said that."

Karen pressed a kiss to his cheek. "Well, it's not on

your looks! Your secret's safe." She stepped back, suppressing a yawn. "I need a shower."

"You need sleep."

"Later." She headed for the stairs. "The factory scene needs documenting while it's fresh, so I'll head to the station first, and then on to the factory."

Zac followed her to the hallway. "At least let me drive you in."

"No." Karen paused on the bottom step. "You have your own stuff to focus on."

"Karen."

"Trust me to know my limits." She turned to face him. "Like I trust you to face your fears about returning."

His shoulders dropped, tension bleeding away. "When did you become so wise?"

"Learned from the best." She climbed another step. "You showed me how to balance duty with self-preservation. Now it's your turn to remember that lesson."

Zac nodded, understanding replacing the anxiety in his features. "The job's part of who we are."

"Not just what we do." Karen continued up the stairs. "Get your notes ready for the board. Show them the strength I see every day."

Hot water eased her aching muscles as Karen showered, though each breath still burned. Matthews' toxic legacy would linger in her system for days.

She rummaged through her wardrobe, choosing loose clothes that wouldn't rub on the worst bruises. Her reflection showed fatigue in every line.

Zac waited by the front door as she descended, car keys in hand. "Sure about this?"

"About work? Yes." She took the keys from his grip. "About you? Always."

"Even when I question myself?"

"Those doubts keep us alive." Karen opened the door. That was the closest he'd come to admitting how much this all terrified him, so she wouldn't push him to say more. Zac pulled her close, mindful of her injuries. "Be careful today."

"Always." She returned his embrace. "You focus on those notes. Show the board the officer I know you still are."

His kiss held promise rather than fear. Karen carried that strength with her as she drove away, watching Zac in her mirror.

51

Two weeks passed before Matthews left the hospital, his body ravaged by chemical exposure. Karen stepped into the interview room at York Police Station, where he sat slumped at the table. His skin appeared pale and papery beneath the lights. Chemical burns marked his neck and throat, the flesh pink and mottled. Dark circles shadowed his eyes.

Ed arranged his notes and clicked on the recording device. "Interview commenced at ten forty-seven. Present are DCI Karen Heath, DC Ed Hyde, and Stephen Matthews. Also present is Mr Matthews' solicitor, James Burton."

Matthews stared at his hands, now scarred from chemical exposure. His court clerk demeanour had vanished, replaced by a man carved hollow by grief and rage.

"Let's discuss what triggered your actions," Karen said, her own throat still recovering from the factory fumes. "You maintained control for two years after Pamela's death. What changed?"

Matthews lifted his gaze. "Sarah Collins. Twenty-seven. Mother of a five-year-old boy." His voice emerged as a whisper, vocal cords damaged. "Hit by a drink driver outside Marks & Spencer."

"The Morrison case," Ed said, checking his notes. "February this year."

"The driver mounted the pavement." Matthews pressed his palms flat against the table. "Blood alcohol three times the limit. Previous drink-driving conviction. But his barrister argued addiction issues warranted leniency."

Karen saw Matthews' fingers curl into fists. "The sentence?"

"Eighteen months' custody. Two-year driving ban. Five-hundred-pound fine." Blood drained from Matthews' face. "While Sarah learned to walk again through agony. Her spine... her legs..."

His solicitor touched his arm. "Take your time."

Matthews drew a shaky breath. "I processed the court papers. Read her impact statement. She can't run with her son any more. Can't lift him. Each step up the stairs brings pain."

Tears slid down his cheeks. "The driver walks free next summer. But Sarah's prison has no release date. No time off for good behaviour. Endless days of watching her boy grow up from the sidelines."

"That case broke your control," Karen said.

Matthews nodded. "I sat in court, recording everything. I saw another drink driver ruin another life. The judge spoke of rehabilitation. Second chances." His voice hardened. "But who gives Sarah a second chance at running with her child?"

"So you chose your targets," Ed said. "Started planning."

"The system protects criminals. Calls it justice." Matthews tugged at his sleeve. "Sarah's boy asked why the bad man who hurt mummy isn't being told off. How do you explain that to a child?"

Karen pursed her lips. "Tell us about the surveillance. The research."

"I knew the patterns. Which judges favoured lenient sentences. Which barristers twisted truth into doubt." Matthews touched the burns on his neck. "Two years of seeing them get away with their crimes while victims suffered. Sarah's case lit the fuse. Something snapped in me."

"Your wife's death consumed you," Karen said. "You couldn't save her. But Sarah's suffering..."

"Showed nothing had changed." Matthews slumped in his chair. "Same excuses. Same legal games. Different family torn apart."

His solicitor pushed a glass of water closer. Matthews ignored it.

"I chose Reeves first. Another drink driver who killed then walked free after five years... five poxy years! Studied his routine. His habits." Matthews closed his eyes.

"But Ashworth was your real goal," Karen said.

Matthews' expression twisted. "Every one of his cases ended with a reduced sentence. He had a way of turning guilt into reasonable doubt."

"You wanted him to confess," Ed said.

"To acknowledge the lives he'd ruined through playing with the emotions of the jury." Matthews touched his throat again.

Karen studied the broken man before her. "Sarah's case pushed you over the edge. But you'd planned this for years."

He nodded. Matthews' voice cracked. "Sarah's

suffering became Pamela's. Every victim's story merged until I couldn't cope any more. I couldn't stay there and see the crocodile tears, pleas for forgiveness, while those evil bastards looked over their shoulders and smiled and winked at their own family members. There was no remorse there. They were playing up for the jury."

He looked at his scarred hands. A tear rolled down his cheek. "But I failed. The system still stands. Sarah still can't climb stairs without pain shooting through her spine."

Matthews reached for the water. "I wanted to change things. Make them feel the pain they'd inflicted." He stared into the glass. "Now I'm no better than them."

"Three families lost loved ones," Karen said. "Your actions multiplied the suffering you fought against."

"I read their files each night." Matthews set down the water untouched. "Told myself they deserved punishment. That I served justice." His voice broke. "But their screams... their pleas..."

Ed pushed a photograph across the table. Reeves slumped in his car, the plastic hood cruel against his skin. Matthews turned away.

"You planned each death," Karen said.

Matthews nodded and pressed his fingers against his temples. "Someone had to balance the scales."

"By becoming judge and executioner?"

"You don't understand," Matthews replied, head bowed.

"I understand your grief and the need to make sense of senseless loss."

"Then you know why..."

"But I also understand the law," Karen cut him off. "Without it, we're ruled by vengeance. By personal judgement of who deserves to live or die."

A Matter Of Justice

Matthews slumped back. The marks on his neck stood stark against his collar. "Sarah Collins will never run again. Never dance at her son's wedding. Never..." He closed his eyes and snarled. "The driver who crippled her serves eighteen months."

"Your wife's death broke you, I get that," Karen said. "But it didn't give you the right to kill."

"They showed no genuine remorse." Matthews' voice strengthened.

"Yet you chose their manner of death," Ed said. "Gas. Chemicals. Fire."

Matthews touched his throat where the burns remained raw. "I wanted them to confess. To acknowledge their crimes before..."

"Before you executed them," Karen finished.

Silence filled the room. Matthews stared at the table.

"You'll appear before magistrates this afternoon," Karen sighed. "We've charged you with three counts of murder, one attempted murder, multiple counts of false imprisonment, and assaulting an emergency worker."

"Ashworth survived?" Matthews' voice cracked.

"He's recovering." Karen gathered her papers. "The courts you despise will now judge you."

Matthews pressed his palms against his eyes. "I see their faces. Hear their final breaths. The system failed them, but I..." His shoulders shook. "I became what I hated."

"This wasn't justice," Karen said. "It was revenge masked as moral purpose."

Matthews' solicitor cleared his throat. "My client understands the gravity..."

"No." Matthews cut him off. "Let her speak the truth. I killed three men. Planned their deaths and used my position to track them down." His voice dropped.

Karen stood. "Interview terminated at eleven fifty-two." She clicked off the recording. "Officers will transport you to court at two."

Matthews remained seated as Ed gathered the photographs. "What happens to Sarah Collins? To others like her?"

"We work to change the system," Karen said. "Through law, not violence. Through reform, not revenge."

"I failed Pamela," Matthews whispered.

Karen paused at the door. "You lost yourself to grief. Let it twist your purpose into nothing more than evil." She met his gaze.

Matthews nodded as Karen and Ed left the room, his shoulders curved with defeat.

52

Karen sat at her desk, staring at Matthews' case file. She should have felt relief. Three dead, one critically injured, a killer in custody. The facts were clean. The case, wrapped. But the weight of it still pressed against her ribs, heavier than the bruises Matthews had left behind. Because justice wasn't always about arrests and convictions. Sometimes, justice came too late.

And that was what unsettled her the most.

Jade entered, dropping into the chair opposite. Her face bore the exhaustion of the past week. She tipped her head back and yawned.

"Keeping you up?"

Jade shook her head, still in mid yawn. "Detective Superintendent Kelly asked me to deliver the forensic report," Jade said, placing a thick folder on Karen's desk. "They found over fifty chemical containers at the scene. Matthews obtained them through a network of industrial suppliers. Paid cash, used false details."

Karen lifted the folder. "How's your throat?"

"Better than yours by the sound of it." Jade leaned

back. "The doctor wants me to go back next week for more tests. Says chemical exposure effects can surface later."

"You did well, you know." Karen set down the report. "Coming back wasn't easy."

Jade tapped her fingers against the chair arm. "That first body at Rawcliffe knocked me down. But each scene after..." She paused. "The work mattered more than the fear."

"You pushed through it. Found connections we needed."

"The court records kept me busy. Looking for evidence instead of..." Jade's hands stilled. "Instead of letting the bodies freak me out."

Karen nodded. The change in her sergeant struck her. Not only the physical recovery, but her renewed confidence.

Jade had walked into this case one version of herself and had come out another. Not broken. Not lost. Just changed. That was the thing about this job—it took from you, piece by piece, shift by shift. But sometimes, if you fought hard enough, it gave something back, too.

"THE OLD JADE would have hidden her panic attacks." A small smile crossed Jade's face. "The new one knows when to step back, refocus, find different ways to contribute... and ask for help."

"Well, I'm glad to hear it. And it's good to have the team together again. They missed you. God knows why?" Karen's throat burned as she spoke.

Jade rolled her eyes and smiled. Silence settled between them, comfortable rather than tense. Years of friendship and shared experiences filled the space.

"Remember my first day back?" Jade asked. "When you found me chucking up?"

"You thought you'd failed." Karen picked up her coffee, grimacing at the cold liquid. "But facing that fear showed more courage than pretending you were fine."

"You gave me space to heal. To find my feet again." Jade stood and moved to the window. "The team followed your lead. No pressure, no judgement. Just support when I needed it."

"The job changes us. But it doesn't define us."

"Matthews was really messed up." Jade said. "Years of plotting revenge while living in a shrine to his dead wife. He couldn't get over that hurdle."

"He was pretty messed up. It had become an obsession." Karen said. "But you faced your demons head-on. Fought through them instead of letting them control you."

"Had a good friend showing me how." Jade's voice carried warmth. "Someone who understood the struggle because she'd fought her own battles."

Karen stood, her bruised ribs protesting the movement. "The friend learned from watching you recover. Your strength reminded her why the job matters."

"Even when it leads us into chemical deathtraps?"

"Especially then." Karen moved to join Jade at the window.

Outside, life continued as officers headed to calls, witnesses arrived for statements, the routine of justice pushed on. The world didn't pause for grief. Didn't hesitate for the broken, the battered, or the ones left behind. Cases closed, new ones opened, and the wheel kept turning.

And that was why they did it.

Not for headlines, not for promotions. But for the ones

who couldn't move forward until someone else stood still long enough to fight for them.

"Some good came from this case," Karen said, returning to her desk. "Ashworth's confession about bribes and fixed cases. The network of barristers trading verdicts for payment. Detective Superintendent Kelly's established a task force." Karen lifted a memo from her desk. "Every case Ashworth handled faces review. Other defence counsels will be under scrutiny. The task force starts Monday." Karen gestured to the memo. "Kelly wants us involved once clearance comes through. Ready to tackle corruption the right way?"

"Always." Jade moved to the door. "That's why we are here."

Karen watched her leave, her heart filled with pride.

JOIN MY READER'S GROUP

If you haven't already done so, then please join my reader's group for your free starter library, information about my writing, share in my journey as I research my next book, as well as news about my latest releases.

Join up to my VIP reader list here

CURRENT BOOK LIST

Hop over to my website for a current list of books:
http://jaynadal.com/current-books/

OTHER WAYS TO STAY IN TOUCH

Other ways you can connect with me:
Like my page on Facebook: Jay Nadal
Email jay@jaynadal.com with any questions, ideas or interesting story suggestions. Hey, even if you spot a typo that we've missed, then drop me a line. I'd love to hear from you.

Printed in Great Britain
by Amazon